Accustomed
to the
Dark

Accustomed to the Dark

A Joshua Croft Mystery

Walter Satterthwait

University of New Mexico Press   ALBUQUERQUE

Library of Congress Cataloging-in-Publication Data

Satterthwait, Walter.
  Accustomed to the dark : a Joshua Croft mystery /
Walter Satterthwait.— University of New Mexico
Press paperback ed.
      p.   cm.
  ISBN 0-8263-3348-6 (pbk. : alk. paper)
  1. Croft, Joshua (Fictitious character)—Fiction.
2. Private investigators—New Mexico—Santa Fe—Fiction.
3. Santa Fe (N.M.)—Fiction.
4. Large type books.   I. Title.
PS3569.A784A64 2004
813'.54—dc22

                            2003018982

This book is for Caroline

ACKNOWLEDGMENTS

Writing is one of the few forms of self-abuse in which a helping hand is sometimes necessary. This book probably wouldn't have been completed without the kind assistance of a number of people. So, thanks to Dana Bramwell in Colorado Springs; Sara Bullington, Senor Pelota, Dr. Roger Smithpeter in Santa Fe; Bill Crider in Alvin, Texas; Mike Stone in Denver; and to Susan Rose at Snoop Sisters, in Bellaire, Florida.

Thanks, also, to Janet McConnoughey, for showing me New Orleans, and to Thomas L. Touhy for the feral women.

And particular thanks to my wife, Caroline, who put up with me while I put this out.

When I first came in, back in '78, I was always in the free world when I dreamed at night, but recently I stopped dreaming about being outside. Now, even in my dreams, I'm in the penitentiary.

—A Voice: Bank Robber, age thirty-nine from *The Hot House,* by Pete Earley

PART ONE

1

WE MADE IT easy for them. We were sitting out on Rita's patio, exposed and vulnerable.

It was a Sunday morning toward the end of May. The winter had been mild and the spring had been milder. Up in the mountains, up toward the ski basin, the fields of aspen were showing pale olive against the dark green bruise of pine. Down in town, iris and narcissus crowded the gardens, purple bursts of lilac and wisteria spilled over the sunbaked brown adobe walls. Here at Rita's house, in the hills overlooking Santa Fe, the air was warm and soft and scented with piñon.

I had cooked breakfast burritos and blueberry muffins, squeezed some oranges for fresh juice. Now the plates and the glasses and the wicker basket lay empty atop the round white metal table.

Rita sipped at her coffee. Holding the mug with both hands, she lowered it to her lap and she smiled at me. "What shall we do today?"

"Why should we do anything?" I was slumped against the back of my chair in a dense, amiable lassitude. My stomach was full and so was my life. There was nothing, anywhere, that needed to be done.

She nodded. "You're a lazy pig," she said.

"Thang you," I said. "Thang you veramuch."

"And you do a terrible Elvis."

"Thang you."

"We could drive up to the Jemez," she said. "Go through Bandelier."

Her hair was loose and it tumbled black as the wings of ravens to her shoulders. She wore a blouse of lavender silk, stonewashed blue jeans, and sandals with thin brown leather straps. She was beautiful, as usual, but I was almost getting used to that.

With an effort I leaned forward and hooked my finger around the handle of my coffee cup. Sighing happily, I sat back. "We could," I agreed. I sipped some coffee. "Or we could hang around here all day. Scratch. Yawn. Maybe belch from time to time."

She smiled. "Be still my heart."

"Too nice a day to go running around the countryside, Rita."

"It's too nice a day to lie around and waste it."

"I'm not wasting it," I said. "I'm savoring it."

"And you couldn't savor it in Bandelier?"

"Maybe. I guess we'll never know." I smiled. I was enjoying this. A few years ago, when Rita was in the wheelchair, it would have been me arguing for a trip out of town. Often it had been.

"I'll drive," she said.

I considered that carefully.

"We'll bring along your Geritol," she said.

"Very droll."

"And when we come to civilization," she said, "I'll wake you up and you can put in your teeth."

I laughed.

We heard the helicopter then, a muffled *chuk-a-chuk* coming from behind us, from over the mountain. We both looked up, and a few moments later the aircraft sailed into view, a monster locust clattering across the sky. It was flying low, only a couple of hundred feet above. It passed over us and a chill shadow slipped across the flagstones.

"The state police," Rita said.

"Probably." It was an Aerostatial Twinstar, and the state police owned one.

"I wonder what they're looking for," she said.

We hadn't listened to the news last night, or this morning. If we had, we'd have known what the state police were looking for.

"Lost tourists," I said. This year, the tourists had arrived early, and this year they were traveling in packs.

We watched the mechanical bug scrape across the blue, its dark carapace growing smaller, its rhythmic chatter fading. It banked and then disappeared off to the south.

Rita turned to me. "So? What do you say, Joshua? Bandelier?"

"You'll drive?"

"Yes."

I shrugged. "Why not."

Smiling, Rita shook her head—in exasperation, probably—and then her head jerked to the left, suddenly, comically, like the head of a marionette, and her mouth opened wide as though she were about to scream. For a moment, a millisecond, I thought she was acting, playing out a piece of uncharacteristic slapstick, and I began to frown, puzzled. The frown froze when I saw the small, perfectly circular hole at the right side of her head, and then she was toppling from her chair and her porcelain cup was twirling off through the air, spraying black coffee. She was halfway to the ground and I was up from my seat and reaching for her when I heard the far-off crack of the rifle.

The sunlight came down hard and flat against the dusty earth and it slammed against the cars slumbering in the hospital's unpaved lot.

I stood there at the edge of the lot, staring off to the east, toward the mountains. The mountains were less than three miles away, but they seemed remote, alien, strange formations on the landscape of a distant planet. I had my arms crossed over my chest, my hands clamped beneath them. I took deep, long, staggered breaths. The air around me had grown thinner, as though it had been leached of its oxygen.

It wasn't the mountains that were alien. It was the creature who stood staring at them, holding desperately onto himself as

5

though parts of him might, at any moment, spin away and go reeling through the ether.

I had nearly lost Rita once before. We had both survived. Since then the two of us had come together in ways that were complicated and elegant but also, I had suddenly discovered, infinitely fragile. I honestly did not know how I would survive if I lost her now, or even that I could.

I remembered her face, pale and drawn, as they wheeled her into the operating room. . . .

I heard a faint sound behind me, the sole of a shoe scuffling at the caliche, and I turned.

Striding toward me between the cars was Hector Ramirez, a friend, a sergeant in the Santa Fe Police Department. He was a bodybuilder, thick and powerful, but he always moved as lightly on his feet as a ballerina. The scuffling sound had been intentional, to warn me of his approach.

"Anything?" I said. "Any news?"

He shook his head. "She's still in the operating room, they told me." The knot of his red silk tie was loose, the sleeves of his off-white shirt were rolled back along his heavy forearms.

I looked at the mountains, took another staggered breath.

"How you doing?" he said.

I turned to him. "What kind of question is that?"

He frowned, lightly ran his hand down over his bandito mustache.

"Shit," I said. I looked off, toward the mountain. "I'm sorry, Hector."

For a moment or two, he was silent. Then he said, "They're doing everything they can. The surgeon, Berger, he's the best in the state. One of the best in the country."

"He'd better be." It was an empty, stupid threat and both of us knew that. Hector had the grace to ignore it.

I said, "I talked to the uniforms. Diego and Monahan."

"I heard."

"It was Martinez who shot her."

6

"Probably. You told Diego you weren't working on anything right now."

"Nothing."

"No threats? No letters? Phone calls?"

"No." I turned to him. "Why didn't you let us know that Martinez was out?"

He frowned. "It only happened last night, Josh. I wasn't even in town. I didn't know about it till a half an hour ago, when I got back. I came here as soon as I could."

I nodded. I stared off at the mountains again.

"Tell me what happened," he said.

I didn't look at him. "I already told them. Diego and Monahan."

"So tell me," he said.

I told him. And I relived everything. Rita's face as the bullet took her, her body spinning from the chair and slapping hard against the flagstones, boneless and slack. My kneeling down beside her, suddenly paralyzed with shock and panic and disbelief. The bright shiny blood trickling down into her hair. Her eyes open but lifeless, staring straight up at nothing.

I wanted to sweep her up into my arms, hold her, protect her from the horrors of the universe, all of them. I wanted to leap to my feet and scream at the bastard who shot her, dare him to shoot me. I wanted to die.

None of that would help her.

I put my fingers to her throat. There was a pulse, fluttery and very faint. My hand was trembling.

The shot had come from the hills to the south. I looked up there. The nearest heavy cover was about two hundred yards away, a thicket of pines, dark green beneath the blue of the sky.

The sky shouldn't still be blue, I remember thinking. The sun shouldn't still be shining.

Down on my knees, I was partially concealed by the balustrade

7

that ran around the edge of the patio. But if he were still there, hiding behind the trees, he could probably see me.

I sprang in a dive through the opened French doors, hit the carpet with my shoulder, tumbled across the living room, ripped the phone from the end table. Dialed 911. Gave the dispatcher everything she asked for. Hung up, darted back to the patio, glanced up at the pine trees, knelt down beside her once more.

There had been no second shot.

I put my fingers on her throat again, lightly. The pulse was still there. I kept my fingers against it and I leaned down toward her ear and I began to talk in an urgent whisper. I told her to hang on. I told her that help was coming. I told her a lot of things.

Her pulse kept up its faint, fluttery beat.

I was still whispering when they arrived to secure the scene, Diego and Monahan, Monahan carrying a rifle. They wanted to talk to me but I waved them away and I kept whispering into Rita's ear as the pulse fluttered beneath my fingers. Diego and Monahan did whatever it was they had to do, and after a while they let in the paramedics, three of them in white coats, with a gurney.

I let them push me aside. One of them talked into a headset while he got her vital signs. In only a few minutes they were moving her.

Even as stupid with shock as I was, I felt a sickening sense of familiarity. I had been through all this before, six years ago—the cops, the paramedics, the limp body rushed into the ambulance.

Outside, in the driveway, three or four police cars were crouched, some with their doors still open. A radio was squawking. Cops were running into the forest. Back in the tall pine trees, someone shouted.

The paramedics didn't want me to come along, but I came anyway. I rode in the ambulance, squatting beside her, whispering again. The paramedic with the headset was still monitoring her, still chattering away.

The doctor—Berger—met us at the hospital. He let me come along as far as the operating room and then he told me that I had to leave her. They would do everything they could, he said. The metal door swung shut behind him.

Back in the lobby, I gave someone all the insurance information. When I was finished, Diego and Monahan were waiting for me. They asked me their questions. It was Diego who told me that Ernie Martinez had escaped from the state penitentiary last night.

"You were pretty hard on Diego," said Hector.

"Yeah," I said. I was still staring off at the green mountains. "I know. I apologized. But someone should've let us know."

"Everyone was busy, Josh. We were, the Staties were. And the thinking, this morning, was that Martinez had already gone. That he'd slipped out of town."

I looked at him. "He tried to kill her before. He shot her, Hector. She spent three years in a wheelchair. Someone should've let us know he was out."

He frowned. He stroked his mustache.

"Would you have called?" I asked him. "If you were here, would you've let us know?"

His broad face tightened and became darker. "You know I would."

"So why didn't—"

"Sergeant!" It was Diego, running toward us. "She's out of the operating room!"

9

2

ALL RIGHT," SAID Berger. "First of all, we recovered the bullet. It appears to be a two-twenty-three." He turned to Hector. "It's in excellent shape."

The doctor had herded Hector and me into a doctor's lounge near the recovery room. Off-white walls, a few framed photographs of Southwest scenes, a long wooden table surrounded by upholstered chairs. At one corner of the table lay a glossy Santa Fe real estate magazine.

Berger sat at the head of the table, Hector to his left, along one side of it.

"What kind of shape is *she* in?" I asked him.

He turned to me. "As I told you, we have her stabilized at the moment."

"Which means what, exactly?"

Short and compact and tidy, maybe forty-five years old, Berger still wore his pale blue scrub suit. He sat back in his chair with his elbows propped on the chair's arms, his hands tented before his chest, the fingers slightly spread. His face was pale and oval and his thinning black hair was combed back from a sharply defined widow's peak over small pale ears that lay flat against his head. He had a pointed nose and slightly fleshy lips. There were faint bags under his eyes. He had looked tired when I first saw him, at the hospital entrance, and he looked more tired now.

On the lower left breast of the scrub suit, just beneath the pocket, there was a small dark brown stain, smeared.

He looked at me over the tented fingers. "We've recovered

the bullet, as I said. It was lodged in the right temporal lobe."
He pursed his lips. "Mrs. Mondragón is right-handed?"

"Yes."

"In a way, then, it's a blessing that the bullet lodged where it did."

"A blessing," I said. I tried to keep the anger from my voice but I don't think I succeeded. I could feel Hector watching me. Dr. Berger hadn't heard the anger. He was staring off, probably watching the operation he'd just performed. His lips were pursed again. He turned back to me. "Yes," he said. "It's a remarkable piece of luck, really. A fraction of an inch in any direction, and Mrs. Mondragón would have been irreparably damaged, or fatally wounded." He cocked his head slightly, curious. "Was she moving at the moment of impact?"

I didn't need to think about it. I had replayed the scene, again and again, since it happened. "She was shaking her head. At something I said."

He nodded slightly, as though that confirmed some interesting theory he'd been mulling over. "Then whatever you said, by saying it you may very well have saved her life."

My glance kept sliding down to that small dried smear on the pale blue scrub suit. "And what's the prognosis?" I asked him.

"Well," he said. "Naturally, it's always difficult to forecast the progress of these cases. There's no question but that Mrs. Mondragón has suffered an extremely serious injury. But I do want you to know that I'm optimistic. Guardedly."

"Guardedly," I said.

He nodded slightly again. "If we can keep down the pressure in the cranial cavity, prevent herniation, I believe there's a very good chance, an excellent chance, that Mrs. Mondragón will recover completely. I've seen it happen before. That's barring any additional complications, of course."

"And if you can't keep down the pressure?"

He gave me a small, tight smile. "We're doing everything we can to keep it down. We've evacuated the hematoma—cleaned the internal area—and we've electrocauterized the wound. She's on a mannitol drip, to dehydrate her and reduce swelling. She's on a respirator. And she'll be under constant monitoring—her heart, her brain, her breathing."

"She's still out? Still unconscious?"

"That's correct."

"When will she regain consciousness?"

"We've no way of knowing. It could be a matter of hours. It could be a matter of days."

"How many days?"

He frowned slightly. "Mr. . . . . Craft, is it?"

"Croft."

"Mr. Croft, the brain is a remarkable organ." He swiveled his tented fingers slightly forward. "Historically, we've had cases of a patient wandering into a doctor's office, complaining of nagging headaches. The doctor examines the skull and, much to his surprise, discovers an entry wound. Later, an X ray reveals the presence of a thirty-eight caliber slug in the brain. The patient had never realized that he'd been shot."

"A thirty-eight," I said. "That's a pistol cartridge."

"Yes. And this was a rifle cartridge. Had the slug been more powerful, had it been traveling more quickly, hydrostatic shock would almost certainly have proven fatal. But this slug was traveling quickly enough to create a very serious trauma. Edema has set in, the brain has swollen. At the moment, the swelling is our primary enemy."

"In what way?"

Delicately, he untented his fingers and shaped them around an imaginary skull. "The cranial vault is rigid. Cerebral swelling could bring pressure against the medulla oblongata, at the stem of the brain." He moved his thumbs slightly, down there at the bottom of the skull. "Herniation. And that would very likely prove fatal."

He dropped his hands and the skull disappeared. He sat up in his chair, smiled a tight, brief smile. "But Mrs. Mondragón seems an extremely healthy woman. And, as I said, we've done everything possible for her. I have good reason to be hopeful."

12

"But you don't know when she'll regain consciousness."

"That's correct. Today, perhaps. Perhaps tomorrow. No one can say."

"Perhaps next month. Perhaps never."

He shook his head slightly. "As I said, I *am* hopeful. I've seen many, many people recover from wounds that were very nearly identical to this one."

"With no residual effects. No permanent damage."

"None." He frowned thoughtfully. "Well." He considered whether to speak, decided to go ahead. He looked at me. "You know that some people consider the right frontal lobe, in right-handed people, to be the seat of the unconscious."

"Drawing on the Right Side of the Brain."

"Exactly. There's a school of thought, not so much in this country as in Europe, which believes that damage to the right frontal lobe may possibly affect certain . . . aspects of the personality."

"Which aspects?"

"The subconscious. Creativity. The so-called artistic impulse."

I thought of Rita's watercolors. Sometimes on summer evenings she sat out on the patio, brush in hand, and she slowly filled sheets of paper with soft, subdued views of the town, of the stands of juniper and piñon, of the distant purple mountains.

"But that's speculation, of course," said Berger. "And it is, as I say, a European school of thought. French, for the most part. In my own experience, and I do have fairly extensive experience with trauma of this type, I've never witnessed any such change."

"Were any of your patients artists, Doctor?"

He pursed his lips again. "Mr. Croft, I assure you that there's every hope of Mrs. Mondragón making a complete recovery. I wouldn't say so if I didn't believe it to be true."

"But no guarantees."

He produced the small, tight smile again. "There are never any guarantees, Mr. Croft. As I told you, however, I believe that Mrs. Mondragón has an excellent chance." He stood up. "And now, gentlemen, forgive me, but I'm afraid I've things to do."

13

Hector and I stood. "When can I see her?" I said.

He frowned, as though displeased by my failure to understand that the meeting was over. "She's still in recovery," he said. "She'll remain there until we're certain that she's stabilized. At which point we'll move her to the ICU."

"And when will that be?"

"A few hours, perhaps." He glanced at his watch. "I'm sorry, but I really must be going."

"I can't see her until then?"

"No. That's impossible, I'm afraid."

As he came around the table, Hector stepped forward and offered a hand. Berger took it. "Thank you, Doctor," Hector told him. "I'll be getting back to you."

Berger nodded, released Hector's hand, held out his own to me. I took it.

"Mr. Croft," he said. I nodded. I glanced again, not wanting to, at the stain.

He escorted us out the door and then he went down the hallway alone.

"A cold sonovabitch," I said to Hector.

Hector looked at me. "And if he weren't?" he said. "Doing what he does? How long would he last, you figure?"

He was right, but I wasn't ready to surrender my dislike. I changed the subject. "Who's in charge over at the state police?"

He looked at me. He frowned. "There's not much point in telling you to stay away from this, is there?"

"No."

"Yeah." He took a deep breath. "Hernandez," he said.

"Hernandez? He's a foot soldier."

"He got promoted."

I nodded. "Okay, Hector. Thanks."

"Don't do anything stupid, Josh."

"Right."

14

3

THE STATE POLICE complex was out on Cerrillos Road, past the commercial district but before the entrance to the Interstate. I parked the Cherokee in the visitors' lot and I stalked along the sidewalk to the entrance, a two-story box of black glass set midway in the long beige wall. I stepped into a small lobby and faced another door, this one locked. To my right, behind a wall of reinforced glass, a young woman with blonde hair took my name and dialed Hernandez. She spoke briefly into the phone, then hung up and told me to go on in. She buzzed open the interior door.

The place was busy. Cops, uniforms and suits, were sprinting up and down the stairs, pacing quickly through the corridor on the second floor. The door to Hernandez's office was open. He was sitting back in his chair, waiting, and he stood up when I walked in. "Croft," he said.

He was in his early thirties and he wore a military crew cut along the top of his square red head, and a pale gray chambray shirt that fit snugly against his broad shoulders. A brown tie, khaki pants. Beneath the desk, he would be wearing a pair of cowboy boots. He always did. "I heard about Mrs. Mondragón," he said. "I'm sorry. How is she?"

"When did you people know that Martinez was out?" I asked him.

He pressed his lips together and nodded toward the door. "Close that," he said.

I stepped back, closed it.

15

"Take a seat," he said, and waved a big-knuckled hand toward a straight-back wooden chair.

"I'm fine where I am."

Hernandez stared at me for a moment. He looked down at his desk and then he looked back up and he sighed. "You gonna feel any better if you dance with me for a couple of rounds?"

"Maybe."

"Yeah, well, you'll have to wait in line." He frowned impatiently. "C'mon, Croft. Don't be a hard-ass. Take a seat and we'll see what we got here. The two of us."

I crossed the room and sat down.

With another sigh, Hernandez lowered himself behind the desk.

He glanced at his watch. "I told them to hold my calls," he said. "We got about fifteen minutes."

I said nothing.

"How is she?" he asked.

"She's in a coma."

"What do they think? The doctors?"

"If she's lucky, she'll pull through."

"Jesus, I hope so." He pressed his lips together and then he leaned back against the swivel seat, lay his arms on the arms of the chair. He nodded. "Okay," he said. "We blew it. *I* blew it. The Captain—Captain Gold—he tells me to make sure Mrs. Mondragón gets a warning. This is last night, maybe an hour after the breakout. He knew all about Martinez. I didn't. Before my time."

I felt my face stiffen.

He waved a tired hand, as though trying to wipe away what he'd just said, and knowing he couldn't. "Yeah, yeah," he said. "So what. Anyway, about then—it's nine, nine-thirty, and I'm up to my kneecaps in shit. I'm in charge, right? I'm 'coordinating' all this. And I'm liaising with the PD and the sheriff's office. We got reports coming in from all over. From everywhere. Santa Fe, Pecos, Taos. Denver, for God's sake. I got twenty,

16

thirty guys out there, on foot, in cruisers, in the chopper. And that's just from this office alone."

He took another deep breath. "Okay, so I'm the one makes the first mistake. I lateral the call. Pass it on. And what happens then, the trooper who's supposed to handle it, call up Mrs. Mondragón, he makes the second mistake. He gets sidetracked. The call gets lost."

He frowned. "Okay, so I'm here all night. A shower, some clean clothes this morning, I'm ready to start all over. Superman. But I never check with the trooper. Then the Captain hears about Mrs. Mondragón—before I do—and he's in here reaming me a new asshole."

He shrugged. "Fair enough. I deserve it. But a reaming, that's like a dose of clap. It's something you can spread around. So I track down the trooper and I ream *him* out. He's a good cop, a damned good cop, but he takes it. Just like I took it."

"Who was the trooper?"

He looked at me across the desk with tired eyes. "You wanna talk to the guy who screwed up, you're talking' to him. I'm sorry about what happened, Croft. It makes me sick. If I could go back and fix things, change them around, God knows I would."

"Yeah. I'll tell Mrs. Mondragón."

He took another deep breath, filled up his cheeks, let the air out between puckered lips. "You wanna take a pop at me? A free swing?" He shrugged. "Go ahead. Get your rocks off."

"Tell me about the breakout," I said.

He stared at me for a moment. He glanced down at his watch and looked back up. He shrugged again. "Six guys. We picked up three of them already, all within five miles of the pen. Picked 'em up right away. We'll probably grab the fourth guy sometime today. He's a nothing. A bookend, like the other three. We figure Martinez and Lucero brought 'em all along to act as decoys. Set 'em loose on the ground, to keep us busy, and then took off. They had a car waiting. We figured they used the car to get out of town before the roadblocks went up. Looks like we figured wrong."

"Looks like it," I said. "Who's Lucero?"

"Luiz Lucero. Not a local. From Denver. From Cuba, originally. A Marielito. One of those guys who landed here when Castro was tossing out the garbage. He's a bug."

"How?"

"He's a psycho."

"What's he do for a living?"

"Deals drugs. Pretty big time, up there in Denver."

"So what's he doing in the New Mexico state pen?"

"Shot a guy down in Albuquerque. Once in the forehead. Then once in each eye." He shrugged. "Kind of showy, but I guess it did the job."

"Why?"

"Why show off, or why kill the guy?"

"Why kill the guy."

"Small-time dealer. He stiffed Lucero somehow. That's what the guy's wife said, anyway. But who knows. Maybe Lucero didn't like the guy's suit."

"What are Lucero and Martinez doing together? Martinez is a street guy, a loser. Sounds to me like Lucero's out of his league."

"They were cellmates." He shrugged. "Maybe they were sweethearts of the rodeo."

I nodded. "How'd they manage the breakout?"

He glanced at his watch again. "Lucero had a pistol, a twenty-two automatic. Overpowered one guard. Got to the control center. Picked up some radios—police band—and some flack jackets, and then they went out over the roof."

"There's razor wire up there. That's what the flak jackets were for?"

"Yeah. They flung 'em over the wire. Tied some overalls together and dropped down."

"What about the exterior wire?"

"Cut. Bolt cutters. From the outside." He smiled sourly. "What we call an accomplice."

"Where did Lucero get the gun?"

18

"I got no idea."

"Come on, Hernandez. I've been to the pen. Visitors are frisked beforehand. Meetings are allowed only under observation. Prisoners are body-searched afterward. Someone looked the other way. A guard. Maybe more than one."

He shook his head. "That's a separate investigation. Not my jurisdiction."

"Lucero have a lot of money to toss around?"

"I got no idea."

I let it go. "How much lead time did they have? After the break."

"Not much. Ten, fifteen minutes." He looked down again at his watch, then back up at me. "Speaking of time. Sorry, Croft. I got a few other things to do around here."

"Will you let me know how this is going? The investigation?"

"No," he said. "I'll let you know when we find Martinez and Lucero."

"You people didn't find Martinez before. Six years ago."

"Yeah, you did. And nearly killed him, I heard."

"Not exactly."

"Banged him up some."

"So he said."

"He said it in court. You could've lost your license."

"I'm still here. So's the license."

"Yeah, well—" The telephone rang. Keeping his eye on me, Hernandez answered it. "Yeah. Yeah. Right. You handle it for now. Gimme a few more minutes here."

He hung up the phone. "Forget about it, Croft. This is a state police investigation. No way I'm gonna jeopardize it for your sake."

"It seems to me that you owe—"

He raised a hand. "Don't push it."

"—that you owe something to Mrs. Mondragón. Will you be talking to Hector Ramirez at the Santa Fe PD?"

He looked at me silently for a moment. Then, finally, he nodded. "Yeah. I'll be in touch with Ramirez, probably."

19

I drove back into town, stopping at the first pay phone I could find. I called the hospital. There had been no change in Mrs. Mondragón's condition. She was still in recovery. She was still stable.

I kept moving, using movement to stop myself from thinking and feeling, to keep my body racing ahead of my brain and my heart.

Rosa Sanchez had moved from the barrio on Santa Fe's west side, where she had lived four years ago. The man who now lived in her tiny apartment had no idea where she was, or who she was.

She wasn't listed in the phone book. I tried information. She had no unlisted number. I went to the office, dragged out the Martinez file, and I made some more phone calls. I learned, from a woman who had once been a friend of Rosa's, that Rosa had gotten married about two years ago. To an Anglo, the woman told me, but she didn't know his name. She hadn't seen Rosa for a while, and thought she might have left town. I called a clerk I knew at City Records and she pulled the marriage license. The groom had been a Mr. Robert Theissen. Not a typical Santa Fe name. I flipped through the phone book. A Robert Theissen was listed at 433 Acequia Court. I dialed the number but no one answered.

Rita kept a .38 Smith & Wesson in the office safe. An Airweight, two-inch barrel, shrouded hammer. I unlocked the safe, took out the pistol, checked it, shoved it into my right pocket. Concealed carry is illegal in New Mexico, but I didn't much care.

Before I left the office, I called the hospital again. No change.

Acequia means ditch in Spanish, and the *Acequia Madre,* the mother ditch that once carried water to the farms and households of the hidalgos who lived here, four hundred years ago, still runs through the old and wealthy part of town, in the shade of the cottonwoods and the pines.

There were no ditches on Acequia Court, and no cottonwoods. The street was part of a new development off Airport Road. Crowded onto both sides of it were boxy one- and two-story frame houses disguised to look like adobe. Each was perched on a small square treeless lot of green grass, and each sat no more than twenty feet from its neighbor. Most of the tiny lawns were carefully fenced along the sides with brown planking—marking off private domains amid all that closeness—and most of them were strewn with children's toys: tricycles, bicycles, wagons, tall plastic dinosaurs lying stiffly on their sides.

There were no toys on the lawn at 433 Acequia Court. Someone had taken good care of the grass, which was almost lush, and someone had planted a neat flower garden along the front edge of the house. Crocus and daffodil, tulip and hyacinth, their colors radiant against the shiny green of the ground cover.

I parked in the driveway behind a Ford Taurus and a Chevy pickup, got out of the Jeep, walked up the asphalt. I noticed that the front curtains were drawn shut.

Drawn curtains at midday. Two cars in the driveway, one for Robert, one for Rosa. And no one had answered the phone.

I slid my hand into my right pocket and I rang the doorbell. I waited. Nothing. I tried the doorknob. It was unlocked.

I slipped out the Smith, held it down by my thigh, and gently pushed open the door with my left hand. I stepped in.

Robert Theissen was in the living room. He was lying on the floor, fully clothed, face up. He had been shot once in the forehead, once in each eye.

I found Rosa in the bedroom. She lay naked and spread-eagled along the big bed. They had done the same things to her, but they had played with her first.

21

4

"So who was she?" Hector asked me.

"Her maiden name was Rosa Sanchez. She was the woman who located Martinez for me. Six years ago."

"When you brought him in," he said.

"Yeah."

We were out on the enclosed back porch, both of us sitting on inexpensive aluminum folding chairs webbed with plastic. I had gone through the house, found nothing, walked out to the car, slipped the Smith & Wesson back into the glove compartment. Returned to the house, carefully picked up the phone, and dialed 911. The police had arrived about an hour and a half ago, first a couple of SFPD cruisers, then an unmarked city Ford carrying two detectives, then a pair of unmarked state police Chevrolets carrying state plainclothes people. I had told my story three or four times, and now the state cops and the locals were trying to figure out who had jurisdiction.

I was telling Hector the same story. He had shown up about five minutes ago. The technical people had lifted prints from in here and they had let me roll open the jalousie windows. But the floor out here was an imitation Mexican tile that held the heat of the sun. The air was warm and motionless.

Hector had arrived wearing a jacket but he was back in shirt-sleeves now. The jacket was draped along the back of another piece of aluminum furniture, a frail-looking chaise lounge.

"She was what?" Hector asked me. "Martinez's girlfriend?"

"Yeah. One of them."

22

Like Dr. Berger, Hector looked more tired than he had the first time I'd seen him. There were small bruises now beneath his dark brown eyes. Maybe I just hadn't noticed them before. "Why'd she give him up to you?" he asked me.

"She was angry at him."

"Yeah, but why you? Why not the police?"

"I happened to be around."

"We never knew about her."

"No."

"If we'd known about her now—"

"She'd still be alive? Come on, Hector. If you'd known last night, maybe. If someone had told me about Martinez last night, yeah, maybe I could've told someone about Rosa. And yeah, maybe she'd still be alive now."

Hector's face was expressionless. "Hey," he said. "I was out of town. Remember?"

I took a breath. "Yeah. Sorry." I was saying that a lot lately.

"You could've told me," he said, "about the woman this morning."

"I didn't remember her then. I was a bit preoccupied. I didn't think of her until a couple of hours ago. And once I did, I knew that I could find her as quickly as you people could."

"You came out here hoping that Martinez was still around."

I shook my head. "I wasn't sure that Martinez knew who'd given him up. But it seemed like a good idea to check on her."

"You had to figure that if Martinez knew, he could've still been here."

"He wasn't."

"If he had been, you could've walked into a bullet."

"Martinez is long gone, Hector. Rosa and her husband are room temperature. They've been dead since last night."

"You didn't know that before you showed up. It was a dumb move."

I shrugged. It wasn't the first dumb move I'd ever made, and it wouldn't be the last.

He frowned. "You're not carrying, are you, Josh?"

23

"That would be illegal, Hector."

"Got something in the car? That Smith of yours?"

"That would be legal."

"Yeah." He sat back, frowning again. "Doesn't make much sense, though, does it?"

"What?"

"Hanging around town. Him and the other one. Lucero. Santa Fe was crawling with cops last night, within an hour of the breakout. Cruisers everywhere. Why didn't they leave when they could?"

"He had a score to settle with Rosa. And with Rita."

"Dangerous for him. Stupid. Especially trying for Rita. And that's something else. You're the one who brought him in. Not Rita. Why shoot *her?*"

"I don't know," I said. "Maybe he wanted to go for both of us this morning. And maybe someone showed up. A hiker. A family. Or maybe he shot her this time because he didn't kill her when he shot her before. I don't know. Have you figured out where he fired the rifle?"

He nodded. "Up above Gonzales Road. We found the cartridge casing. Berger was right. It was two-twenty-three. Two pairs of footprints. Not prison shoes—they both found themselves some nice new boots somewhere. We've got casts of the prints. One of them fired the rifle, and then the two of them walked down to Gonzales. Had a car waiting. Nothing on the car yet."

"That's something else to think about."

"The car. Yeah."

"They're getting around too damned easily, Hector. You've got at least three people here—Martinez, Lucero, and whoever cut the perimeter fence at the pen. Like you said, the town is crawling with cops. Why hasn't anyone spotted them?"

He nodded. "Maybe not a car. A van. A utility vehicle."

"Maybe." I stood up. "We done?"

He nodded. "Where you going?"

"Back to the hospital."

"Hey, Rita," I said.

She lay still. Her eyes were shut.

They had moved her to Intensive Care. In the square, sterile room she lay on the pale green sheets looking small and frail and lost. A white bandage covered the top of her head, wires and plastic tubes snaking from beneath it. Another tube ran from her nose. To my left a respirator rasped slowly, in time to the soft rise and fall of her chest. Above her head, a color monitor displayed her vital signs. Heartbeat, brainwaves, the interior pulse and rhythm of her life, the muscular contractions, the spikes of electrical energy, reduced to bright banal lines on a television screen.

There was a sculpted black plastic chair to my right. I picked it up, set it down beside the bed. I sat down on it and leaned toward her, my hands clasped together between my knees.

Only her face and neck were visible. Usually, even in winter, her skin was the color of café au lait. Now it was translucent. I could see a small blue vein throbbing gently at her throat.

"Rita?" I said.

She lay there.

A month before this we had been in California. We had spent a weekend on Catalina, a birthday present to Rita from Ed Norman, the head of a PI agency in L.A. We had become tourists. We had rented a golf cart to explore the narrow streets of Avalon. We had admired an art deco movie theater. We had strolled through a botanical garden. We had ambled along a shingle beach. We had ridden a crowded bus past a small herd of lumpish, impassive buffalo. At night, we sat at a restaurant by the edge of the sea and ate steamed clams and broiled swordfish while we looked out at the cheerful yellow lights of the small yachts lounging in the sleek black harbor.

She had loved all of it. But what she had loved most had been the moonlit ride in the undersea boat. Specially designed, looking from topside like a cartoon submarine, the craft had room for maybe sixty passengers. We sat on tiny, uncomfortable plastic seats along the walls of a metal tube beneath the waterline and peered out through portholes into the sea. Powerful lights from above us, on the deck, shot down through the darkness and showed us the slowly swaying fronds of kelp, the ragged rocks, the drifting golden motes of plankton.

And the fish.

"Look!" Rita had cried, and tugged me over to her porthole. "Joshua, look look *look!* What *is* that?" Her eyes wide, she tapped a finger at the glass.

"That's a shark."

"Oh it is *not!*" she said, and laughed, and thumped her elbow against my arm.

"Okay," I said. "It's a squid."

"It's *not!* Wait! Wait a minute!" She flipped open the thin brochure we'd picked up at the dock. "It's a rock bass! It says so right here."

"Well, Rita," I said, sitting back, "if you'd rather trust some silly brochure than a trained professional investigator, you go ahead. But that's definitely a shark. Or a squid."

She laughed again, and then the laugh became a smile and she slid her arm around my shoulder and leaned closer and she looked into my eyes. "This is fun, isn't it?"

I smiled. "Yeah," I said. "This is fun."

"We should do it more often."

"Fine by me."

Her glance slid away from mine and out the porthole and suddenly her eyes went wide again. "Oh, *look,* Joshua! Look at *that!*"

Now she lay on the small bed, silent and still, hooked up to machines, trapped within herself, her face wan and slack, drained of color and all animation.

"Rita?" I said again.

She lay there. In the background, the respirator wheezed like a rheumy old man.

I spoke to her with a voice that was as near to normal as I could manage. "I've talked to the doctor," I said. "He says you're going to pull through this. I'd appreciate it if you'd do that pretty soon, because I'm not much good at all that computer stuff. Records and things. I'll make a mess of it all."

I sat back against the rigid plastic chair and took a deep breath. "Okay," I said. "Here's the situation. It was probably Ernie Martinez who shot you. The same guy who shot you six years ago. He and five other men broke out of the state pen last night. The state cops picked up three of them already, and according to Hernandez—you remember Hernandez? the state cop?—they'll probably get a fourth guy soon. He's not so sure about Martinez. Martinez is running with a guy named Lucero, a drug dealer out of Denver."

I inhaled. "You remember Rosa Sanchez, Martinez's girlfriend? I told you about her. The one who gave him to me? She got married a couple of years ago. Last night, someone, probably Martinez and Lucero, killed her and her husband. Martinez and Lucero, they've got some way to move around without being spotted. A utility van, maybe. I'll find out. But whatever it is, they used it to get close to your house this morning. They parked it on Gonzales Road, walked up through the trees, and one of them fired at you with a two-twenty-three. Probably Martinez."

I took another deep breath. "Hector can't figure out why Martinez shot you, and not me. There was plenty of time for him to get off another shot. But I think I know why. I think he wants a replay of six years ago. He wants me to come after him again. He wants to pull it off this time, and he thinks he can."

I leaned toward her. "Okay," I said. "I know what you'd tell me, if you could. You'd tell me that I'd be a fool to go after him. And maybe you'd be right. But I can't do anything to help you right now, and this sitting around is driving me crazy. So I've decided to do what he wants. I'm going after him."

I kissed her cheek. "But listen. I'll be fairly smart about it. If they've gone out of state, Martinez and Lucero, I'll need some way to stay in contact with Hector, so he can keep me up to speed on what the cops are doing. On what's happening here in town. And I'll need to stay in contact with the hospital, so these people can let me know when you're okay. I'll talk to Leroy about it. He's outside, along with the rest of your family. You've got cousins I never heard of. Seems like half the town is out there. I gotta tell you, Rita, it's a much better turnout than I would've gotten."

I kissed her again. "Anyway. I don't want you to worry. I'll be okay. And I'll be in touch. I'll call here as often as I can. You just get better. I'll talk to you soon."

I said a few more things, and then I kissed her again, and then I left.

5

WHEN I GOT back to the office, I saw that the red light on my answering machine was blinking. I slumped into the chair and I tapped the Play button.

A message from an insurance claims adjuster, who wanted to know if I was free to check up on a claim he suspected was fraudulent.

A message from a friend who hadn't heard about Rita, asking if I was free for lunch tomorrow.

Some messages from friends who had heard, their voices hesitant, made tight and awkward by worry.

A message from a reporter at *The New Mexican* who wanted to discuss "this awful tragedy." His voice was coated with a smooth sincerity that didn't quite conceal his eagerness.

He had a job to do. But then so did I, and mine didn't include helping him do his.

I opened the desk drawer, tugged out the address book, flipped it open. Found the number I wanted, picked up the phone, dialed it.

At the other end, the phone was answered by a woman who sounded young and well educated. "The Montoya residence."

I said, "May I speak to Mr. Montoya?"

"Who may I say is calling?"

"Joshua Croft."

"One moment, please."

I was put on hold. I swiveled the chair around, away from the desk. I looked up, out the window at the mountains. There was still snow up there, at their tops, startling white beneath the cobalt sweep of sky. Over the next few weeks and months, slowly, it would melt and trickle down the slopes, down the gullies and ravines, down the arroyos, until it joined the swollen brown surge of the Rio Grande and began its tumbling journey toward the faraway Gulf of Mexico.

The world was indifferent. It kept moving on, implacable, flowers growing, leaves sprouting, rivers flowing, no matter how badly you wanted it to stop.

"Mr. Croft?" The gruff, smoky voice of Norman Montoya. "Hello."

"I heard about Mrs. Mondragón. This is a terrible thing. How is she?"

I had met Montoya a couple of years ago, and now I pictured him as he had been then, sitting in an enormous hot tub, before a broad double-glazed window that looked out over a steep spectacular northern New Mexico valley. He was small and hard muscled and he had the profile of a Roman emperor.

"She's in a coma," I told him. "The doctor thinks she'll pull through."

"I am most pleased to learn that. Most pleased. I was in fact going to telephone you when I heard, but I felt that perhaps you would be too involved with other matters to accept an offer of help."

"As a matter of fact," I said, "I'm calling to ask for your help."

"There is no need for you to ask, Mr. Croft. Any assistance I can provide is yours, of course, and with no reservations. I am in your debt. I have not forgotten what you did for my niece."

"How is she?" For a second or two I couldn't remember her name. Then I did—Winona.

"Excellent," he said. "She is excellent. And very happy where she is, I'm pleased to say. She received straight A's on her most recent report card."

Norman Montoya was rumored to be many things—among them, the Godfather of New Mexico—and probably he was everything he was rumored to be. At any other time, the thought

30

of his being so delighted by a young girl's report card might have been charming. But there was nothing in me, just now, that could respond to charm.

As he'd sometimes done in the past, Norman Montoya seemed to read my mind. "Forgive me, Mr. Croft. You have more pressing concerns. How may I help?"

"You know that it was probably Ernie Martinez who shot Mrs. Mondragón this morning?"

"So I understand, yes."

"Martinez was in the pen for six years. There may be someone around town, someone who's out now, who knew him up there. Or someone who knew Lucero, the man Martinez is running with."

"This is quite possible. You would like me to initiate inquiries as to who that someone might be?"

"If you could, yes. I'd like to talk to anyone who knew them. Either one of them, or both. Both would be better, if that's possible."

"Very well. Consider it done. Is there any other way in which I might help?"

"No. Thank you. Not right now."

There was a brief silence. And then: "Mr. Croft?"

"Yeah?"

"May I make a suggestion?"

"Sure."

"I believe that at the moment you are perhaps operating almost entirely from your emotions. You are no doubt very distressed—and understandably so—about what has happened to Mrs. Mondragón. Is that a fair appraisal?"

"That's a fair appraisal, yes."

"Mr. Croft, I commend to you the idea of meditating before you act. The tendency in your situation, particularly for a man such as yourself, a man inclined, I believe, toward action, is to respond physically, and with as much force and speed as he might possess. But I suspect that in this case such a response might prove counterproductive."

31

"Uh huh." Montoya was a Buddhist, and I suppose that this was the kind of advice a Buddhist would give.

"If you can, Mr. Croft, try to find some time to sit quietly by yourself. Experience your thoughts, your emotions. Let them fill you. Examine them quietly. And only then, after you have done so, permit yourself to act."

"Right, Mr. Montoya. Thanks. I'll do that."

"Ah, Mr. Croft," he said. "I can hear the hunger for action in your voice. Well, so be it. But please, let me know if I can assist you in any other way."

"I will. Thanks."

"Where might I be able to reach you?"

"I'll be here at the office for a while," I told him. "Later, I'll probably be at home." I gave him both numbers.

"Very well," he said. "Good-bye, Mr. Croft."

"Good-bye, Mr. Montoya."

While I waited for Leroy to show up, I made some more phone calls. Rita had been working on a couple of assets searches for Ed Norman, and I called him and told him what had happened. He was concerned. He offered to send one of his people to New Mexico to help—he couldn't come himself. I told him it wouldn't be necessary. He asked me if I were going after Martinez. I said that I was. He told me to be careful, and to call him if I needed anything. I said that I'd do both.

I called the claims adjuster and let him know that I couldn't take any new business at the moment. He hadn't heard about Rita, and I didn't tell him. I gave him the name of a local investigator who was good at claims.

Just as I hung up, someone knocked at my door.

"Come in."

Leroy shuffled into the office, carrying a black leather briefcase.

Rita had once said that Leroy could make you rethink your position on evolution, whatever your position might be. Somewhere in his thirties, squat and dark, he moved in a simian crouch, his long arms dangling almost to his knees. His heavy forehead was ridged, his eyes were deeply set, his gaunt jowls were blue with a beard that couldn't be shaved away. He looked like someone who swung on vines, yet he knew more about electronics than most of the engineers at Sony.

He was wearing what he'd worn when I'd talked to him at the hospital, khaki work pants tucked into black motorcycle boots, a silk Hawaiian shirt printed with green palm trees and pink flamingos. He seemed as stricken now as he had seemed then.

"Hey, Leroy," I said. "Grab a seat."

He sat down in one of the client chairs and lay the briefcase along his lap. Sitting back, holding onto the case as though it were a life preserver, he shook his head. "This is a bitch, man. This is really a bitch."

"How's the rest of the family doing?"

"Okay, I guess. I dunno. Most of them, you know, they haven't been, like, real close to Rita for a couple years. Since William died. They couldn't handle the idea of her running the agency, a detective agency, a woman and all, you know? They're like real traditional people, mostly. Women should stay in the house and cook and all. But they're hurting now, man. They're seriously hurting." He frowned. "She looks pretty bad, doesn't she?" He shook his head again, remembering. "Jesus, I felt so bad for her. Useless. Helpless, you know?"

I knew. "The doctor thinks she'll be all right," I told him.

He raised his head and nodded. "Right, man, right. And he's like one of the top guys in the world, I hear. He should know, right? If anyone does. Right?"

"Right." I nodded toward the briefcase. "What've you got for me?"

He drew the briefcase toward himself, protectively. "You're going after the guy, right? The guy who did it?"

"Yeah."

"You gotta promise me something."

33

"What?"

"You gotta promise me, man, you find him, you give me a call. I want to be there when it happens. I wanna help you bring him down."

"I can't promise that, Leroy. I don't know where I'll be. I don't know what the situation will be."

He set his mouth in a thin line. "No, man. No way. You got to promise."

"I can't," I said. "But I can promise you this. I'll find him. And I'll find him with your help or without it. But with it, maybe, I might be able to find him a little bit faster."

It was manipulative and it was callous. But like a lot of behavior that was manipulative and callous, it worked. He stared at me for a moment and then he looked away, his shoulders slumping in defeat. "Shit," he said.

"What've you got, Leroy?" I asked him.

He looked back at me. He nodded. "Okay." He lifted the briefcase, set its bottom along his thighs and unzipped its top. He peered inside the case, reached in, pulled out a small cellular phone. "You said you wanted to keep in touch. This is top of the line, man. Cutting edge. Weighs three point nine ounces. The battery that's in here now, you got eight hours standby time, one hour talk time. Another battery in the case, gives you three hours talk time. You can recharge 'em both from the AC or the cigarette lighter in your car. You don't want the phone to ring, you flip a switch and it vibrates instead. Case you're in a situation where you want to keep things quiet, right?"

I nodded.

"Okay," he said. "See this?" He pointed to the bottom of the phone. "That's where you hook up the computer."

"What computer?"

"This one, man." He lifted the case, stood up, walked to the desk, put down the case, unzipped it down along the sides. "Okay. Here's the computer. Pentium chip, one hundred thirty-three megahertz. Thirty-two megs of RAM. Gigabyte hard disk. Active matrix screen. Right here, that's your PC slot, and what's inside there is a cellular fax/modem. Rated at fourteen thousand baud, but it's more reliable at ninety-six hundred. It works on landlines, too." He turned to me. "You understand what I'm saying here?"

"No. Sorry. Listen, Leroy, I don't need all this."

He gave me a pained look. "Hey, man. You don't know what this stuff is, how can you know you need it or not?" He took a deep breath, drawing in patience with the oxygen. "Okay, look. Say someone wants to send you a photo, right? Of a suspect, right? A contact, whatever. I dunno, doesn't matter. They get to a fax machine, they call your number. You hook the computer to the phone, you receive the fax, you print it out with this. That's your printer. Thermal. Weighs less than a pound. Take you about a minute to print out a fax."

"Fine. What's this?"

"Portable scanner, man. Three hundred dpi. You use that when you want to fax something to someone. And all this stuff, everything, works off rechargeable batteries. Like with the phone. It's all connected to the same line. For the AC outlet, you use this plug. This one's for the cigarette lighter. Whole thing only weighs twelve pounds. But part of that's the case. It's padded—see?—and it's lined with Kevlar. You know what they use Kevlar for?"

"Bulletproof vests. Leroy, I really don't think—"

"Shit, man. This is Rita we're talking about, remember? Even if you think you don't need it, man, you take it anyway, you hear me? Just in case. You don't want to be in a situation, you need it but you don't have it."

I nodded. "Yeah. Show me how it all works."

6

I SPENT A couple of hours with Leroy at the office, learning how to operate the equipment. The phone rang five or six times, but I let the machine answer it. I listened as it did, and none of the calls came from Norman Montoya. I didn't want to talk to anyone else, and I didn't.

Before Leroy and I left, I called the hospital again. No change.

I reached home at about five o'clock in the afternoon. There were more messages waiting for me on the answering machine here, so I played through the tape. No calls from Norman Montoya.

I found a leather carryall and I packed it with clothes. I took my own Smith & Wesson from the shoebox in the closet. I unloaded it, cleaned it, oiled it, wiped it dry, reloaded it, wound a sheet of Glad Wrap around it, stuck it in the carryall.

For a few minutes I just sat there on the living room sofa, as Norman Montoya had suggested, and I examined my thoughts and my emotions. But I didn't much like them, so I put on a jacket and went outside to the Jeep and climbed in.

I couldn't sit by myself, but I couldn't sit with anyone else, and especially not with anyone I knew, so I drove south on St. Francis Drive, away from the center of town. The sun was setting, the blue was fading overhead. There were more cop cars than usual on the road, prowling like sharks between the other vehicles. Off in the distance, high up, the state police helicopter was slowly quartering the sky, still searching for needles in the barren haystack of scrubland to the west of the penitentiary.

I started drinking at Fox's, on St. Michael's. It was a new place, built only a few years ago, but it had the feel of an old neighborhood tavern. Low ceilings, neon beer signs, dark walls. Everyone knew everyone else, and no one knew me, and just then that was exactly what I wanted. Men in blue collars and men in white collars, women in denim and women in raw silk, sat and stood and nestled at the bar, prolonging that sweet empty space between their escape from work and their return to home, between one reality and another. Rita once told me that the Aztecs spent five days a year very carefully doing nothing while they waited for the lunar calendar to realign itself with the solar calendar. It was a time out of time, a period when chronology stopped. We have the cocktail hour.

I found a thin slice of unoccupied bar near the end, two women in suits on my right, two men in suits on my left, and I ordered a Jack Daniel's on the rocks. The air smelled of perfume hastily applied, and of beer and tobacco smoke. No one in here had read the warning label on their cigarette packs, or seemed likely to.

That first drink went down well, and quickly, and I ordered a second. I told myself that the alcohol wasn't having any effect, but it was, because with the second drink the bar lights grew brighter and more intense, the background rumble of conversation grew louder and more distinct and I could make out some of its individual elements.

Everyone was talking about the prison break. For the two women on my right it provided an opportunity to express fears that in some women, maybe in all women, swim beneath the surface of their feelings for men, fears of assault and of sudden violence, overpowering and deadly. "I heard it on the radio," said one of them, a slender Hispanic. "They raped her before they killed her. And it only happened a few miles from here, out near Airport Road. They could be *anywhere* now."

It seemed to me that she said this with a certain amount of

relish, as though a perverse pleasure secretly shivered beneath her concern. In the mirror over the bar, the thin attractive face beneath the shiny black bangs was narrowed with worry, but her large brown eyes were bright.

For the two men on my left, the prison break provided an opportunity for them to explain how much more efficiently the world would operate if they were in charge of it. "Fry 'em all," said one of them. "Slap 'em in the chair and turn on the juice." There was no doubt about the relish in his voice.

He was facing me as he talked, a tall fleshy man in his mid-forties with razor-cut thick blond hair artfully coiffed back from a shiny red face. Powder blue linen shirt snug against the round comfortable belly, silk Countess Mara tie loosened at the neck to signal that his exceedingly important business day had ended and that he was once again a regular guy.

Something else Rita had once said: all overheard conversations sound inane, because we have nothing invested in them.

He noticed me watching him and he raised his chin slightly and held my stare. Which left me three choices. Look away, join the conversation, or keep staring until something happened, probably something physical. I looked away.

He took that as a ratification of his position, and he said, more loudly, "Burn 'em like the fuckin' animals they are. Am I right, Johnny?"

Johnny thought so, energetically.

I felt a sudden surge of fury, partly because I'd looked away, and partly because at that moment I agreed with him, and he wasn't someone I would ever want to agree with. I swallowed my pride and my anger with the rest of my drink, tossed a couple of singles to the bar, and I left.

I drove for a while, going nowhere in particular. Evening was settling around the town. Off to the west, beyond the low rolling ridges of the Jemez range, flat bands of cloud were aglow with pastel reds and yellows, the colors beginning to fade now into the cinder gray they would become. To the east, where the mountains were nearer and higher, the sky had deepened to a dark glossy purple.

Cerrillos Road was packed with cars as I headed north, everyone in a hurry to get somewhere. More police cruisers glided among them, the men inside watchful and alert.

I cut onto St. Francis, slipped off it at Agua Fria, followed that for a few blocks, then turned right on La Madera, toward the river. This was one of Santa Fe's Hispanic neighborhoods, and the houses were mostly frame, all of them neat and trim beneath carefully cropped trees. Their windows were lit up, giving me brief vignettes through lace curtains of busy kitchens, cozy dining rooms, snug living rooms blue with the electric glow of the television.

I turned left at Alto, drove past the house where Sally Durrell, a lawyer friend, had once lived, a tiny adobe crouched behind a low adobe wall. Turned right on Camino Alire, right again on Alameda, followed that to Guadalupe, turned left. Turned right on San Francisco, up the gentle incline into the Plaza. It was early in the evening still and there were very few pedestrians on the streets.

In the darkness, the Plaza looked not much different now than it had looked fifteen years ago, when I first saw it. A dark square of grass, a few broad trees rising above it, their leaves billowing from black to green in the yellow glare of the street lamps. But in those days, the shops facing the Plaza had been family businesses, bookstores, pharmacies, restaurants. Since then, most of the commercial buildings had been gutted and converted into mini-malls crammed with slick little shops that sold overpriced Navajo jewelry and beaded buckskin jackets, blue corn pancakes and jalapeño sorbet.

I hooked a left at the floodlit brown facade of Bishop Lamy's cathedral, hooked a right at Palace Avenue, drove past the compound where my office was located, and I hooked another left onto Paseo De Peralta. I made the right at Marcy, swung back onto Hillside, and eased the Jeep into a parking space at the base of the hill. I got out of the car, locked it, and walked along Paseo to the stairway entrance. There was no sidewalk on this side of the road, and a car honked, loudly and insistently, as it swerved around me. I ignored it.

Fifteen years ago, when I first climbed the hill, on a quick visit to Santa Fe, the path had been uneven, hard-packed dirt, and it had been lighted only by the moon. Now it was notched into the slope with cement and brick, the mass of the hillside held back by a restraining wall of stacked flagstone. Sconces set along the wall illuminated the brickwork, and tall metal lamps drew pale ocher circles upon the landings where the path switched back on itself as it rose.

There was no one at the top when I got there. A wind was picking up from the north.

Before me stood the towering white Cross of the Martyrs. It was a memorial to the Franciscan priests who had been killed throughout New Mexico's Indian pueblos during the seventeenth century. There were quite a few names on the plaque at its base, representing quite a few deaths that stretched over quite a few years. Neither the priests nor the Indians had ever learned anything from their encounters. There were times, like tonight, when I wondered whether anyone ever did.

I turned away from the cross and looked out. Up here, I stood above the entire town. I could see the walls of The Round House, our state capitol building, beaming brightly about a half a mile away. I remembered what a friend had once told me: that they kept the capitol lit at night so the politicians wouldn't sneak back in and steal the furniture.

A bit farther out, I could see the thin, brilliant necklace of streetlights strung along St. Francis Drive. Still farther out, beyond the radiance of the buildings and the darkness of the trees, I could see the finely etched line of the Interstate, where a narrow rivulet of faraway headlights flowed inexorably toward Santa Fe, sliding down that long gradual slope from the top of La Bajada Hill.

Back then, fifteen years ago when I'd first stood here, the town

40

had been a small cluster of lights clinging to the hem of a huge sheet of blackness flung out to the ragged horizon, a blackness broken only here and there by the tiny light of an isolated house bravely gleaming in the distance, like a solitary star. Now, from east to west, left and right as far as I could see, out to the line where the earth met the graying sky, a gaudy Milky Way covered the land.

And every day new houses were being built, new people were flowing into town—Texans, Californians, New Yorkers, all of them hungry for their slice of the stylish Santa Fe pie.

The world keeps moving on. Flowers growing, rivers flowing, people multiplying.

Back then, on that first visit to Santa Fe, seven years before I actually moved here, I had climbed up this hill to get some sense of the town, its layout, its physical reality. I suppose I thought that I might, by understanding its geography, somehow understand its spirit. It hadn't worked.

Tonight, maybe, I'd come up here to get some sense of my connection to the place, to this beautiful and tawdry town in the high desert that over the centuries had been home to American Indians, Spanish hidalgos, French trappers, Union soldiers, railroad men, politicians, cowboys, whores, gamblers, gunfighters, artists, writers, speculators, spies, flower children, junkies, remittance men, movie stars, private detectives, real estate agents, crystal gazers, tarot readers, fakirs and fakers, hustlers and grifters and drifters of every persuasion, and even the occasional saint.

And this hadn't worked, either. I felt removed from it all, from the town's past and from its present, from the people who lived in it and from everything they did, and everything they had done. I felt remote and adrift, more a part of the darkness that surrounded the place than a part of the glittering, relentlessly cheerful lights that made it up.

I didn't stay up there for very long. The wind was growing colder. And I was having trouble breathing again.

★　★　★

41

I did some serious drinking. I ran the Cherokee over to the lot on Water Street, parked it, called the hospital from a pay phone, learned there had been no change, and then hit a couple of nearby bars, places I'd never been to before. Despite the early hour, despite this being a Wednesday, in both bars the smoky air was dense with the buzz and clatter of wall-to-wall people. Most of the people looked maybe twelve years old, their faces bright and mobile and hopelessly unguarded. But they moved with assurance and grace, and they laughed heartily, and they spoke with conviction, and already they had apartments and jobs and serious long-range financial goals. They were getting good at impersonating grown-ups. Soon, like the rest of us, they would forget that it was only an impersonation.

No one was talking about the prison break and the dangers it might represent. Despite their grown-up postures, and impostures, these people were still immortal, and danger of any sort was irrelevant.

I don't remember how much I drank. I thought about Rita. I thought about Rosa and her husband, Robert. I thought about Ernie Martinez. Sitting there at the bar amid the warmth and the crush of young bodies, I grew slowly more remote and adrift, and more bitter. By the time I returned to the car, I was surly. I was also staggering. I shouldn't have driven, but I did. When I reached home, the telephone was ringing. It was Norman Montoya, calling to tell me that he'd located someone who had known Ernie Martinez and Luiz Lucero in the state pen.

7

FROM DEEP UNDERWATER I could hear a distant beckoning chime. The sound insinuated itself around my body, a thin glistening wire, and slowly it grew taut. I couldn't see the faraway surface, but I knew that it shimmered up there like quicksilver, bright and blinding and lethal. I burrowed deeper into the sand, sliding my hands into it, against the grains of it, clutching, squeezing. The chime pulled at me, tugged at me, then abruptly it jerked me loose. Pale yellow sand drifted from the tips of my fingers like clouds of falling stars as I rose upward, slowly, relentlessly.

I opened my eyes and I pushed myself off the bed. Groggy, I fumbled my robe from the dresser and fought my way into it.

I didn't have a hangover. I had drunk so much the night before that my body hadn't had a chance to burn off the alcohol. I was still drunk, and I was feeble and dizzy with it.

I shuffled through the living room to the front door, peered through the peephole, and pulled open the door.

Jimmy McBride looked me up and down and his narrow features went concerned and he said, "Hey, Mr. Croft. I can come back. You want me to come back?"

"No," I told him. "I want you to come in."

I stood aside to let him pass and I closed the door.

McBride stood in the center of the room, looking around, nodding at everything with an admiration that needed a little more practice. "Real nice place you got here. Very livable, you know?"

"Yeah. Sit down."

He sat on the sofa, a small skinny man in stained and wrinkled blue work pants and a wrinkled blue work shirt with an oil company logo on the pocket. His forehead was balding, thin wisps of hair above the shiny scalp forming a spidery outline of his former pompadour, like an afterimage. The genes that had stripped the hair from his head had grown a fine thick crop everywhere else. A single long eyebrow furred the ridge above his close-set brown eyes and his large irregular nose. Stubble darkened his hollow cheeks and his receding chin. A thick black pelt curled up his knobby Adam's apple and spilled over the limp neckband of his gray T-shirt.

He had been sent to prison for beating his three-year-old daughter so badly that he nearly killed her. It hadn't been the first time he'd beaten her. I had met him once or twice, before he went up, and I knew that he wouldn't have come here if he hadn't been frightened into it.

"It's a real shame," he said, "about what happened to Mrs. Mondragón." He was sitting forward on the sofa, his thin forearms on his thighs, his hands clasped tightly together. The bony wrist of his left hand was circled by an expandable gold-plated watch band. Coils of black hair were trapped between the tiny golden slats. "It's terrible," he said, and he shook his head.

I nodded. "I'll be right back," I told him.

I padded across the carpet, down the hallway into the bathroom. I stood at the sink and threw some cold water on my face, cupped my hands and sucked some up. I toweled myself dry and stared at the mirror. Gray pouches of flesh sagged against my cheekbones, bright red blood vessels forked through the whites of my eyes. I needed some coffee, but it would have to wait. Fear had herded McBride into my living room, and this wasn't the time for me to play Mother Hubbard.

McBride had eased back onto the sofa, but he sat upright when I returned to the room. I sat in the chair opposite him. "Okay," I said. "What've you got?"

He leaned forward, confidentially. "Well, see, Mr. Croft, what

I was told, I was told you'd slip me a little something—you know, a consideration—if I came through for you. Which I plan to do, naturally."

"A consideration."

He nodded seriously. "Yeah, right, that's what I was led to believe, yeah."

"You were misinformed," I said.

He stared at me blankly for a moment, then he raised his head slightly. "Come on now, Mr. Croft," he said, his voice thin and wheedling. "You gotta understand my position in this thing. I took time off from work to get over here. I'm supposed to punch in at nine. I got a good job now—over at the Texaco, on Cerrillos?—and my paycheck's gonna get docked."

That voice of his was squeaking along the edge of my nerves like a Magic Marker on cardboard. I said, "You were told to come here and cooperate. By someone connected to Norman Montoya. You want me to put out the word that you didn't cooperate?"

"Hey," he said, and raised his hands to show me his palms. They were pale and surprisingly clean. "I'm here, right? I'm cooperating, right? You can't say I'm not cooperating, Mr. Croft."

"I haven't heard anything so far."

"I only just got here, just now. But I'm absolutely ready to go with this, you know?"

"So go."

"Right," he said. "Sure." He slapped his breast pocket, took out a crumpled pack of Viceroys. "You mind if I smoke?"

"I don't care if you burn to a crisp."

"Right," he said, and smiled weakly. He looked around the room for an ashtray.

"On the table," I told him. I hadn't smoked for years, but I had friends who still did.

"Right, yeah, thanks." He stuck the cigarette in his mouth, pulled a chrome-plated Zippo from his right pocket. He flashed his left hand over the top of the lighter, slapping it open, and then flashed the hand back again, smacking the striker. He leaned forward and dipped the tip of the cigarette into the flame, puffed smoke from the side of his mouth, sat back, flicked his wrist to snap the lighter shut, slipped it into his pocket again. In Jimmy's circles, a routine like that was probably a valuable social skill.

He exhaled a blue plume of smoke. "Okay," he said. "What is it, exactly, you want to know, Mr. Croft?"

"How well did you know Martinez and Lucero?"

He shrugged his thin shoulders. "Well, you know how it is. In the joint, I mean. Everybody knows everybody else, right? It's one of those closed societies, you know? And Lucero now, well, shit, everybody knew who he was. He was famous, you know? Big-time drug dealer, lots of cash on hand, plenty of pull, and the way he killed that guy down in Albuquerque—you heard about that?"

"Yeah."

"Shooting him in the eyes." He shook his head with something that was supposed to look like dismay but may have been envy. "But he's got a set of balls on him, you got to give him that. A real set of balls." He heard himself, and backtracked. "But basically, you know, he's one of those psychopaths. No regard for human life, you know what I mean? Like that Hannibal Lecter guy. In the movie?"

"Was Lucero dealing drugs up there?"

He shrugged again. "Sure. I mean, not directly, not his own self. He had guys, you know, did it for him. Associates."

"How was he getting the stuff in?"

He held up his right palm, like a traffic cop, and his expression became infinitely sorrowful. "See, Mr. Croft, this is where things could maybe get complicated, you know? Maybe right here is where we come up against a brick wall. I mean, I tell you what I know, and maybe Lucero finds out about it, down the road, you know, and life could get kind of rough for me all of a sudden."

I smiled. "It could get kind of rough for you right now."

"Right, right. Sure, Mr. Croft, I know you're not the kind of guy to fool around with. But that's the point I'm tryna make here, exactly. I appreciate your position, I really do. The thing is, you gotta appreciate mine. I got to balance my priorities. I got to make sure I'm making a decision that's not detrimental in the long run, you know? For yours truly."

I nodded. "Let me see if I can clarify your priorities for you, Jimmy. My partner is lying in a coma in a hospital room. I'm very unhappy about that. I'm going after Martinez and Lucero. If you don't tell me what I want to know, I'll pound the shit out of you." I shrugged. "How's that?"

He held up both hands now. "Hey now, Mr. Croft. There's no need for that kind of talk at all. I came here of my own free will. All I'm tryna do is establish—"

Maybe it wouldn't have happened if I hadn't been surly and impatient, and sodden with last night's liquor. Or if Rita hadn't been in the hospital.

I stood up. He was out of the chair before I'd taken two steps, but there really wasn't anywhere for him to go. He flailed his hands at me spastically, like a child, when I grabbed the front of his shirt. I pivoted on my left heel, swung him as hard as I could toward the south wall, where he wouldn't break anything, and let go. He yelped as he sailed backward, his eyes wide, his arms pinwheeling. His shoulders smacked hard against the wall, and then his head did, and he gasped. I came toward him.

His body was crouched away from me and his hands were up again, pushing frantically at the air. "Hey hey *hey!* Okay *okay!*"

My heart was thumping against my ribs. My palms were damp. Adrenaline overload. I took a breath, tightened the belt of my robe, jerked my head toward the sofa. "Sit down, Jimmy."

I stalked back to the chair, feeling extremely proud of myself.

He was close to being subhuman. If I were smaller and weaker, if I were a three-year-old girl, he would have had no compunctions about using violence on me. He understood violence. It was a form of currency for him. Probably he was a scrupulous debtor, and he had spent most of his life trying to pay back the violence he had been paid. Probably he hadn't succeeded, and probably he never would.

47

But I outweighed him by as much as he outweighed his daughter. My brutalizing him wasn't all that different from his brutalizing her, and it had left me feeling sickened and soiled.

And I knew that I had just enlarged the size of his personal debt.

He was sitting forward on the sofa, looking aggrieved, wincing as he ran his hand along the back of his scalp.

I sat down, crossed my legs. "How did Lucero get the drugs into the pen?"

He was still stroking the back of his head. He winced again. "Jeeze, Mr. Croft, you don't have—"

"Jimmy?"

Once more, quickly, he held up the hand. "Okay, okay." He looked down, frowned, whisked the hand down the rumpled front of his shirt, flattening it. He sighed with elaborate hopelessness. He had been backed into a corner. He was always being backed into corners, left with no choices. By events. By people like me. People like his daughter.

"Okay," he said. "There's a guy in the joint. Miller. Ronny Miller. Doing a nickel for B and E. He's got this sister. Sylvia. She's the one who brought it in."

"How?"

"Visitation. Once a week."

"Balloons?" A female mule carried the balloon into the prison concealed in her vagina, transferred it to her mouth, passed the balloon over when she kissed the prisoner. The prisoner swallowed it and retrieved it later. Disregarding the possibility of being caught, which was minimal in a busy prison, it was still a dangerous practice. Balloons can break.

"At first," McBride said. "What I heard, I heard that later she passed it by hand. Lucero paid off the guards."

"What was she moving?"

"Coke, mostly. Some smack."

"Why? To help her brother?"

"Nah." He said this as though no one, anywhere, would want to help a brother. "She's got the hots for Lucero."

48

"How does she know Lucero?"

"She doesn't, see, that's the thing. She never even met him, in actual fact." He became almost professorial as he explained it. "She's one of those straight chicks you read about, they get turned on by hard guys, you know? They get infatuated. She went to his trial every goddam day, I heard. Drove in all the way from Las Vegas." He shook his head in contempt, and the contempt seemed real. "Women, right? Who can figure?"

"The cops must know about her."

"No, see, that's where Lucero was smart." He had forgotten that we weren't friends. He leaned forward again, so he and I could better share the moment. "She gets word to her brother, Ronny, see, that she wants to meet him. Lucero, I mean. So Ronny tells Lucero, but Lucero, he comes up with this better idea. She moves the dope for him, and he gets together with her later. After he gets out."

"And she went along with that."

"Like I said. She was infatuated."

"How did Lucero know he could trust her?"

He shrugged. "He started small, is what I heard. A joint or two. Some hash. Then he moved her up to coke."

"And Sylvia could've given Ronny the gun Lucero used in the break."

He sat back and he shrugged again. "Sure," he said with a conviction that was casual but absolute. "Had to go down that way, I figure."

"How old is she?"

"Forty-something. Not bad looking. If you like the librarian type."

"What type is that?"

"You know. Kind of dried up and stiff."

"What color hair?"

"Brown. That mousey brown. You know."

"What kind of build?"

"Skinny."

I nodded. "You said Las Vegas. New Mexico or Nevada?"

49

He made a face. "Come on, Mr. Croft. Even a crazy chick, she's not gonna drive every day all the way from Nevada."

I nodded. "Her last name is Miller?"

"Yeah."

"All right. Lucero and Martinez were buddies up there."

"Right, yeah. They had the same cell."

"Were they more than buddies?"

"Was one of 'em punking, you mean? Nah. These are tough guys, both of them."

"What kind of visitors did they get?"

"No kind. Nobody."

I spent some time asking him some more questions, but he didn't have anything else.

I stood up. "All right, Jimmy. You can go now."

He rubbed at the back of his head again, to remind me that we were connected now. "Jeeze, Mr. Croft, you don't think you could maybe come through with a little something? For my troubles, you know?"

He had lived long enough to know that other people sometimes felt guilt, and now he was playing me, manipulating mine. My understanding it didn't prevent it from working.

"Wait here," I told him.

I went down the hallway into the bedroom, found my pants, dug out my wallet, slipped loose a twenty. He was standing up when I returned. I handed him the bill.

He looked at me. "Only a twenny?"

"You don't want it, Jimmy, you can always give it back."

"No no, I'll take it." He slid it into his pocket before I could change my mind. He studied me for a moment, an amateur anthropologist examining an alien species. "You're really gonna go after Lucero and Martinez, huh?"

"Yeah."

He shrugged. "Well, okay, it's your funeral, I guess. But I'll tell you something. And this is for free, Mr. Croft. You better be real careful. Martinez is one bad motherfucker. You already know that, I guess. And I guess you know he's got a hard-on for you. But that Lucero, he's something else. He's one of those psychopaths for real. He is one very spooky guy. You talk to him and he keeps changing on you. He does impersonations and stuff. Like that Jim Carrey guy, in the movies."

"I don't think Jim Carrey's all that spooky."

"Yeah, well, Jim Carrey, he won't pull out a gun and shoot you in the eyes. Lucero will, and he won't even think twice about it. He'll be having a good time. So the two of 'em together, Martinez and Lucero, they could cause you some real hurt." Running through the melodrama in his voice I thought I could hear a faint thread of vengeful hope.

8

AFTER MCBRIDE LEFT I called the hospital. Rita was still unconscious.

I dialed New Mexico information and got a phone number and an address for Sylvia Miller in Las Vegas. There were no other Millers listed at that address, so presumably Sylvia lived alone.

I tried the number. No answer.

I made some coffee, took a shower, realized I hadn't eaten anything for twenty-four hours, and put together a sandwich. It went down like raw cotton and turned to lead in my stomach. I washed it down with a glass of milk, thick and chalky.

I kept an emergency stash under a loose floorboard in the bedroom, hundred-dollar bills, ten of them, that I hadn't touched for almost a year. I scooped them up, slipped them into my wallet. I lugged the carryall and the computer out to the Jeep, stowed them behind the front seat, went back to the house and shut down the gas and the hot-water heater. I called the phone company and arranged for all the office phone calls to be forwarded to the cellular in Leroy's briefcase.

Chuck's Garage sat back from the roadway on West Alameda, not far from Siler, a low building walled with metal siding painted a sickly yellow. Beyond a chain-link fence, a small herd of aging automobiles slept in the forecourt, most of them blotched with primer, a few sagging to the side as though mortally wounded.

The door to the garage was open and Chuck was in there, standing beneath an ancient Chevy truck perched high on the pneumatic lift. There was a smell of motor oil and old metal, but the cement floor was spotless.

He turned when he heard my footsteps. "Joshua. Haven't seen you for a while. How's it going?"

"Fine. You?"

"Can't complain. What brings you by?"

"I could use some help."

He glanced past me, at the Jeep. "Not running right?"

"Not that kind of help."

He nodded. He wore dark blue cotton coveralls and he was an inch or so taller than I was. He had deep-set dark brown eyes beneath a wide craggy forehead. His long hair was black, pulled back in a ponytail, and he wore a black beard that left his long upper lip bare, like a Mennonite. It made him resemble a young, handsome version of Abraham Lincoln.

"What do you need?" he asked me.

"Something clean and reliable."

He nodded again. "I heard Mrs. Mondragón got shot."

"That's right."

" 'Kay," he said. "Let's see what I got."

He pulled a pale blue rag from his back pocket, used it to wipe his hands, tossed it to a metal workbench. I followed him to a door set in the east wall of the garage, waited while he found the right key on his key chain. He opened the door, leaned into the room to pull the string for the overhead light, then stood back and gestured me forward. He trailed behind me, pulling the door shut as he entered.

It was an office, cramped and windowless. To the left, at one narrow end of the room, sat a gray metal desk. To the right was a narrow wall that held only a Michelin calendar. Chuck went toward this, pushed gently against its side. The wall swung open, and behind it was another wall, this one made of Peg-Board, and hooked on each of the pegs was the trigger guard of a handgun. There were twenty or thirty of them, and most of them were semiautomatics. Lying along the base of the wall were a Ruger .223 carbine and a black Mossberg shotgun with a plastic stock and an extended cartridge tube.

"I got a forty-caliber Smith," he said. "Brand new, very nice. More stopping power than a nine mil. Lot of your cops these days, that's what they're carrying."

"Ten-round clip?"

"That's the law now. Courtesy of those assholes in Washington. Your tax dollars at work." I didn't know Chuck well, but I'd always suspected that politically he stood somewhere between Pat Buchanan and Jesse James.

"You want more firepower," he said, "I got this Beretta." He lifted it from its peg. "Model Ninety-two-eff. Almost cherry. Got a pre-Carter clip—fifteen rounds. Sixteen pellets in the piece if you keep one up the spout." He handed me the pistol.

It was heavy, and it would be heavier when it held fifteen or sixteen cartridges. But it wasn't so heavy that I couldn't carry it.

"Cock it," he suggested.

I worked the slide. The action was flawless.

"It's okay to dry fire it," he said.

Holding the gun so its barrel pointed toward the wall, I pulled the trigger. Snap.

"Smooth as silk," he said. "Double-action. Spring-loaded safety. Reversible mag release. A very tasty piece of equipment."

"Spare clip? Ammunition?"

"Sure. You want Glasers?" Glasers were cartridges with slugs that blew apart on impact.

"No," I said.

He smiled. "Oh yeah. I forgot. You're a liberal."

"How much?" I asked him.

"For anyone else, six. But I owe you, so I'll make it five. Including the ammo. Bring it back in good shape and I'll buy it off you for three-fifty."

I smiled. "Only three-fifty?"

"Gotta replace the barrel." In case I had left any slugs lying around—in someone's stomach, for example—that a ballistic test might match with the barrel the gun now held.

I asked him, "Is it sighted in?"

"Sure. For standard nine-mil ammo. But I'd play with it before I used it."

"How much for the shotgun?"

"Three."

"You have any shells?"

"Double ought and deer slugs."

"I'll take the shotgun, too. And a box of each."

At both entrances to the Interstate, one opening onto the north and one to the south, there was a line of cars nearly fifty yards long. Here at the northern entrance, two State Police cruisers had been angled across the roadway to permit only one vehicle through at a time. Two troopers leaned against the side of one of the cruisers, arms crossed over their chests, while two others waved the cars up, stopped them, spoke with the drivers, and checked inside the trunks.

When it was my turn, the trooper tipped the brim of his Smokey the Bear hat at me. "License and registration, please, sir." I knew a few state cops, but I didn't recognize this one. I didn't recognize the other trooper, either, the one who strolled around to the back of the Cherokee, hand on the butt of his Glock, and peered in the tailgate window.

The shotgun and the boxes of shells were under the rear passenger seat, the Beretta was under the front passenger's, Rita's .38 was in the glove compartment. But these two weren't looking for guns.

I handed over the papers. The first trooper glanced through them, glanced at me to make sure I matched the photo on the license, then handed them back. "Thank you, sir. Sorry for the delay."

"No problem." I drove off.

It didn't seem possible that Lucero and Martinez had gotten through roadblocks like these. But it didn't seem possible that they had run around Santa Fe, from the penitentiary to Airport Road to Rita's house. And they had.

PART TWO

9

AFTER LEAVING SANTA Fe, I-25 heads southeast for a while, looping through the foothills of the Sangre de Cristos before it gradually swings toward the north and Las Vegas. Up there the mountains are on the left—the easternmost slopes of the Rockies, only rolling ridges nearby, speckled with piñon and juniper, but growing larger and darker and more massive off in the blue distance. To the right is prairie, the Great American Plains, looking as flat as a plate but slowly descending off to the east as far as the eye can see, and a lot farther, down through the Texas panhandle, through Oklahoma and Arkansas, all the way to the Mississippi River.

The weather was clear again, the sky was the color of turquoise. The road was nearly empty. I passed the turnoff for Lamy and Eldorado, passed the turnoffs for Glorieta and Pecos, but I really wasn't paying attention. Out of habit, partly, and partly out of hope, I kept playing in my head the conversation I might have had with Rita.

"It seems to me," I told her, "that the way to find Martinez and Lucero is to find whoever brought in the drugs. And that's Sylvia Miller. If she brought in drugs, she could've brought in a gun. And she could've been the accomplice who cut the perimeter wires at the pen."

"If she brought in the drugs," said Rita. "You have only Jimmy McBride's word for that."

I pictured us sitting out on the patio at her house, the sun shining, the air warm. She was wearing a long white cotton skirt and a silk blouse that matched the sky. At her throat was a small golden cross that some-

59

times caught the light and flashed at me like a tiny beacon. No one had fired a rifle at this Rita, and no one ever would.

"I think McBride was telling the truth," I said. "He was pretty motivated at the time."

She raised an eyebrow. "Oh? What provided the motivation, exactly?"

"I leaned on him a little."

"That must have been very rewarding for you."

"No. Not very."

She nodded. "Do the police know about Miller?"

"I don't think so. Jimmy McBride says not."

"And Jimmy McBride was motivated."

"Yeah. It doesn't matter whether they know, Rita. If they do know, they won't be telling me. The only option I have is go ahead with what I've got."

"Why not give it to them? Tell them about Miller?"

"They've already screwed up. Twice. First, they let Martinez get loose. Then they didn't tell us about it."

She frowned. "Joshua, Hector didn't let Martinez escape. Neither did Robert Hernandez. Why punish them by withholding the information?"

"I'm not punishing anyone."

"No? Then what are you doing?"

"I'm trying to locate Martinez and Lucero."

"But why you, Joshua?"

It always came down to that. Why me?

The cops had more resources. They had more equipment, better communications.

But that didn't matter, finally. I was searching for Martinez and Lucero because right now it was the only thing I could do. I would've gone insane sitting around the house, sitting around the office, waiting to hear from Hector or Hernandez.

And it was Rita's life, and mine, that had been violated by that rifle bullet. It was up to me, so I told myself, to find the men responsible.

And perhaps I sought them because a part of me believed that if I found them—if I found Martinez, as I'd done five years ago—I could somehow guarantee Rita's recovery.

I was thinking such thoughts as I drove along that empty highway when, with no warning at all, the world abruptly shifted and it occurred to me that this was nonsense. That nothing would guarantee Rita's recovery. That, no matter what I did, no matter what anyone did, Rita was not going to recover.

The thought of her death took on a sudden inescapable weight and reality, and I was hit in the center of the heart by a blackness that was unbearable.

I pulled over to the shoulder and I stopped the car. Once again, I couldn't breathe.

For a few moments I was lost deep within a bottomless pit. Rita was gone, forever, and everything had changed.

Grief revises life, rewrites it forward and back. Evoke a small brittle hope, and grief blots it out. Summon a bright remembered joy, and grief twists it, transforms it into a dark swollen pain that seems, through some venomous magic, preordained.

Grief grants you only the aching timeless present, this wretched inescapable moment, and it insists that you will be snared within this, alone, for the rest of time.

All you can do is slog your way through. Or try to.

I told myself that Rita was still alive. That the doctor believed she *would* recover.

I got my lungs working again, and I filled them with air once or twice. I had put Leroy's telephone on the passenger seat. I picked it up, flipped it open, dialed the number for the hospital.

Rita was in a coma still. But she was alive.

I flipped the telephone shut, put the car into gear, and I drove back onto the highway.

I was just passing the Ribera turnoff, about twenty miles south of Las Vegas, when the telephone began to chirp. It had chirped three or four times before. Friends, offering condolences and help, and one caller who had simply hung up.

I lifted it from the seat, flipped it open. "Hello."

"Joshua. Where are you?" Hector Ramirez.

"On the road," I said.

"You're using a cellular phone."

"Yeah."

"I just got a call from the Staties. From Hernandez. He says he got a report that you're heading north on the Interstate."

I hadn't recognized the trooper, but apparently he had recognized my name.

"So I called the office," he said, "and I got you. But you're not at the office. Call forwarding?"

"Yeah."

"Where are you going?"

"North. Like the trooper said."

"Why?"

"To check something out."

"What?"

"Not sure yet. I'll fill you in when I am."

"Jesus, Joshua, do you always have to be an asshole?"

"Yeah."

"Yeah," he said. He paused.

I glanced around me. Foothills to the left, pasture to the right, clusters of fat cows happily grazing on emerald grass.

"I talked to the hospital," he said. "There hasn't been any change."

"I know. I just called."

He paused again. "All right. Listen. Keep in touch. Asshole."

"I'll do that, Hector."

I reached Las Vegas at about one o'clock that afternoon.

Money had come in with the railroad, back in the 1880s, and the people who brought it out here to the Wild West had used it to re-create the East they'd left behind. They had built the grand Victorian houses of wood and brick and stone that still sat back on bright green lawns, spacious verandas cooled by towering oaks and elms. Driving down those broad shaded streets, I could have been in Vermont or New Hampshire or upstate New York.

The address I had for Sylvia Miller was on a small side street. The house was smaller than the Victorians on the main drag, a white frame bungalow with a screened-in porch. There was no garage, and no car in the narrow asphalt driveway. A hedge of juniper ran down each side of the neat rectangle of lawn, hiding it from the houses on either side. The house across the street, a small brick cottage, seemed empty.

I drove past the house and parked a couple of blocks beyond it.

I was wearing a blue oxford shirt, a pair of tan corduroy slacks, a pair of Tommy Mahan ostrich-skin boots. I swiveled around, reached over the console, wrestled my carryall to the backseat, opened it. Slipped out the flat leather wallet that held the picks, stuck in it my back pocket. Slipped out the blue blazer, and then a tie of red and navy blue silk. I shut the suitcase.

I turned back around and admired myself in the rearview mirror as I wrapped on the tie. I looked a bit less degenerate than I'd looked this morning.

I put on the blazer. Then I bent down and retrieved the Beretta from beneath the passenger seat, shoved it between my belt and the small of my back. I picked up Leroy's phone, flicked the switch that turned off the ringer, dropped it in my blazer pocket.

The clipboard was beneath the driver's seat. I bent over and pulled it free.

Carrying the clipboard, I got out, locked the Jeep, and walked down the shaded sidewalk to Sylvia Miller's house. I ambled up the driveway, up the cement steps to the porch, pulled open the screen door, stepped inside, rang the bell.

No one answered it. I could see nothing through the heavy lace curtains that hung like veils beyond the window. I tried the door. Locked.

I left the porch and walked around back. The hedge concealed the entire rear of the yard. Unless someone had seen me approach the house, I was fine. I didn't think that anyone had seen me.

A tall galvanized metal garbage pail stood to the right of the rear door. I lifted the lid. A bulging black plastic bag, its top tied with string in a tidy square knot. I put back the lid.

I went to work on the lock at the door. I'm not very good with locks, but this one didn't take me long. In only a few minutes I was inside the house, standing in the kitchen. I lay the clipboard on the counter, pulled out the Beretta, and I listened for a while. I heard nothing. After a few moments, I started to poke around.

The kitchen was an exhibit dedicated to the 1950s, stocked with aging artifacts, all well preserved and spotlessly clean. Floors of dark green linoleum. Cabinets of pale wood, yellowed now by countless coats of varnish. Crouched along countertops of red Formica were bulbous appliances—a fat toaster, a squat waffle iron, a huge old Mixmaster, its circular stand supporting three porcelain bowls carefully nestled one within the other.

The gas stove and the refrigerator were bulky and their once-white enamel had cracked and yellowed, but they were as immaculate as everything else. On one of the stove's burners sat an old coffee percolator. It had been scoured inside and out. In the refrigerator I found only a few jars of condiments. No milk bottles, no leftovers, nothing in the vegetable crisper except a single limp gray shred of lettuce. The freezer compartment held two empty aluminum ice trays and three Weight Watchers TV dinners. There were no dishes in the rack beside the sink. Sylvia had tidied up before she left.

So did I. I lifted the wash towel that hung from a hook attached to the refrigerator, and I used it to wipe off the prints I'd left.

Carrying the towel in my left hand, the pistol in my right, I moved from the kitchen into the tiny dining room. The light filtering through the lace curtains was dim, like light at the bottom of an ancient well. There was a scent of lemon oil and pine in the air, but lying not far beneath those was a musty smell, a smell I associated with maiden aunts and dried flowers.

Atop the dark hardwood floor, four mahogany cabriolet dining chairs stood rigidly at attention around a shiny mahogany table. The table was draped diagonally with a scallop-hemmed lace tablecloth, and perched in the exact center of that was a mahogany bowl piled with wax fruit. I wiped the towel lightly along one of the apples. No dust.

The living room was the same. Murky light, the smell of lemon and must. Embroidered throw rugs, an upholstered brown sofa, square mahogany end tables supporting shiny brass reading lamps shaded with parchment. A plump leather club chair aimed comfortably toward an old boxy television console. I had the feeling that if I turned on the TV, it would be playing *The Honeymooners*.

Beneath the window ran a low, glass-fronted mahogany bookcase that held what looked like every *Reader's Digest Condensed Book* ever published. Positioned in the center of the lace runner that protected the top of the bookcase was a framed black-and-white photograph. A man, a woman, a young boy, a young girl, all in their Sunday best, standing out on a lawn, a thick hedge forming a backdrop. Probably the hedge that surrounded the house.

The woman, in her early thirties, slight and short and wiry, grasped the girl's hand in her right, the boy's in her left. The boy was looking up toward her, expectantly, his mouth parted. The girl was staring at the camera, and the expression on her round bland face was unreadable. The woman was gazing steadily in the same direction with a smile that seemed fixed and maybe a little forced. A long-ago breeze was ruffling her permed dark hair and fluting the hem of her white summer dress.

The man stood apart. Stocky and powerful, he wore a dark two-piece suit and a dark tie. His arms were crossed over his chest and his heavy jaw was upraised, as though his patience with all this were beginning to wear thin.

Presumably the children were Sylvia and Ronny Miller, and the adults were their parents.

It didn't look like a happy family to me. Everyone in it seemed somehow isolated from everyone else.

But maybe I was reading too much into a single photograph, a single moment snipped from a long history of moments.

I glanced around. There were no other photographs in the room, no pictures on the ivory-colored walls. No knickknacks anywhere. No magazines on the end tables. No books other than those trapped behind their glass cage.

It was the kind of house that seemed to be designed not for inhabitants, but for custodians and curators. I got the feeling that it had been kept this spotless and sterile for years.

I set down the photograph and I went down the hallway.

In the master bedroom there was a big brass double bed, a mahogany dresser, a walk-in closet crowded with clothing and the smell of camphor. The right half held a man's clothes, the left half held a woman's. All of them had been manufactured before the eighties. If Sylvia Miller lived alone, and I believed she did, then these topcoats and suits and dresses and frocks must have belonged to her parents.

In the small adjoining bathroom, on the counter beside the sink, someone had arranged, carefully and recently, a man's toilet items—an old Gillette safety razor, a badger-bristle brush, a round cake of cracked shaving soap nestling on a wooden plate. They looked like relics in a shrine, and they made me uneasy.

The bedroom opposite had probably belonged to Ronny Miller, at some time before he became a guest of the state. The single bed was spread with a cotton print of the American flag. Thumbtacked to the walls were posters from horror movies. Vampires, werewolves, knife-wielding killers wearing hockey masks. The dresser drawers were empty, but in the footlocker at the base of the bed, among the plastic guns and the metal trucks, I found an old stash of battered wrestling magazines, the covers bright with spurting blood from squashed noses and ripped scalps. Ronny's interest in violence had evidently begun early.

I went back into the hallway. Looked into the second bathroom. Clean, functional, and at least thirty years out of date.

No soap in the soap dish. No shampoo, no conditioner along the rim of the gleaming bathtub. I glanced into the medicine cabinet. No perfumes, no cosmetics, no hairspray. No toothbrush, no toothpaste. No aspirin, no tampons, no diaphragm. Either those things had never been there or Sylvia had cleaned them all out.

The entire house made me uneasy. Despite its almost manic cleanliness, there was nothing that suggested that it had been occupied recently. There was nothing that suggested that a young woman had recently been taking up space here. It could have been buried beneath ashes and lava since the seventies, then excavated and painstakingly cleaned so we moderns could marvel at the everyday details of a distant reality.

The door to the final bedroom was locked. I was bending down to use the picks when I caught a whiff of something. It was a smell that didn't really surprise me. At some level below consciousness, I suppose, I had been half-expecting it. It was the smell of decay.

10

I DIDN'T BOTHER with the lock. I leaned back, raised my foot, and I slammed it into the door, just below the knob. The door smashed open and the smell exploded out, a stench of rot and refuse and human filth. My throat cramping, I forced myself to walk in.

There was no body. In a way, I almost wished there had been.

Sitting on the smeared dust of the nightstand, next to a TV remote, was an empty glass, its sides and bottom lined with milk that had dried and cracked. Curled beside that were the remains of an old apple, black and shriveled.

The nightstand was the cleanest part of the room.

Alongside the bed, piled haphazardly on the wooden floor, were aluminum TV dinner trays, most of the food only half-eaten, some of it so old it was furred with green mold. The blanket and top sheet had been tossed back from the bed to the floor. Where the bottom sheet clung to the center of the sagging single mattress, most of the cotton was dark gray and nubby, as though it had never been washed. In the center were several large irregular yellow stains, overlapping each other.

Gray cobwebs drooped from every corner of the ceiling. The wall beside the bed was streaked with grime where greasy fingers and greasy hands had wiped themselves clean. The floor was strewn with candy wrappers, milk cartons, pizza trays, empty cardboard ice-cream pints, crumpled paper towels crusted with unidentifiable slop.

There was more garbage on top of the big stereo television.

Paper bags from McDonald's and Dairy Queen. Powdery fragments of cake, desiccated crusts of bread. A piece of chocolate that had melted and run out along the walnut veneer before it hardened again. A glass bowl of something that might once have been cereal and milk, its sunken surface blistered and filmed.

Weeks must have passed, maybe months, for the room to get this foul. And Sylvia Miller had obviously been living in it all the while.

I had a sudden vision of her moving from room to room through the rest of the house, relentlessly cleaning and polishing, sweat breaking out on her forehead as she vacuumed and swept and dusted—until at last, finished, she retreated here, to her lair. Where perhaps she collapsed in relief to the filth of that bed, happily sucked in that dense, choking, poisoned air.

Had she lived like this as a kind of balance to the feverish cleanliness of the other rooms? As a kind of revenge?

But why the cleanliness? Why that neurotic balance?

Worse than neurotic. Both of them, the filth and the cleanliness, the balance itself, seemed finally self-denying, life-denying.

Had she reveled in her hidden squalor? Had it been one of those dark secrets that some damaged people clutch to their hearts with a kind of fierce bitter pride?

I looked around the room. The closet door was open, and the floor in there was littered with clothing. To the right of the door stood a square birdcage on a tall brass pole. I walked over to the cage. The feeder and the water supply were full, the foil liner was scattered with seeds and bird droppings. But there was no bird. It had flown away, perhaps, with Sylvia.

I spent over an hour in that house, most of it in Sylvia Miller's room, but I found nothing that would tell me where she might be now. There was no diary, no calendar, no revealing doodles scribbled on the front cover of the phone book, or anywhere else. There was a telephone, buried beneath the bedroom rubble, but there was no answering machine attached.

There were no personal records, no insurance papers, bank statements, sales receipts, checkbooks, utility bills. Sylvia had not only disappeared. She had never, it seemed, even existed.

I returned to the antique kitchen, washed my hands, dried them on the wash towel. I stuck the Beretta back beneath my belt, lifted the clipboard from the counter, and then I left, using the sleeve of my blazer to wipe the prints from the doorknob.

When I came out from behind the house I saw that the neighbor, across the street, was out on her lawn, lightly hosing the rose bushes that ran along the brick front of her house. Her back was toward me, but she must have sensed my presence, because abruptly she turned around, eased off on the hose nozzle, and stared at me with open curiosity.

I waved, called out "Hi," and walked toward her. I strode up the paved driveway, carefully avoiding her well-tended lawn. I loosened the muscles of my shoulders, loosened the muscles of my face, found a smile somewhere and stretched it over teeth that ached from having recently been clenched.

She was in her sixties but trim and slender in a pair of blue Nikes, gray sweatpants, a hooded gray sweatshirt. Her hair hugged her head in soft white waves. She stood with the gun-shaped nozzle pointed downward, away from me, but I sensed that she thought of it as a weapon, and that she was ready to turn it on me.

"My name is Croft," I told her. "Joshua Croft. I'm looking for Sylvia Miller."

"And why would you be doing that?" she asked me, her voice giving away nothing. Bright blue eyes, a thin nose. Laugh lines along the sides of her mouth, even though she wasn't laughing at the moment. Just below her left cheekbone, a small smudge of dirt stood out against her pale skin like a fading bruise.

I had a story prepared. An insurance investigation, Sylvia a witness to an accident.

But snooping through Sylvia's house had worn me out, and the woman's frank blue eyes belied the wariness of her face. I had been fooled by blue eyes before, but I felt—or I told myself—that I might get more from her with the truth. I relaxed my face and the false smile faded away to wherever it was that false smiles went. "There was a prison break down in Santa Fe," I said. "I think Sylvia was involved."

Her expression didn't change. "Sylvia? It wasn't her brother who escaped."

"No. I think she was involved with one of the men who did."

"And you're . . . what? Not a policeman."

"A private detective."

"Representing whom?"

"No one. My partner was shot by one of the men who escaped."

She nodded. "A woman? Rita Something? One of those lovely old Spanish names. It was on the radio."

"Mondragón."

She considered this. She said, "I didn't see you go up to Sylvia's house."

"No, ma'am," I said. "I've been poking around out back for a while."

She considered that. "Do you have any identification, Mr. . . . ?"

"Croft." I took out my wallet, handed it to her. She examined the driver's license, the photocopy of the PI ticket. She handed them back to me. She said, "Sylvia's in trouble?"

"I think so, yes." I thought that Sylvia had been in trouble for quite some time.

She hesitated for a moment, and then she made up her mind. "I'm Betsy Rudolph." She switched the nozzle to her left hand and held out her right. I took it. Her grip was firm. "Maybe we should go inside," she said.

Sometimes the truth can be useful.

She asked me if I'd like some tea and I said I would, and I waited while she prepared it.

It was a relief to be in a house that hadn't been mummified.

Here in the living room, the gray curtains were open at the picture window, and sunlight poured into the room and streamed over the dark Colonial furniture and the white shag carpeting. On the end table beside the sofa lay issues of *Psychology Today* and *Newsweek* and a copy of the latest Elmore Leonard thriller.

There were more books in the pair of matching cherry-wood bookcases along the wall opposite the window. I stood there for a few moments, glancing over the titles. Mysteries, more thrillers, biographies, poetry anthologies, a couple of shelves of psychology texts, some expensive coffee-table art books, Vermeer, Rembrandt, Renoir.

"I just called the bank," she said behind me.

I turned. "Excuse me?"

She held a dishtowel in her right hand. Her face was concerned, eyebrows lowered, mouth tight. There was still a smudge of dirt on her cheek. "The bank. The First National, where Sylvia works. She wasn't there. They said she was on vacation. Friday was the last day she worked."

I nodded, waiting.

"It's not that I don't trust you, Mr. Croft," she said. "I'm sure you're who you say you are, and I'm sure you believe everything you've told me. But I've known Sylvia since she was a little girl." She held the dishtowel with both hands now, twisting it gently and probably unconsciously. "The idea of her being involved in a prison break . . . It's just so bizarre." She frowned and she looked off at something, maybe at the past and the young Sylvia she remembered.

"Did the bank say when she'd be back?" I asked her.

"Two weeks, they said." She shook her head slightly, as though shaking herself back into the present. "But Sylvia never mentioned anything about a vacation, and I spoke with her just last week. It doesn't—" She blinked, and then she frowned. "I'm terribly sorry. Where are my manners? Please. Sit down." She gestured toward the sofa. "The tea is brewing. It'll be ready in a minute."

"Thanks," I said, and I sat down and leaned back. The big

Beretta reminded me that it was there by digging into my spine.

She sat down in the armchair opposite me, leaning forward, her knees together and bent slightly to the side, as though she were wearing a cocktail dress and not that prosaic gray sweat suit. Her right arm rested along her lap and the length of the dish-towel hung down along her leg, trembling slightly as she kneaded it.

11

THE PSYCHOLOGY BOOKS," I said. "They're yours?"

She was staring at the floor. She looked up. "What? Oh. No, they were my husband's. He taught psychology at Highlands." The state university here in Las Vegas. "He died four years ago."

"I'm sorry."

She nodded, still distracted, and then she looked directly at me. "Please, Mr. Croft," she said. "Tell me about Sylvia."

"I don't know very much, Mrs. Rudolph. I was hoping you'd be able to tell *me* about her."

"But what makes you think she was involved in that escape from the prison?"

"An informant told me she was bringing drugs into the place. She could have also brought in a gun. And someone helped the men escape afterward, cut the perimeter wires at the penitentiary."

"Drugs?" she said. "But Sylvia's never been involved with drugs. She doesn't even drink. And a *gun?*"

"Apparently she handed the drugs over to her brother Ronny. He handed them over to a man named Lucero. What kind of car does Sylvia drive, Mrs. Rudolph?"

She frowned again. "Well, for the longest time she owned an old station wagon, a Ford. It had belonged to her father, and she'd had it for years. Mr. Miller died in nineteen eighty, and even then it wasn't new. But I thought she'd never get rid of it."

"But she did?"

The woman nodded. "She bought one of those big—what do

74

they call them? Not a trailer. One of those big, self-contained things. With a stove and a bathroom?"

"An RV?"

"An RV," she nodded. "Sylvia bought it just last week. That was when I spoke with her. It was . . . let's see . . . a week ago Saturday. I saw her drive it into her driveway. I was just coming back from my walk—I walk every day, in the evening—and I thought it was someone visiting. Visiting Sylvia, a guest. And that surprised me, you know, because Sylvia *never* has guests. But then Sylvia stepped out of it. I called to her and she came over to say hello. She told me she'd just bought it, that day. The RV. I was stunned."

"Stunned?"

"Well, Sylvia's a very reserved woman. Repressed, my husband used to say, and I suppose he was right. I don't mean that she's not pleasant and well spoken, because she is. But coming from the kind of background she did, it's not surprising that she might be repressed. And the idea of her *camping,* and in a big old thing like that RV . . . It just seemed so completely incongruous."

"Did you ask her about it?"

"Well, yes, of course. As I said, it seemed so out of character. She told me she was thinking about taking a long trip this summer. Getting away from it all. And that surprised me, too, naturally."

"But she said this summer. Not next week."

"No, not next week."

"Did you happen to notice the brand name on the RV?"

"No." She shrugged lightly, apologetically. "It never occurred to me to look."

"Was it new?"

"I don't think so. I don't know anything about them, of course, but I don't think so. It looked very clean, very well cared for, but I think it was used."

"And she sold the car. The Ford."

"I assume so. I never saw it again."

75

"When was the last time you saw the RV?"

She thought a moment. "Friday. Friday morning. At about seven in the morning. I happened to look out the window and it was there, in the driveway. When I looked out again—that would be around nine or so—it was gone. But Sylvia had usually left for work by then, so I didn't think anything of it."

"It wasn't in the driveway over the weekend?"

"No." She sat up abruptly, blue eyes wide, and for a moment I thought she had remembered something crucial. "The tea," she said. "I'm sorry. I'd forgotten it." She stood. "I'll be right back."

And, a few moments later, she was, carrying a black lacquered tray that held a blue porcelain teapot, matching cups and saucers, matching sugar bowl and creamer. She set it in front of me on the coffee table. "Would you like milk or sugar?"

I noticed that the smudge of dirt was gone. "Sugar, please. Thanks."

She poured for me, handed me the cup and saucer, then poured for herself. She carried her tea back to the armchair and sat down carefully. "I apologize, Mr. Croft. This has all been . . . unsettling."

"I understand. And I apologize for imposing on you like this."

"It's no imposition. It's just that I find it difficult to believe that Sylvia could have done the things you say she has. I know she had an oppressive childhood, and I've always felt that she was basically an unhappy woman, but I never . . ." She let the sentence trail off and she shook her head. She took a sip of tea.

"You mentioned her childhood before. You knew Sylvia's parents?"

She nodded. "Yes, but not terribly well. Neither my husband nor I were very fond of Frank—Mr. Miller."

"Why was that?"

She frowned again, organizing her thoughts. "He was one of those people who believed that a man's home is his castle, and that everyone in it was a servant. And he was a brutal man. I don't like saying this, but I think that he abused them all. Doris—Mrs.

Miller—and Sylvia and Ronny. I could be wrong, of course, but my husband thought the same thing. I'm not talking about sexual abuse—although God knows, we're finding out that there's more of that than anyone ever suspected, aren't we? But I did think that he beat them. They looked, all of them, as though they were walking around on eggshells. Sullen, but watchful. Do you know what I mean?"

"Yes."

"Both Doris and Sylvia seemed to accept it. Ronny was the only one who ever really stood up to him."

"And how did he do that?" I took a sip of the tea. Earl Grey, and strong.

"He left. Ran away, really. I didn't know about it until my daughter told me. Ruth. She's married; she lives in Pagosa Springs now. She heard about it from Sylvia, and she told me. Ronny went to Santa Fe. I gather that he started getting into trouble down there."

"Sylvia was close to Ruth?"

She sipped her tea, pursed her lips. "Not close, not really. She and Ruth went to the same high school. They came home on the same bus. They talked."

I nodded.

"After high school," she said, "Ruth went up to Boulder, to college. Sylvia stayed here and took some courses at Highlands. She dropped out two years later, in nineteen seventy-five, when her mother died."

"Sylvia's always lived at home?"

"Always. I think that after Doris died, Sylvia just took over for her. Assumed her role, in a way. She cleaned the house for her father, did all the shopping, all the cooking. Except for her job, I don't think Sylvia had any real life outside that house. No men friends, no women friends."

She frowned. "I'm making her sound like some sort of terrible basket case. She wasn't. As I said, she was very polite, very well spoken. She always dressed well—not fashionably, really, but well, and she was always very nicely groomed." She glanced down at her sweat suit, looked up, smiled a faint smile. "Unlike some people we might mention."

I smiled back.

"And she's a responsible woman," she said. "She's the head teller at the bank. She's worked there for nearly twenty years, and I doubt that she's taken a single day off."

"Did you speak with her often?"

She frowned again. "It's terrible to admit this, but I'm afraid I didn't. I doubt that I've been over there, to Sylvia's house, more than three or four times in the past five years. And Sylvia's never come over here."

"Why is that?"

"It was my fault, probably. She was so very reserved, so very . . . self-contained. It was as though she didn't need anyone. Didn't want anyone. Whenever I went over to say hello, I felt as though I were intruding. And she kept that house looking exactly the way it had looked while her parents were alive. She never even rearranged the furniture. It was clean—she always kept it very clean—but it was like some sort of gloomy . . . crypt. I hate to admit this, but it always made me uncomfortable. I invited her over here, many times, but she always found some reason to beg off. Finally, I stopped inviting her." She raised the teacup to her lips, stopped herself, lowered it. "Have you ever read Emily Dickinson?"

"Not recently."

"There's a poem of hers that I've always associated with Sylvia. 'We grow accustomed to the Dark.' Do you know it?"

"No. Sorry."

" 'We grow accustomed to the Dark,' " she quoted, " 'when Light is put away.' " She smiled. "I don't remember the entire poem, but it ends something like 'Either the Darkness alters, or something in the sight adjusts itself to Midnight—and Life steps almost straight.' I've always thought that Sylvia had grown accustomed to the dark—to her own Dark, the Darkness within that family, within that awful house—and that she was never really able to experience the Light again. Happiness, I mean. Whatever that might be, however you might define it. Even just the simple, ordinary day-to-day pleasures of life." She smiled, embarrassed, and she shook her head. "I'm probably being very silly."

"I don't think so," I said.

"It was as though she'd been pressed beneath the weight of that house, like a flower." She paused. "I would've liked to help her. I did try to help her, over the years. But it's terribly difficult to help someone who doesn't really want your help, isn't it? And eventually, out of a kind of moral laziness, I suppose, you stop trying." She shrugged, embarrassed again, at the sadness in her voice, perhaps, or at her failure.

"I have a feeling," I said, "that there wasn't much you could've done to help Sylvia."

She shook her head. "But it's all so dreadful. Drugs, guns. Helping prisoners escape." She looked at me. "Convicted killers. That's what the radio said."

"That's right."

"It's so dreadful." She shook her head again. "What on *earth* is she doing?"

"I don't know. Do you have any photographs of Sylvia, Mrs. Rudoph?"

"No. I'm sorry."

I nodded.

"What are *you* going to do?" she asked me. "Will you be calling the police?"

"I don't have any real evidence against Sylvia. Just the word of a man whose word isn't very good."

She narrowed her eyes. "You broke into Sylvia's house, didn't you? To look around. To investigate. You were inside while I was watering the roses. That's why I didn't see you come up."

I smiled. "If I admitted to that, Mrs. Rudolph, I'd be admitting to a felony."

Her face was serious. "But if you *had* gone through the house, hypothetically speaking, and if you'd found anything helpful, then you wouldn't be talking to me."

I smiled again. "I'm not so sure that's true. But you've been very helpful yourself."

She waved that away. "But what are you going to *do?*"

"Sylvia left a bag of garbage in her backyard. I'm going to go through it."

"Garbage?" She blinked.

"People sometimes get careless about what they throw away. Maybe Sylvia did."

"But is that legal? Going through someone's garbage?"

"Once something's been put in the garbage, it essentially becomes public property." Essentially, this wasn't true. According to the Supreme Court, the garbage had to be on a public thoroughfare. Technically, by lifting the garbage from Sylvia's lawn, I was guilty of trespass.

She thought about that for a moment. "Well," she said finally, "if you say so." She didn't seem entirely convinced. "But I think I should be with you when you do it."

"Why?"

"You've really only this man's word, you said. About Sylvia. And his word isn't necessarily good, you said. Suppose you're wrong, suppose Sylvia had nothing to do with the jailbreak. Or the drugs. Or any of it. Maybe there's some other explanation for all this. The RV, the vacation. Everything. I'm sure your heart's in the right place, Mr. Croft, and I don't mean to be obstructive. But it seems to me that someone should be there with you, someone who can . . . protect Sylvia's interests." She frowned once more. "Does that sound silly?"

"No, it doesn't," I told her. "Do you have a plastic tarp?"

She didn't, but she had some large garbage bags of her own. She also had a pair of rubber gloves, and she lent them to me. She walked along beside me as I carried everything across the street and behind Sylvia's house. I unfolded the bags, four of them, and spread them out along the lawn near the garbage can. I put on the gloves, lifted the lid, set it on the grass, hauled the garbage from the can, set it down on the outspread bags. I used my pocket knife to cut the string. Carefully, I began to shake the trash loose from the bag.

"Oh!" said Mrs. Rudolph.

I had seen it, too. A small yellow bird, a parakeet, had been lying at the top of the garbage. It tumbled out across the black plastic and onto the grass and it lay there, stiff and still, like a child's discarded toy.

12

I LET GO of the bag, squatted down beside the bird, picked it up. Its soft yellow feathers were smooth and unruffled but its opened eyes were filmed with dust.

Mrs. Rudolph said, "Sylvia had a parakeet?"

I lay the bird down on the ground and I stood. "Not anymore."

"But why . . . how did it die?"

"Its neck's been broken."

She sucked in a sharp breath. "She *killed* it?"

"Someone did."

"But that's so . . . so heartless. So *cold*. How could *anyone* do something like that?"

"I don't know," I said. But I thought I did. The parakeet had been put into the bag last, and it seemed likely to me that it had been put in there by Sylvia. Maybe this had been the last act she'd performed before she drove away in her dandy new RV. Maybe she had hesitated before she killed it. Maybe she had told herself that she was doing the best thing, the only thing. But in the end she had broken its neck, swiftly and firmly, as though she were breaking the link between herself and her past.

Mrs. Rudolph was thinking the same, perhaps. "Poor Sylvia," she said sadly.

"Yeah," I said.

She took in a long deep breath. "It's such a waste. Such a terrible waste. She was such a sweet little girl. Years ago. She really was. I felt so sorry for her, living in that house. And I just stood by and watched her grow older and more and more . . . enclosed." She lifted her chin. "I *still* feel sorry for her."

"So do I," I said. I bent down, lifted the bag, began to shake the garbage loose again.

It was clear from what she'd left behind that Sylvia had made a break with her past. I found the kind of things I had expected to find in the medicine cabinet: a can of hairspray, a bottle of Midol, some old lipsticks, a tube of toothpaste squeezed flat. Amid the limp fruits and vegetables I found her credit cards, American Express, Visa, and Master, all three neatly scissored into quarters. Next to these I found her driver's license, some folded grocery coupons, and a receipt, dated two weeks ago, for the purchase of a Colt Python and a .22 caliber Beretta semiautomatic. Probably she had emptied her wallet, cut the cards, and then tossed everything into the trash. I set the receipt aside, on the grass.

I looked at the small picture on the driver's license. A thin woman, a sharp nose, a narrow mouth, brown hair swept back over her ears, hiding them. I put the license beside the receipt.

Stuck to an empty milk carton I found a slip of paper with a phone number scribbled across it. I recognized the area code—Denver. Above the number, someone had scrawled, "Call Lyle Saturday!!!!" The phrase had been underlined twice, and the handwriting resembled the signature on the driver's license. I put the slip on the grass.

Lucero and Martinez had escaped from the penitentiary on Saturday night.

Toward the bottom of the bag, beneath some coffee grounds, I found a sodden mass of what had once been photographs. They had been set alight, left to burn for a while, then doused with water. A few charred corners of prints remained, some black-and-white, some color. There wasn't enough left of the photographs for me to identify anything. But I assumed that they were more family photos, more moments snipped from a long and probably complicated lifetime, and that Sylvia had burned them deliberately.

I stripped off the gloves, picked up the license, the receipt, the slip of paper, and I stood up.

Mrs. Rudolph came over to me, looked down at the number on the paper. "Do you think that's important?" she asked me.

"I don't know," I said. "Let's find out." I took out Leroy's tiny phone, flipped it open, tapped in the numbers. The phone rang. Once, twice, three times.

"Hello?" A woman's voice.

Mrs. Rudolph was watching me. I signaled for her to come forward and I held the phone away from my ear, so both of us could hear. She leaned carefully toward me, craning her neck.

"Hello?" said the woman again.

I said, "Sylvia?"

"I—who *is* thi—" And then suddenly a dial tone. The woman, or someone else, had hung up the phone.

I looked at Mrs. Rudolph. "Was that Sylvia?"

She made a face. "I don't know. It could've been." She cocked her head, listened to her memory. She winced with frustration. "It *could've* been." She raised her hands. "I'm sorry. Really I am. I just didn't hear enough."

"That's okay. Excuse me." I raised the phone again, tapped in Hector's number.

He answered it himself. "Ramirez."

"Hector, Joshua. I'm in Las Vegas and I may have something."

A brief pause—probably while he found something to write with. "Okay. Go ahead."

"I think that a woman named Sylvia Miller was the one who brought the gun into the pen for Lucero. Before that, she was bringing in dope for him, and delivering it to her brother, Ronny."

Watching me, Mrs. Rudolph frowned. She looked down at the garbage spread out along the black plastic, at the small yellow bird lying on the grass.

Hector asked me, "Where are you getting all this?"

"You want me to go on?" I said.

He sighed. "Right," he said. "Go on."

"She's gone now, and I think she's gone for good. But a couple of weeks ago she bought herself a Colt Python and a twenty-two Beretta."

A pause. "Yeah?"

"She also bought a used RV."

"An RV," he repeated.

"If she had it modified, she could've hidden both of them in there. Lucero and Martinez. Under the seats, under the floor."

"And with a woman," he said, "maybe some of the uniforms wouldn't search as carefully at the roadblocks."

"Maybe."

"You got the make and model?"

"No."

"Okay. I'll get it from Motor Vehicles."

"You may have a problem."

"How's that?"

"She's tossed her driver's license. And her credit cards. I think that maybe she picked up new papers and a new name. The RV may be registered to that one."

"This woman would know how to get new papers?"

"Lucero might."

"Shit. Right. What else you got?"

I looked down at the phone number in my hand and for a brief moment I considered not giving it to him. But I was hours away from Denver. If that had been Sylvia who answered the phone, I had alerted her.

"A Denver phone number." I read it to him. "I just called it and a woman answered. Could've been Sylvia, could've been someone else. Whoever it was, she hung up."

"You already called?" His voice had tightened. "You check to see who owned it first?"

"No. Could be someone named Lyle."

"Lyle. Terrific. What else?"

"A possibility."

"These are *all* possibilities, sounds like."

"Another one, then. Sylvia worked at the First National here. She was the head teller. She had access to the bank's money."

A few feet away, Mrs. Rudolph started. She looked at me with her eyebrows lowered, her mouth set in disapproval.

"You're telling me," Hector said, "that she dipped into the till?"

"It looks like she's burned all her bridges, Hector. She might have burned that one, too. She told them at the bank that she was going on vacation last Friday. Today's Monday. Maybe it's a slow day. Maybe they haven't checked the vaults. Maybe they should."

"Okay, yeah, I'll make a call. That it?"

"I don't think she kept her personal records here at the house. She may have a safe deposit box somewhere. At her own bank, maybe at another one."

"Okay. You're at the house now?"

"No," I said. "I'm gone, Hector."

"Hold on. I'm gonna call the Las Vegas cops, bring them in."

"Give me fifteen minutes. The house'll still be here."

"Shit."

"Hector, I'm the one who found her. And I didn't have to call this in."

"Shit, shit, *shit.*"

"Is that a yes?"

I heard him take a deep breath. "Fifteen minutes. Don't screw around with the evidence."

"Thanks, Hector."

"They must've given you a special plaque when you graduated from the Asshole Academy."

"I keep it with the bowling trophies."

"I know a better place for you to keep it." He hung up.

I flipped the phone shut, slipped it back in my pocket.

"You had no reason to say that," Mrs. Rudolph told me sternly. "About Sylvia and the money at the bank."

"I may be wrong," I admitted. "But like I told my friend, I think that Sylvia's left for good. Maybe all that money was a temptation."

"But you don't know Sylvia. You *could* be wrong about everything you've said. It's all . . . conjecture, isn't it?"

"Yeah, it is. Mrs. Rudolph, I'm sorry, but I have to leave. The police'll be here any minute, and there are things I need to do. If you want to stay out of this, you should probably—"

"I'll wait for them." She lifted her chin again. "Here. Someone has to look out for Sylvia."

I nodded. "Why don't you give them these?" I handed over the receipt, the slip of paper, the license. I could get a copy of the license from Motor Vehicles.

She took them, looked down at them unhappily.

"Thank you for your help," I said. "I apologize for getting you involved in all this."

She took a breath. "I suppose," she said sadly, and looked around her, at the house, the yard, the hedge of juniper, "that I've always been involved in all this."

"Good-bye, Mrs. Rudolph."

"Yes," she said, and then once again she looked down at the garbage scattered across the black plastic bags.

I turned to leave.

"Mr. Croft?"

I turned back.

"Would you let me know what happens? If you find her. Would you call me?"

"I'll call you," I said.

I drove back onto the Interstate, heading north again, toward Denver. I phoned the hospital and learned, once again, that there had been no change.

For a while, I kept my eye cocked toward the rearview mirror. After half an hour, when no one had stopped me, I let myself relax a bit. There had been a possibility that the state police would want to talk to me. Hector had evidently headed them off.

I passed the turnoffs for Watrous and Valmora. Horse and cattle country on either side of me now, bright green and empty.

I thought about Sylvia Miller.

"She brings the gun into the penitentiary somehow," I said. "She hands it over to Ronny. Ronny gives it to Lucero. On Saturday night, Lucero and Martinez organize the breakout. Outside, they dump the other four men—decoys, like Hernandez said—and they head for the RV, where Sylvia is waiting. They hide inside it. Sylvia drives them into town."

"To Airport Road?" Rita asked me. The sunlight sparkled off the small cross at her throat. "To the house of Robert and Rosa Theissen? Or do you think they dropped her off first, at some motel, on some neutral ground?"

"They needed Sylvia," I said. "She was their passport. Driving the van themselves would be too dangerous."

"So. What did Sylvia do while Martinez and Lucero walked into Four-thirty-three Acequia Court? While they were in there, shooting Robert Theissen, then abusing and shooting Rosa?"

"Maybe she came inside and joined the fun."

Rita frowned.

Sylvia Miller. A quiet, reserved woman who had taken care of her father until he died. Who worked at the same place for nearly twenty years. Who was responsible. Polite, well spoken.

Who looked like a librarian, Jimmy McBride had said.

But I had seen the inside of Sylvia Miller's house. I had seen that razor and brush carefully positioned on the bathroom counter, in memory of a dead, and probably brutal, father. I had seen her own room and its filth. If the condition of our surroundings reflects the condition of our souls, then Sylvia Miller had possessed a very troubled soul.

13

I WAS APPROACHING Raton, green mountains crowding the sky ahead, when the telephone began to chirp from the passenger seat. There had been three more calls since I left Las Vegas. Two of them were from other friends, with more condolences, more offers of help. The third was another hang-up.

I picked up the phone. "Hello?"

"Well, Sherlock, you really opened up a can of worms." Hector.

"How so?"

"First off, that phone number you gave me."

"Yeah?"

"Belongs to a guy named Lyle Monroe. Well, *belonged* is probably a better way to put it, because Lyle's dead. He was shot. The Denver cops found him in the basement of the house."

"When was he shot?"

"Sometime today. Not more than an hour or two before they found him."

"They were there. Lucero and Martinez. And Sylvia Miller. That was her on the phone."

"Yeah. Prints all over the place, Lucero's and Martinez's. The Denver cops say it looks like they took off in a hurry. Probably right after your call. The cops were there fifteen minutes after I called them."

He waited a few seconds for me to figure it out. I didn't need a few seconds. "I screwed up," I said.

"Looks that way."

I made him an offering: "If the cops up there can locate that RV, they can bring all three of them in."

"That's the second thing. You were right about the bank."

"Yeah? How much right was I?"

The prairie had fallen away behind me and now the Jeep and I were climbing up toward Raton Pass, into the pine trees. Big pine trees, ponderosas, looking primeval and indestructible, like they'd been here forever and would be here forever. They hadn't, of course, and they wouldn't.

Hector said, "Sixty-eight thousand dollars, they figure."

"Pretty big money for a small town bank."

"Friday, payday, they carry a surplus. I called the honcho at the bank right after I talked to you. Like you said, Monday was slow, no need to check the vaults. He called me back about a half an hour ago. Not a happy camper. But he sounded less angry about the money being gone than he was about Miller taking it. A huge betrayal of trust, is the way he put it."

"The money was insured. His self-esteem wasn't."

"Sixty-eight grand, that could take a pretty big chunk out of your self-esteem. Something else."

"What?"

"Sylvia's personal account. She's been depositing some hefty checks lately. Hold on." I heard the rattle of paper. "Five thousand last week, seven thousand the week before. A total of twenty-three thousand over the past month and a half."

"Who signed the checks?"

"Different name every time. But they were all drawn on Denver banks."

"Lucero's been running his money through her account."

"Or maybe she's been selling Mary Kay."

"Did she clean it out before she left?"

"What do you think?"

"What about a safety-deposit box?"

"She's got one, there at the bank, but the Staties need a court order to open it. Won't take them long to get it, I figure. Anyway, Lucero and Martinez have probably dumped the RV. That much cash on hand, they can buy themselves a couple new cars."

"Maybe they already had one lined up."

"Maybe. Looks like they thought this thing through. So when are you getting back here?"

"When Lucero and Martinez are on ice."

"Come on, Josh. The FBI is working on this. We're working on it, down here. And now the Denver cops are working on it. You think you can get something that everybody else can't? Never mind. I forgot who I was talking to. Look, you're on your way to Denver?"

The road kept climbing and climbing, winding higher and higher into the trees as though it wouldn't stop until it had left them and pierced the faraway blue film of sky.

"Yeah."

"Guy to see up there is a Sergeant Labbady. He's expecting you. Says he can't wait to talk to the hotshot private detective. Your reputation precedes you, it seems."

"Okay, Hector. Thanks."

"You know she's still the same? Rita?"

"I called a little while ago. And the hospital has my number."

"All right. Listen. Keep in touch."

"Yeah. Thanks again."

I flipped the phone shut, tossed it to the seat.

A good cop, Hector. And a good man. Over the years he'd been a better friend than any private detective had a right to. Not too long ago I had shot a man. The man hadn't given me much choice, and he had survived, but for a while I had felt the weight of his life, and his death, on my soul. Hector had walked me through it.

I looked around. The forest was dark and thick, impenetrable. Not just pine trees now but oaks and elms. It was as though I had entered not only a different landscape but a different planet.

I remembered the first time I'd driven the Raton Pass. It was in September and I'd been coming from the other direction, riding down the long slide of the slope through the lush green forest when suddenly the flat brown prairie opened up like an enormous fan beneath me, stretching off to the edge of the world. I had been on my way to Santa Fe then. To live there this time, and not merely visit.

When I arrived in town after I got myself a room at the De Vargas Hotel, downtown, Hector had been one of the first people I'd spoken to.

"Croft, right. I got a phone call from my cousin," he'd said.

I nodded. "Bernie said he'd call."

"Sit down."

I sat.

We were in Hector's old cubicle in the Violent Crimes Division. This was back when the police station was on Washington and Marcy, where the public library is now.

The man sitting on the far side of the worn wooden desk was squat and muscular. His jet black hair was short and curly and combed back from a blunt widow's peak. His dark, hooded eyes and his drooping mustache made him look a bit like the Frito Bandito. I decided not to mention this.

He wore a pulled-down blue silk tie at his opened collar, and a white-on-white striped cotton shirt that had been cut to display the clean line of powerful pectorals. The sleeves were rolled back, maybe to display the clean line of powerful forearms. Bodybuilding is hard work, painful and tedious, and sometimes the people who do it like to show off what they've accomplished.

"Bernie says you used to be a cop," Hector said.

"A long time ago."

"Why'd you leave?"

"I didn't like the hours."

"That's not what Bernie says."

"What does Bernie say?"

"He says you slugged a lieutenant."

"We disagreed about the hours."

He smiled faintly. "This is amazing," he said.

92

"What is?"

"I was just sitting here, sending up a little prayer that God would deliver a wiseass PI into my life."

I smiled. I stood up. "Thanks a lot, Sergeant. It's been a pleasure talking to you."

He grinned. "Bernie said you were kind of a hard-ass."

"Bernie said a lot."

"Well, he's a talkative guy, you know. That's our shared Hispanic heritage. We're a very talkative people, we Hispanics." He waved a hand at me. "Sit down and we'll talk a while."

I sat again.

"Bernie also says you're okay," he said.

I shrugged.

"But Bernie's wrong a lot of the time."

"Yeah," I said. "He told me you were okay, too."

He laughed, and then he looked at me across the desk with those sleepy eyes. "You're a pretty tough hombre, are you, Croft?"

"You'd have to ask Bernie."

He smiled. "You were a PI there in . . . where is it?"

"Fairfield."

"Right, Fairfield, Connecticut." He shook his head. "Beats me how a cousin of mine ended up in Fairfield, Connecticut."

"It's not a bad town."

"Yeah, right." He was clearly dubious. "You were there how long?"

"Ten years. Two as a cop. Eight as a PI."

"Why'd you leave?"

"I wanted something new."

"Why Santa Fe?"

"It was something new."

He gave me another faint smile. "I've got an idea. Why don't we pretend that you're not the clever guy you really are, and then you can go ahead and give me some straight answers. How would that be?"

"I was here a few years ago. Passing through. I liked it."

"The Land of Entrapment."

"It came down," I said, "to a choice between here and Oregon. I know some people there." I shrugged again. "If this doesn't work out, I can always go on to Oregon."

"Lot of redwood trees in Oregon. Nice, if you like redwoods."

"Yeah."

"You get a lot of work, over there in Fairfield, Connecticut?"

"Enough to get by."

"Your license up to date?"

"The license and the carry permit."

"No carry permits in New Mexico. No such thing." He looked me over, casually but thoroughly, to make sure I wasn't carrying a weapon now. It wasn't something I usually did when I went into a police station.

"How do I shoot the bad guys?" I asked him.

"You don't. You give us a call and we leap into a car and dash over and we shoot the bad guys for you."

I smiled. "What a deal."

"Or we shoot you, depending."

"Well," I said, "you can't have everything."

He smiled again. "Let's see what we can do here." He reached out, picked up his telephone, dialed it. After a moment, he said, "William? Hector. Still alive, thanks, and you? . . . And how's Rita? Good, good. Listen, you still looking for a hired hand? I've got a guy in my office, PI, just came in from the East. Connecticut license. My cousin Bernie's worked with him . . . No, Carmen's son, he's a cop in Connecticut, in Fairfield. Says this guy's okay . . . I don't know, hold on."

He looked over at me. "You bondable?"

I nodded. "And reverent and clean."

"Yeah," he said into the phone. "He's also kind of a wiseass . . . Right. Joshua Croft . . . Right, I'll tell him. No problem. You take care. Say hello to Rita . . . Right, bye."

He hung up the phone. "William Mondragón," he told me. "He and his wife run an agency here in town. They've been looking for someone. The office is over on Palace." He picked up a scrap of paper, picked up a pen, scribbled something. He pushed the scrap across the desk. "That's the address."

I leaned forward, took the piece of paper. "Thank you, Sergeant."

He stood. So did I. He held out his hand and I took it. "I'll tell Bernie you showed," he said.

"Give him my regards. And I appreciate the help."

He nodded. "Keep your nose clean."

14

SOUTH OF TRINIDAD, ten or fifteen miles into Colorado, I
dialed information, got the number for the Denver Police. I dialed that, asked for Sergeant Labbady. After a few long minutes
of cellular charges, he came on the line. "Labbady."

"This is Joshua Croft, from Santa Fe. I was just talking to Hector Ramirez—"

"Oh yeah, the famous private detective." A New York accent. "You're the guy that warned the scumbags, right? Let 'em
get away?"

"Yeah. That's me."

"It's a real honor to talk to you, pally."

"I—"

"Where are you?"

"In my car. Just below Trinidad, on my way to Denver. Are
you—"

"That's three or four hours away. I'm on my way outta here.
You know where the main station is? Downtown?"

"I know where it is."

"Be here tomorrow morning at eleven."

"Have you—"

He hung up.

It was only seven o'clock in the evening by the time I reached
Pueblo, but the day had been a long one and I was tired and there

was nowhere I had to be. I pulled off the Interstate at the Pueblo fast-food alley—a quarter mile of quarter pounders and fish fillets—and grabbed some food at a Wendy's. The hamburger didn't taste any better than the sandwich had tasted this morning. I stopped at a liquor store, picked up a bottle of Jack Daniel's, found a motel, asked at the desk for a wake-up call at seven the next morning, and unloaded everything into the room. Everything except the shotgun. Motel managers sometimes get a little nervous about shotguns.

Inside, I poured myself a stiff drink, added a splash of water, and I called the hospital. Once again, there had been no change.

I called Leroy and asked him to do some favors for me. I told him I'd call him again tomorrow.

I lay on the bed. Sipping the drink. Remembering.

Eight years ago, the office had been located in the same Palace Avenue complex in which it was located now. I climbed up the narrow stairs to the door at the second floor. Into the frosted glass, in a broad neat script, was etched THE MONDRAGÓN DETECTIVE AGENCY. I knocked on the door.

"Come in," a man's voice called out to me.

I opened the door and stepped in. The door sighed slowly shut behind me.

He was sitting behind a large antique wooden desk in front of a window that looked up at the mountains. His features were somewhat obscured by the light behind him, and I was pretty sure that the desk had been put there for that reason. His elbow was notched against the desk's green blotter as he leaned forward, his ear to the telephone receiver. He sat back and he smiled at me, an easy smile that seemed to hold a lot of teeth, then he waved me in with his free hand, waved the hand at one of the two padded leather client chairs. I sat down.

"I understand," he said into the phone. He sat back, smiled at me again, and held up a finger to tell me he'd be off the phone soon. I nodded.

"I understand," he said again. "But you hired us to do a job, Mr. Cronin. We did it."

I had heard discussions like this one before. I had been a part of them.

I glanced around the room. All the furniture was antique—the desk, the chairs, a low sideboard, a bookcase filled with law and reference books. The carpeting was thick gray pile and it ran from wall to wall. Either the agency was doing well now or it had started out doing well.

To my right was a wooden door, unmarked.

"That's an interesting observation, Mr. Cronin," said the man behind the desk. "I'll certainly bear it in mind. But I have company at the moment and I'm afraid we'll have to continue this at some other time." He glanced at me and he smiled—more to himself, I thought, than to me. "Perhaps I'll send one of my associates out to discuss the matter with you. Yes, I'll be sure to convey that to him."

He hung up the phone and he stood, holding his manicured hand across the desk. I stood and took it.

"Joshua Croft?" he said. I admitted I was. "William Mondragón," he said. "Please. Sit down."

He was slender and tall, about my height, and his broad shoulders and narrow hips were neatly gift wrapped in a tailored three-piece tropical-weight light gray wool suit. His silk tie was taupe, his silk shirt was cream. His thick black hair, nicely grayed at the temples, was swept evenly back from a broad square forehead. He had dark eyebrows, long dark eyelashes, dark eyes, and a dark mustache beneath a thin aristocratic nose. His mouth was wide and sculpted. His movements were graceful and fluid and he was good looking in a way that was almost, but not quite, feminine.

He sat back in his swivel, lay his arms along the arms of the chair, crossed his legs comfortably. "You were a private investigator in Connecticut?"

"That's right."

"For how long?"

"Eight years."

"With an agency or on your own?"

"On my own."

"A lone wolf?"

I shrugged. "It just worked out that way."

He smiled. "Do you think you can get along in an office, working with other investigators?"

"I like to think," I said, "that I can get along with just about anyone, more or less." Which didn't mean I had to like them. I was getting along with Mondragón, more or less, and I wasn't sure yet that I liked him.

He smiled again, nodded. "We're not that large an agency. At the moment, there's only me and my wife, Rita." There was a hint of promise, or maybe merely a hint of hope, in his *at the moment.* "We do a bit of everything. Missing persons, accident investigation, some security work. We also do a fair amount of white-collar business—asset searches and personnel background—but Rita handles most of that. Our rates vary with the type of job we do, but I think it's fair to say that we charge a reasonable fee. If you worked with us, you might not get rich, but you wouldn't starve to death."

I nodded.

"We also do a certain amount of divorce work," he said. "Do you have a problem with divorce work?"

"Not an insurmountable problem."

He nodded and looked at me as though I'd disappointed him in a way he had almost been expecting to be disappointed. "But you're less than enthusiastic about it."

I shrugged again. "People can get intense."

He nodded again. "And we do some collecting. Have you done any collecting?"

"Some."

Another smile. "But you're less than enthusiastic about it."

"For the same reason."

Another nod. "The gentleman on the telephone was a man named Jack Cronin. He owes the agency five hundred dollars. His daughter ran away and he hired us to find her. We found her. She was down in Albuquerque, mainlining heroin and working twelve hours a day on Central Avenue. I pried her away from her pimp and brought her back. She ran away again, and Mr. Cronin has decided that this has negated his debt to us."

"Not very sporting of him," I said.

"No, not at all. How would you feel about giving Mr. Cronin a visit? Asking him if he'd reconsider?"

I smiled. "Is this a test?"

He smiled back. "I suppose you could see it that way."

"What kind of work does Mr. Cronin do?"

He sat back and a flicker of interest passed over his handsome face. "He's a building contractor," he said.

"He works out of an office?"

"Out of his home."

"He's there now?"

"Yes."

"Does his wife work?"

"As a housewife."

"What kind of a neighborhood do they live in?"

"A new development off Zia Road."

"Middle class? Upper class?"

"Middle. With a pretension or two. Do you know where Zia is?"

"I can find it," I said. "I'll need a van."

"A what?"

"A white van. Doesn't matter what year, so long as it runs."

"A white van," he repeated.

"Gray's okay, but I'd prefer white."

He smiled again. "I can arrange one for you in fifteen minutes."

"Fine," I said. "What's my legal status?"

"Your Connecticut license isn't valid here. You're a civilian. Simply someone I've asked to collect a debt."

I nodded. "One more thing."

"What?"

"What was it that Cronin wanted you to tell the 'associate' you sent out there?"

"That he'd better bring along an army." Once again he smiled that easy smile.

I gave him one of mine. "A contractor, you said. He's worked construction?"

"Mr. Cronin is perhaps a half a foot shorter than you are, and perhaps a foot wider. He seems in fairly good shape. Is that what you're asking?"

"Pretty much, yeah."

Another smile. "You're welcome to change your mind, if you like."

"Would I still get the job?"

It was his turn to shrug. "I'd take it under advisement."

I nodded. "Where do I pick up the van?"

He grinned at me and reached for the telephone.

Two and a half hours later, I was knocking on the office door once more. He called out for me to come in. I did, the door sighing behind me again, and I walked across the room to the desk and put the five hundred dollars on the blotter. I was showing off a bit, but I wasn't the one who'd set this up.

He picked up the money, counted it, grinned. He looked at me. "Have a seat. Tell me the story."

I sat down and I told him.

After a while, he was laughing. It was a good laugh, and I decided that maybe I did like him after all. "Wait," he said, and held up a hand. "Wait. I want Rita to hear this." He leaned to the side, pushed a button on his intercom. "Rita? Can you come in here for a minute?"

He sat back, grinning at me. After a moment, the door to my right opened.

There are some women who immediately own every room they enter, who take it over simply by the force of their presence. They seem to attract the available light and somehow crystalize it around their bodies, so they move through space and time within a bright, clear, immutable nimbus. They don't need to be beautiful, but they all share a kind of intensity that comes from a rock-solid sense of their own identity and purpose. This woman had that, and she was also beautiful.

She was wearing a pale blue silk blouse, a black skirt, a pair of black pumps. Her long hair, black as the wings of a raven, tumbled loose and thick to her shoulders.

Mondragón and I stood up. "Rita, this is the man I told you about. Joshua Croft. Joshua, my wife, Rita."

Smiling, she held out her hand. I took it, half-expecting to receive an electric shock when my flesh touched hers. I didn't. Her eyes were large and black and her stare was difficult to meet.

"I'm pleased to meet you," she said.

"Mrs. Mondragón," I said.

"Grab a seat, Rita," Mondragón told her. "You really have to hear this."

She smiled at him, looked at me, raised an eyebrow expectantly, and then she sat down, crossing one slim tanned leg over the other.

Mondragón and I sat. She was still looking at me, still expectant.

I said to her, "It's not that big a deal."

I'd be shuffling my feet next, like Jimmy Stewart, and blushing, and scratching at the back of my befuddled head.

"I told you," said Mondragón, "that I sent Croft out to talk to our friend Cronin."

She nodded, turned to me, smiled. "Why the white van?"

"He painted a sign on it," Mondragón said, grinning. "Black watercolors, both sides, in big letters. 'Jack Cronin is a liar and a welsher.' Then he drove it out there and parked it in front of

Cronin's house." He turned to me. "How long did it take for Cronin to notice it?"

I turned to face him, but along the skin of my face I could still feel the pressure of Mrs. Mondragón's presence, as though I were sitting along the edge of some force field she gave out. "Cronin's wife noticed it first. I saw her in the window. Then Cronin came out to discuss it with me." Barreling across the lawn at about thirty miles an hour with a sledgehammer held at port arms.

"To discuss it," said Mrs. Mondragón.

I turned back to her. "He felt that I should move the van. I told him that I planned to. That I planned to drive it around the neighborhood all afternoon. And maybe all day tomorrow, too."

She smiled.

"It was fairly simple after that," I said. "His wife convinced him to pay up."

"What's that?" said Mrs. Mondragón, lightly touching the tip of her fingers to her own cheekbone. "On your face. It looks like the beginning of a bruise."

I rubbed at my cheek. "I banged it on something." On the handle of Cronin's sledgehammer, when I took it away from him.

"I see," she said. "Mr. Cronin isn't bruised, too, is he?"

"No." The knee I'd planted in his stomach probably hadn't left any bruise at all.

"Well," she said, "that was very enterprising of you, Mr. Croft." She smiled, and suddenly I got the feeling that she'd seen everything that had happened at Cronin's house as clearly as if she'd watched it on television.

I shrugged. I think that probably I *was* blushing.

Her husband said to me, "How'd you like to start work tomorrow?"

"Sure," I said. "Tomorrow would be fine." But I knew that tomorrow wouldn't be fine. I knew that by tomorrow I'd be on my way to Oregon. I would call Mondragón later today and tell him.

She said, "Is it Josh or Joshua?"

103

"Joshua," I said.

She smiled. "Welcome to the firm, Joshua." She held out her hand again, and again I shook it. Her fingers were slender but her grip was firm.

I wondered how long it would take me to get to Portland.

15

THE DENVER POLICE Administration Building was on Cherokee Street, a six- or seven-story complex of tan buildings that
took up a whole block between Thirteenth and Fourteenth Av-
enues. I presented myself at the desk at eleven o'clock exactly.
The policeman behind the counter made a phone call, listened
into the receiver, then hung up and told me to wait down here
until Labbady arrived.

I thanked him and then I wandered around the huge lobby.
Beneath the high ceiling, along the walls, in the corners, displays
had been set up to provide little snippets of Denver Police history. In one corner there were three motorcycles, among them
an old Harley trike. On the north wall, behind glass that looked
reinforced, there were rows of weapons—including a 30.06
Sedgeley rifle, a 12-gauge pump Winchester, some lethal-looking
tear gas grenades.

On the west wall hung a chart that described how various
drugs affected their users. I was reading how marijuana, after six
hours, caused paranoid anxiety and suicidal tendencies, which
wasn't exactly the way I remembered it, when someone tapped
me on the shoulder.

I turned.

"Croft?" He was maybe five foot ten and he was maybe fifteen pounds overweight. His receding black hair was wired with
gray and there were dark pouches under his small brown eyes.
A blue suit, a white shirt, a blue tie. Basic Cop, down to the thick
soles of his black brogues.

"Yeah," I said. "Labbady?"

He nodded glumly. "C'mon."

I followed him out the front door and to the right across the sunlit concrete plaza. The headquarters building also housed the Pre-Arraignment Detention Facility—the jail—and it was surrounded by old private homes, frame houses two and three stories tall, that had been converted into offices for bail bondsmen. Some of the buildings were painted in bright festive colors, blues and pinks and yellows, presumably to make arranging bail a merrier affair.

Not saying a word and not looking back at me, Labbady led me a block or two down Thirteenth and up the stairs of a small restaurant. The hostess knew Labbady, gave him an affable smile, then seated us at the bar. There were a couple of other cops, plainclothes officers, sitting in there already. For all I knew, everyone in the place, including the hostess, was a cop.

The bar was decorated to look like a British pub. The walls were dark and one of them held a dartboard. We sat in a booth beside a mural of old sailing ships. A cardboard tent on the table advised me that Guinness was available on tap. But for some reason I didn't feel as though I had been transported to Picadilly Circus.

"You're paying," Labbady told me, and picked up his menu.

"A pleasure," I said.

He glanced over at me, to see if I were mocking him. He decided that I wasn't, apparently, but he frowned anyway. "You're not off the hook," he said. "That was a dumb move, calling the house."

I nodded. "I know."

He said, "I talked to your friend in Santa Fe again this morning. Ramirez. He filled me in a little, about you and your partner. She still in a coma?"

"Last I heard." I'd called this morning, before leaving Pueblo, and again when I arrived in Denver.

"Tough break," Labbady said. "But she's lucky, in a way."

This was the second time someone had said that, and I didn't like it any more than I had the first time. "In what way?" I said. I was careful, once again, to flatten the level of my voice.

"Most of the people who run into Lucero," he said, "the ones he doesn't like, they end up dead."

"I don't think it was Lucero who shot her. I think it was Martinez."

He nodded. "The other one. Ramirez says you brought him in, what? six years ago?"

"Yeah."

A waitress materialized at the table. Labbady ordered a cheeseburger and a salad and a Fat Tire beer. I ordered the same. I still wasn't hungry but I knew that I needed the fuel. And the beer might help with the headache and the dehydration that had come after sleeping with a bellyful of Jack Daniel's.

When she left, Labbady said, "Tell me about Martinez."

I told him about Martinez. By the time I finished, the food had arrived.

I took a sip of my beer and said, "You know anything about Lucero?"

Leaning forward, Labbady had the cheeseburger halfway to his mouth, holding it in both hands with his elbows on the table. He smiled glumly and he said, "What I don't know about Lucero, it isn't worth knowing. I been following his career with interest for years." He took a huge bite of the burger.

"Which part of it?" I knew he was either Homicide or Narcotics.

He chewed the food over to one side of his mouth, and out of the other side he said, "Drugs." He swallowed, washed it down with a long gulp of beer. "You know he was a Marielito?"

I nodded, took a bite of my hamburger.

Labbady dipped a french fry in ketchup, popped it into his mouth. "He did real well for himself in Miami when he showed up there. Got himself hooked up to a Colombian family, the Ortegas. Part of the Cali cartel. Started pushing, street level stuff. Then he found his true calling. Shooting people."

He took a bite of cheeseburger, chewed, swallowed, drank

107

some beer. "Luiz is real good at shooting people. He does this little trick, where he shoots them in the eyes and the forehead? You know about that?"

"Yeah. A trademark."

Labbady nodded. "Yeah. Anyway, he started off by wiping out a couple of soldiers from another family of Colombians. He moved up the ladder after that. He's a maggot, Luiz, he's crazy as a loon, but he's no moron. He's got some real administrative skills. Aside from shooting people, I mean. But shooting people, that can be a good administrative skill, right? Helps motivate the troops." He took another bite.

I nodded, sipped again at my beer.

"They sent him to Dallas," he said, "in nineteen eighty-six, to handle their distribution here. They were having problems. Lucero shot some people and solved the problems. He came here in nineteen ninety-one."

"What kind of a record does he have?"

He drained off his beer. "None at all. Officially. Not till he got busted down in Albuquerque."

"If he's no moron, how did that happen?"

"He doesn't like being cheated, Luiz. He gets very upset about that. The guy in Albuquerque, guy named Carlyle, another maggot, he stiffed Lucero on a big order. Luiz went down there, to take care of it personally. Thing is, Carlyle heard he was coming. He got the sweats and he talked about it. Cops down there heard the story and staked him out. Even so, Lucero almost got away with it. He made his way in there, into Carlyle's house, shot the guy, and almost managed to make it back out."

The waitress materialized again and asked us if we'd like another beer. Both Labbady and I said yes.

"Tell me about this Miller bimbo," Labbady said. "On paper she looks like a straight civilian."

I told him what I knew about Sylvia Miller. The waitress brought two more beers, cleared away the plates. I told him some more about Sylvia.

"So she's a filbert," he said. "A gun groupie."

"Looks like it. What's the story on Lyle, the man who was shot?"

He lifted his beer, took a long swallow. "Lyle Monroe. We don't have much on him. No record. Some kind of film producer. Documentaries. He had money, but he didn't make it off any kind of movies. It's family money. His house was over by the country club, near Cherry Creek. You know the area?"

"I've been there."

"Big old stone house, fifteen or twenty rooms. Lawn the size of Nebraska."

"What was his connection to Lucero?"

He shrugged. "No idea. Drugs, probably, but we haven't nailed it down."

"Did any of the neighbors see the RV there?"

He shook his head. "There's a stone wall around the property. You can't see jack from the street. But I wouldn't be surprised to hear that Lucero dumped the RV before he got there. Neighborhood like that, an RV would stick out like a sore thumb. He probably had a car waiting for him somewhere. Him and the others."

"Sylvia had a Ford."

"We found it. She sold it, weeks ago. They had another car."

"But no one saw it," I said.

"We haven't found anyone yet."

"Where do you think they are now?"

He shrugged. "Texas, maybe. Florida, maybe. Lucero's got connections in both places. I had to put money on it, I'd say he's on his way to Florida. That's where he started. That's where he hung out the longest."

"Do you think they'll try to leave the country?"

"Nah. I don't think so. Not Luiz. To him, that'd be like running away. Like going back to his beginnings, when he was nothing." He shrugged. "But who knows? Things are pretty hot for him right now. Maybe he'll take off for South America."

"Colombia?"

"I don't think Colombia. He's a Cuban, don't forget. The Colombians are all pretty tight with each other. Luiz was always kind of an outsider, even when he was a honcho. That's the way I read it, anyway."

I nodded. "Thanks, Sergeant. I appreciate all the help. Would you mind if I poked around in Denver for a while?"

"Yeah," he said. "I would mind that a lot." He smiled and leaned forward and clasped his hands together on the table. "You know why I'm being such a prince of a guy here?"

"No," I said. "Why's that?"

"I'm giving you a break because your friend Ramirez says you're kosher. And because of your partner. I got a partner, too. So I can understand how you got a personal involvement in all this. But that also means you can make mistakes, right? Like you already did when you called up Monroe's house. That was primo, pally. That was classic. So here's the deal. I don't want you hanging around and maybe screwing things up again. You go on back to Santa Fe. Or go to Texas. Go to Florida. Go anywhere you want, but get out of Denver."

"Or what happens?"

Raising his hand off the table, he sat back. "Hey, who knows? It's a complicated world, right? Almost anything could happen. What I'm saying, things could get difficult for you. In general, you know?"

"Right."

"Right," he said. "And I wouldn't want to think that you and me, we screwed up this fantastic rapport we got established here. You follow me?"

"Like a caboose."

"Good. And like I say, I'm sorry about your partner. I mean that sincerely. I hope it all works out."

"Thanks," I said.

"Okay," he said. He stood, I stood, we shook hands. He nodded toward the bill. "Don't forget," he said. "You're paying."

★　★　★

110

I needed a place to operate from, so I drove up to Colfax and followed that east, until I found a generic motel a few miles past Monaco Parkway. After I hauled the computer into my room, I used the cellular phone to call the hospital. No change.

I called Leroy. He told me that the photos were ready, and I hung up. I connected the phone to the computer, turned on the machine, and brought up the fax software. In just over two minutes, the phone rang and the computer answered it. The machine hissed and beeped, whirred softly for a maybe a minute, hissed and beeped some more, went through the cycle again, then clicked off.

A few minutes later, after I'd told the computer what to do, and it had sent the information to the portable printer, I had fairly good paper copies of photographs of Ernest Martinez, Luiz Lucero, and Sylvia Miller, all facial views. As Leroy had told me, the photo of Sylvia was less clear than the other two. He had gotten a copy of her photo from Motor Vehicles and enlarged it. Although he had used his own computer to enhance the enlargement, the picture was still blurred and grainy.

I called Leroy, told him everything had come through all right. Then I lay down on the bed, called the New Mexico State Police, and asked for Robert Hernandez. He came on the line gruffly. "Yeah?"

"This is Joshua Croft."

"You don't listen good. I don't have anything else to say to you."

"Right. But you already said something. When we were talking before."

"What?"

"You said that after the breakout, you were getting phone calls from all over."

"Yeah, so?"

"One of them came from Denver, you said."

"So?"

"So I'm in Denver. Do you have a record of who made the call?"

"It was junk. The Denver PD already checked it out."

"Then they won't mind if I check it out again." This was something less than the truth, but Hernandez didn't have to know that. "If it's junk, what difference does it make? But if it isn't, it might help me locate Martinez and Lucero."

"And that whacko Miller woman. How'd you get onto her?"

"An informant."

"Pretty good work," he said. "Too bad you blew it by calling the house in Denver."

"I made a mistake. It won't happen again. Do I get the phone number?"

"You know, Croft, you really are a major pain in the ass."

"I've heard that before."

"I'll bet. Look, I'm busy right now. How do I get back to you?"

I gave him the cellular phone number. He hung up.

I flipped the phone shut and tossed it to the mattress.

The two beers at lunch had made me slow and fuzzy. I lay there, staring up at the dingy false ceiling, listening to the sound of the traffic whizzing through the thin walls. After a while, I thought back to the time I'd been lying in my room in the De Vargas Hotel in Santa Fe.

The De Vargas used to be on Water and Don Gaspar. It doesn't exist any longer. It's been gutted and refurbished and transformed into the Hotel St. Francis, a sleek and stylish place where you can order your breakfast in French. Back then, when it was the De Vargas, it had been the only cheap hotel in downtown Santa Fe. My small room had cost something like thirty dollars, but even at that price I had been overcharged. The grimy window looked over a service courtyard littered with garbage. The air was tainted with the smell of old cigar smoke and Pine Sol. The bedcover was as thin and frayed as the prospects of the hotel's guests.

112

It hadn't really mattered to me. By tomorrow I would be gone. I had already called Mondragón to tell him. Neither he nor his wife had been there, and I had been cowardly enough to feel relieved. I had left a message on his machine. It was early evening now and the nightstand lamp was on, casting a jaundiced yellow light through the thin shade, imitation parchment decorated with clumsy paintings of cowboys busting broncs. I was lying there in my clothes, trying to decide what to do with myself. I could go to the Bullring or the Pink Adobe, over on the Old Santa Fe Trail, and have a drink. Or maybe stop by the Palace. Back then there weren't as many places to get drunk as there are now.

I had decided on the Palace when someone knocked at the door. I was puzzled. I hadn't been expecting anyone.

I got up, crossed the tiny floor, and opened the door.

She stood there in the hallway, wearing the same pale blue blouse and the same black skirt she had worn earlier today. She held a flat black leather purse under her right arm.

"Mrs. Mondragón," I said.

She smiled. "May I come in?"

There was no polite way to refuse her. "Of course," I said, and I stepped aside to let her pass. As she did, I could smell the fragrance she wore, something faintly astringent and faintly sweet that reminded me of citrus flowers.

I was abruptly conscious of how cramped and shabby the room was. The thin bedspread, the worn brown rug, the peeling wallpaper—everything seemed to have become, in an instant, even more sleazy and pathetic than it had been before. I turned to her, leaving the door slightly ajar. I didn't know who I was protecting by doing that, or what I was protecting them from.

She stood in the center of the room. Over the years, maybe a hundred times, I've thought about this scene. Rita Mondragón standing in the center of that small seedy room.

She smiled again. "Joshua—"

★　★　★

113

The telephone rang, hurling me from one cramped room to another.

I grabbed Leroy's phone, flipped it open. "Yeah?"

"Croft? Hernandez. You ready? I got that information."

16

It was a gated suburban development to the west of Denver. But probably the home owners here would take umbrage at the word *development*. Probably the home owners here would take umbrage at a lot of words. Like *poverty*, and *hunger*, and *desperation*. The houses were mostly huge mock-Tudor castles and they sat comfortably back among imported trees on bright green land-scaped lawns that looked as though they should be crowded with pavilions and banners and jousting knights, and with motion picture cameras.

I found the house I wanted, drove the Jeep into the circular driveway, parked under a tall maple. I climbed up the flagstone walk, up the flagstone stairway, thumbed the buzzer. The door was pine, roughened and stained to look almost exactly like old oak, and it was banded with strips of anodized aluminum hammered to look almost exactly like wrought iron. There was a small casement window set into the wood, and through the artistically pebbled glass I could see someone moving toward me, like a fish gliding through murky water.

The door opened and the lady of the manor appeared. She was a blonde, and had been since at least Friday. Her face had the healthy glow that comes from a good diet, a good conscience, and an excellent bank account. She was probably in her mid-fifties but she was very fit and she wore a bright red blouse and a short black skirt that proved it. People probably told her fairly often that she had good legs. They were right. She had good arms, too, strong and wiry below the carefully back-folded cuffs of her blouse. It was my guess that there was a tennis racquet lurking around somewhere.

"Mrs. Albert?" I said.

"Yes," she said, and with the back of her slender hand she brushed away a lock of hair that had slumped a couple of millimeters out of place. Her nails were long and flawless and, like her lips, they were painted the same color as her blouse. "Are you Mr. Croft?"

"Yes."

"May I see some identification?"

"Certainly." I slipped out my wallet, showed her the ID. "Did you call Robert Hernandez at the New Mexico State Police?"

"I did, yes. But you can never tell, can you? Someone could be wandering the streets, pretending to be you."

No one was that stupid, I thought. But I smiled pleasantly.

"Please come in," she said.

I tucked the wallet back into my pocket and I stepped into the foyer. She glanced swiftly down to make sure I hadn't tracked any socialism onto the parquet floor. "This way," she said. "He's upstairs. He has his own suite of rooms."

I thought that must be very jolly for him.

I followed her along the edge of a living room that wasn't quite as large as the L.A. Coliseum. Stone walls, square beams overhead, a huge fireplace, dark wooden floors brightened here and there by throw rugs that had probably been woven in quaint Third World countries. Off in the distance a short Hispanic woman was plumping up the cushions of a white sofa the size of a tugboat. Mrs. Albert told me, "The policeman who came here before said that it was a waste of time."

"You can never tell," I said. Words to live by.

We came to a broad balustraded stairway, more pine, more stain. Mrs. Albert turned to me. "You won't take terribly long, will you? The house is a mess and we've got some people coming over tonight. Consuelo and I are trying to get everything ready." She brushed her perfect hair back again. This time I realized that the gesture was designed to demonstrate that her competence, usually invincible, was a tad harried at the moment.

I smiled pleasantly again. It's easy when you know how. "I doubt it," I said. "I'll try to be out of here as quickly as possible."

She nodded, not at all surprised that life would proceed as she expected it to proceed. "He's just up there," she said, pointing up the stairs. "The door all the way at the end, on the left."

At the end of the long hallway, I knocked on the door to my left.

It was opened by an elf. He had to be at least seventy years old, and possibly he was older, but he looked about sixty. He was a thin inch over five feet tall and he wore a double-breasted gray wool suit with the jacket buttoned shut, a white shirt, and a neatly knotted black tie. His face was shiny and red and his wavy hair was thick and white. So were his eyebrows. His eyes were blue. "Are you the PI?" he said.

"Yes," I said. "Joshua Croft."

"Terrific," he said, and beamed at me. "Terrific." He held out a small red hand and I took it. The small red hand wrapped around mine and crushed it. "Charlie Niederman," he said. "Come on in."

I stepped into a small parlor filled with antique furniture that seemed too bulky for the space it occupied. A rambling upholstered sofa printed with a floral pattern, a pair of bulky matching club chairs, an elaborately carved coffee table, matching end tables, tall matching bookcases along one wall. It reminded me for a moment of the furniture in Sylvia Miller's house in Las Vegas, but all of this had been lived-in, for a long time. And probably it had been lived-in somewhere else, before it had been crowded into this room.

"I dressed up for the occasion," said the elf, cocking his head and running his thumbs along the broad lapels of his jacket. "Whatty ya think?"

"Very dapper," I said.

"Yeah? You think dapper?" He turned to look at himself in a full-length mirror mounted on the wall. "Dapper, sure, why not?" He nodded to the mirror. "Dapper's good." He raised his head slightly, giving himself another half an inch of height, turned to the side, and lightly ran his hand down the front of the suit coat as though he were stroking a cat. "Forty years I got this suit, and it fits me like I only bought it yesterday. Like a glove." He turned to me. "You know why?"

I smiled. "You had it altered?"

"Altered! Whatty you, a jokester? *Fitness,*" he said, and thumped his fist against his chest. *"Fitness.* I take care of myself, fella. You don't take care of yourself, who's going to, huh?" Squinting at me, he raised his hand and twitched a finger, beckoning. "C'mon, Mr. PI. Lemme show you something."

We went into the next room, smaller than the parlor and set up as a home gym. Plastic mats on the floor, a stationary bicycle, a rowing machine. Beneath the window, an orderly row of gray dumbbells, pairs of them in weights from fifteen pounds to forty.

He pointed to the plastic mats. "Every day," he said, "one hundred sit-ups. And one hundred push-ups. *Every day.*" He eyed me thoughtfully. "You look pretty healthy. You work out?"

"I swim a little."

He nodded. "Swimming's good. Cardiovascular. Good. Weights are good, too. You do weights?"

"Not if I have a choice."

"Weights are good. Here. Look." He danced over to the dumbbells, bent over at the waist, grabbed a forty-pound weight in each hand, straightened his body and did a quick, smooth curl with his right arm, then another with his left. His face went from red to purple. "Muscle mass," he said through clenched teeth. He lowered the dumbbells. "Muscle mass is good." He curled his right arm. "Muscle tissue burns calories all day long." He curled his left arm. "Fat just lies there. Not good." I thought I saw a bead of sweat suddenly blister his forehead.

"Mr. Niederman," I said, "I came here because I was told you might have information about Luiz Lucero."

"Lucero, okay. Forget the weights." He lowered the dumbbells to the floor, then turned to me. He was puffing slightly, but both of us ignored it. "I'm a nutcase," he said, and he grinned. "But I *know* I'm a nutcase. When you know it, it's good. When you don't know, not so good. Okay. You want information. Follow me, Mr. PI." He twitched the finger at me again.

I followed him into the third room. This was a bedroom. Against the far wall stood a huge four-poster. Just inside the door, carefully positioned atop a small white table, was a computer setup—keyboard, monitor, printer, some other equipment I couldn't identify. To the left of the table was a black wooden rocker. In front of the table sat a gray swivel chair. To the right was a white metal file cabinet.

Farther to the right was the window. He led me there. From a hook beside the sill, on a leather strap, hung a Minolta camera with a long telephoto lens.

Mr. Niederman pointed out the window to the mock-Tudor castle across the street. "See there?" he said. "That's his house."

"Whose house?"

"*Whose house,*" he said, and snorted. He squinted up at me. "How long you been a private detective?"

"I'm just starting out."

"I can believe it. *Whose house,* you ask me. So who's the guy you wanna know about? Luiz Lucero, that's who. That's *his* house. He moved in there about five years ago. And I been doing surveillance ever since."

"Surveillance."

"Look at this baby." He lifted the camera off its hook, cradled it gently in his small hands. "I can shoot a fly from half a mile away. I can watch him drool."

"But Lucero's not living there."

He scowled with impatience. "What am I, a dummy? Lucero was in prison, *I* know that. Where he belonged, the pig. But see, one of his henchmen is taking care of the place. Another drug

119

pig. Fella named Carillo. He's Lucero's right-hand man, see. He moved in when they put Lucero in prison, down in New Mexico. And I been keeping records."

"What kind of records?"

Carefully, he hung the strap over the hook. "C'mon."

He danced over to the computer. "Grab a seat," he said, and pointed to a black wooden rocking chair to my right. "Make yourself at home." He jumped into the swivel chair, rolled it forward, and tapped at the keys. "You know computers?" He grabbed the mouse on the tabletop and began to skate it around the white surface.

"I'm just starting out," I said. I maneuvered the rocker closer to the table and sat down in it.

He was leaning forward, peering into the monitor. "Yeah? Whatty ya got? What kinda chip?"

"A Pentium, I think."

He looked at me as though I'd stolen his dog. "You got a Pentium?"

"It was a gift," I said. Apologetically.

"A Pentium," he said. It seemed to me that his shoulders had slumped within the suit jacket. "I been telling Moira for months I need a Pentium. Moira, my daughter. You met her? Downstairs?"

"I met her."

"You gotta keep up, I tell her. You gotta keep abreast. How many megahertz?"

"I'm not sure. What's good?"

"Anything over a hundred is good."

"Nothing like that," I told him. "Twenty, I think."

"Oh, well," he said, and he seemed to relax. "This is a 486-DX4-100, see. That's the top of the line for the 486. Very fast. Faster than a sixty megahertz Pentium, even."

"A lot faster than mine."

He nodded happily, pleased with himself and his machine, and also with me. "But twenny megahertz is good. Don't get me wrong. In a Pentium, twenny megahertz is very good. That's a terrific little chip, that Pentium." He turned back to the screen. "Okay. Here we are. Now watch."

I watched. I was looking at some sort of tabular arrangement, information arranged in rows and columns.

He said, "On the left, see, we got dates. On the right, we got descriptions." As he slid the mouse around the tabletop, the computer's cursor zipped around the screen. "Okay, look, that's Friday, right? Ten A.M. The day before the prison thing. The escape, right? Okay, so what does that say?"

"Three men. Mercedes."

He nodded. "So now we know you can read. Good. That's very good. Now watch. I click on this, right?"

The tabular screen was abruptly replaced by a screen that held five small color photographs against a gray background. Three of the photographs were of Hispanic men, facial shots. The fourth was a shot of a silver-gray four-door Mercedes, one of the newer models. The fifth was a shot of the car's license plate.

"These are thumbnails," he said, swinging the cursor around the screen. "All I got to do is click on one . . ." He moved the cursor over one of the facial shots, clicked the mouse. The thumbnails vanished and the screen slowly filled, from top to bottom, with an enlargement of the shot.

"That's why I need a Pentium, see," said Mr. Niederman. "A Pentium, you wouldn't have to wait."

The picture was slightly blurry, as though the camera hadn't been completely still when the frame was exposed. But the man's features were clear enough.

"Who is he?" I asked him.

"Who knows?" he said. "Another henchman." He turned to me. "That's how come I called the police. This meeting, see? Carillo doesn't get that many visitors. So when I see these guys on Friday, and then on Saturday I hear about the prison break," he leaned toward me, winked, and tapped his forehead, "I put two and two together, right? These guys, drug pigs, they're *planning* the prison break. Right there, right across the street."

"What did the police say?"

"The police," he scowled. "Whatta *they* know? The guy they sent out here was a dummy. Very polite, yessir, nosir, but I could see what he's thinking—we got a nutcase here. Okay, so I'm a nutcase, I admit it, but I'm no dummy. The guy never even called me, afterward, to keep me abreast—I had to call him."

"And what did he say?"

"Said he talked to the guys involved. Said it was only a poker game. *Thank you very much for your assistance, sir.* A poker game!" he sneered. "At ten o'clock in the morning?"

I nodded. "Mr. Niederman, you've been taking these pictures for five years now?"

"Right, right. Since Lucero moved in over there. I got a darkroom down in the basement, a very nice setup. Top of the line. I put it together myself. I print out the shots, see, then I run them through this baby here." He reached out toward an oblong beige box on the desk, patted it paternally. "My scanner."

I nodded again and I took from my jacket pocket the photographs I'd gotten from Leroy's computer a few hours ago.

"What I really need," he said, "is a digital camera. One of those new Canons. That way, see, I could download the pictures directly into the computer. That would be better." He shrugged, held out his hands—what's a guy to do? "I been telling Moira *that* for months now, too."

I handed him the picture of Sylvia Miller. "Have you ever seen this woman?"

He studied it, shook his head. "Not a very good print. A blowup." He looked at me. "What is it, off of some kinda ID thing? A driver's license?"

"A driver's license."

He studied the picture some more, finally nodded. "Maybe, yeah. Could be. Could be her." He turned back to the machine, fiddled with the mouse. The photograph disappeared, replaced by the tabular screen. He jerked the mouse and the lines went whizzing down the screen. The screen stopped. He clicked the mouse. The screen showed another series of thumbnails. None of these were a picture of a woman.

"Damn," said Mr. Niederman. "Wait. We'll get there."

The tabular screen showed again. Mr. Niederman clicked his mouse.

Four small photos showed on the screen. A man, a woman, a silver-gray Lincoln Towncar, the car's Texas license plate. The photograph of the woman was about the same size as the photo on a driver's license, and it was a photograph of Sylvia Miller.

Mr. Niederman turned to me and grinned. "Good, huh?"

"Very good," I told him.

PART THREE

17

INTERSTATE 70 HEADS directly east into the plains from Denver until it reaches Strasburg, where it dips toward the south for a while before it levels out at Limon and heads east again, aiming straight at Kansas. The land around me was flat and mostly empty. Some of it was open range, a few gaunt and solemn cattle grazing in the sparse scrub grass. Some of it was farmland, acres and acres of winter wheat coming up pale and thin. Now and then, off in the distance, a tiny complex of farm buildings huddled against a lonely clump of elms. Now and then, a faraway copse of cottonwoods clung to a thin ribbon of stream. Now and then, every twenty or thirty miles, signaled by the silhouette of a water tower against the blank blue sky, a small town clung to the thin ribbon of highway.

It seemed bleak and desolate to me and I wondered how they did it. How those people, whoever they were, lived out here in those isolated farmhouses, those isolated towns, surviving over the years at the mercy of the weather and the water and the finance companies.

Maybe they had MTV.

"You're being snide, Joshua," Rita told me.

"I honestly don't know how they do it," I said. *"I'd go crazy in a week."*

She smiled. We were on the patio again. The sunlight was winking off the gold cross at her slender neck, sliding along the black of her hair and the blue silk of her blouse. "Perhaps that indicates that you've some fundamental flaw. Some problem with confronting yourself."

"Maybe. I've got plenty of flaws, fundamental and otherwise. But I don't even like driving through a place like this."

"Why do it, then? Why drive to Texas?"

"Those pictures of Mr. Niederman's. He got a good shot of Sylvia Miller, and a good shot of the license plate of the car she was in. It's registered to a Thomas Thorogood of Carlton, Texas. Carlton is a few miles west of Wichita Falls. This is the best way for me to get there."

"But why drive? Why not take an airplane?"

"I keep my mobility. Maybe, somewhere along the line, I'll have to turn around and head back to Santa Fe."

We didn't discuss why I might have to do that.

"Why do you think Sylvia was in Denver with Thorogood?" she asked me.

"I think that Carillo, who's apparently some kind of lieutenant to Lucero, was arranging for the flow of funds into Sylvia's account."

"And why was Thorogood there?"

"I don't know. Maybe he had business with Carillo and it was convenient for him to pick up Sylvia along the way."

"And why would he drive all the way from Texas?"

"Maybe he was transporting drugs."

She smiled. "That's fairly thin, isn't it?"

"Maybe. We'll see."

"And you really think that Lucero will be taking Martinez and Miller to Carlton?"

"It's the only lead I've got," I said.

"It's not much of one."

"Following it is the only thing I can do right now."

"You can give it to the police."

"Then I wouldn't have anything to do. And they had their chance. The Denver cop who came by Mr. Niederman's. If he'd looked through all the pictures in that computer, he'd have seen the picture of Sylvia Miller."

She smiled again. "It wouldn't have meant anything to him. You know that. No one knew about Sylvia Miller until yesterday. When was that picture taken?"

"Two months ago. But he'd still have seen the picture of the car with the Texas license plate. He could've checked it out with Texas Motor Vehicles, just like I did, and found Thorogood."

"He would've had no reason to. Without the Sylvia Miller connection, Mr. Thorogood was just a simple visitor."

"The cop still should've checked him out."

"Joshua." She smiled again. "What's the real reason you're driving to Texas? Why won't you come back to Santa Fe?"

I tried to find an answer that made sense, and one that put me in something like a good light. But that particular answer didn't exist. I was refusing to return to Santa Fe because I knew I would be helpless there. I would be unable to do anything but sit by her bedside and wait for her to recover. Or to die.

Hurtling through the grim flat prairie, with Thorogood and Carlton as goals, I could at least persuade myself that I was doing something. Even if I suspected that the goals, when I reached them, would prove to be phantoms.

And, like a phantom, the image of Rita slowly faded away, smiling as it did, smiling at the answer I had failed to provide, had been unable to provide, until all that was left was the empty prairie on either side of me, and the tent of dull blue sky, and the stuttering white line of the highway, racing toward the car like a volley of arrows.

I took a deep breath, blew it out.

Rita hadn't been a phantom that time, eight years ago, when she stood in the center of my shabby room at the De Vargas.

"Joshua," she said. She smiled at me. "I found your message on the answering machine."

Still standing by the partly opened door, leaning against the wall with my arms crossed, I only nodded.

She pointed to the rickety wooden chair in front of the rickety wooden desk. "Do you mind if I sit down?"

I smiled, I think. "Have you had a tetanus shot?"

I know that she smiled. She had the kind of smile that I could feel in my chest, even eight years later. "Not recently," she said, "but I'm willing to take a chance."

"Then be my guest," I said.

She lifted the chair, turned it around to face the room, and sat down, her knees together, her hands holding her purse on her lap. She looked up at me and she raised her eyebrows, amused. "Are you going to keep standing there?"

The only other place to sit was the bed. It was foolish of me not to sit there, but I've often been a fool. "I've been sitting all day," I told her. "I'm fine."

She nodded, then pursed her lips, looked down for a moment at the threadbare carpet. I don't think she saw it. She was a woman who was used to speaking her mind, it seemed to me, and who was frustrated now because, for whatever reason, this was proving difficult. She looked up at me, smiled faintly. At herself, maybe. At the difficulty, maybe. "My husband," she said at last, looking up, "is usually a very cautious man."

I nodded.

"Not in the physical sense," she said. "Physically, he's as brave as any man I've ever known. I've accused him, more than once, of being foolhardy."

I nodded again. This was her scene, it seemed to me, and there wasn't any way I could help her with it.

But maybe, at bottom, I didn't really want to help her. Maybe I resented her for showing up here, and for reminding me of all the reasons I hadn't wanted to see her again. Maybe I was punishing her.

I've often been a fool.

"Let's call it," she said, "a kind of emotional caution. He seldom takes people at face value."

"That's generally a good way to go," I said, "for a private detective."

"Generally, yes. But sometimes William lets the caution seep over into his personal life. He sometimes finds it difficult to trust anyone at all. Not simply clients. Anyone he meets, in whatever circumstances."

I nodded some more. "An occupational hazard."

Smiling again, wryly now, she shook her head at my deliberate obtuseness. "You're not making this any easier."

"What are you trying to say, Mrs. Mondragón?"

She looked at me directly. "What made you decide not to work with us?"

I shook my head. "It wasn't that. I just decided that I'd be happier in Oregon."

"Why?"

"The redwood trees."

She winced briefly, annoyed. "Oh, for goodness sake, Joshua. Stop being so difficult."

"What would you like me to tell you?"

"Something that made sense."

"I changed my mind. That's all. So far as I know, it's still legal in this country."

She looked down at her purse for a moment, then looked up at me. "William trusted you. Immediately. That's the point I'm trying to make. He may not have shown it, he's sometimes not . . . quite as good at that as he could be, but he trusted you. And he enjoyed you. We've been looking for someone for months now. We've talked to retired policemen. We've talked to dead-end PIs. We've talked to bouncers from the Bullring. And William hasn't liked any of them. With good cause, usually."

I smiled. "Are you trying to find him someone to play with?"

She looked at me for a moment and then she smiled. I could feel it in my chest again. "Yes," she said. "In a sense I am. I'm trying to find someone he can like, and someone with whom he can enjoy working. There's too much business for him to handle on his own. And I can help with only a certain amount of it. He needs someone he can rely upon. And he felt that you were that person."

"Mrs. Mondragón—"

She pursed her lips. "His sending you out on that collection—perhaps that upset you. The manner in which he did it. Perhaps it struck you as . . . arrogant. William is not an arrogant man, but I can understand how some people might perceive him as such."

I was so busy admiring her language skills, and the black depths of her large eyes, that she caught me off guard when she suddenly stood up. "I'm not going to beg you, Joshua. But I am going to remind you that you told him you'd be there tomorrow. I know that William would be extremely surprised, and extremely disappointed, to learn that you'd gone back on your word."

"That's not entirely fair, Mrs.—"

She came toward me. "I've erased the tape on the answering machine," she said. She stood only a foot or two away and again I could smell the citrus and floral scent of her perfume. "I hope I'll see you in the office tomorrow. I'll be expecting you. So will William. In a few weeks, or even in a few days, if we all find that we can't work together, then I'll understand if you decide to leave. But I think you should give William a chance. After all, he gave one to you."

She smiled once more, briefly and without humor. "Thank you for hearing me out," she said. And then she left, sliding through the opened door, phantomlike.

Later, I went to the Bullring and sat there among a jostling throng of red-faced New Mexican politicians, amid the sound of heavy masculine laughter and the sour smell of stale beer. As I nursed my drink, it occurred to me how strange it was that she had come to me. All right, fine, they needed another hand at the ranch. But were they so desperate for help that she had to plead with the first drifter who passed through town?

It occurred to me, too, that by not telling William about my message on the answering machine, she was keeping secrets from her husband. And that if I stayed, if I went to work with them, this would be a secret that we shared, she and I.

And, according to her, William had a failing or two. He was

foolhardy. He was distrustful. He was sometimes perceived as arrogant.

Maybe the marriage of Mr. and Mrs. Mondragón was not an altogether happy one. And maybe, if I hung around for a while . . .

I felt, within me, a sudden queasy flutter of self-disgust. It's always unpleasant to discover that you're still capable of thinking like some theoretically lower form of life. A weasel, for example.

Forget it, I told myself. Even if the marriage wasn't perfect, what difference would that make to you?

I drank there for a while, and after a few hours I convinced myself to give the job a try. As she had pointed out, I had said I would. As she had pointed out, I could always leave in a few days, a few weeks.

I convinced myself that I would take the job despite her, and not because of her. I convinced myself I'd be able to handle being in the same office, day after day, with Rita Mondragón.

She was, after all, just another woman.

I've often been a fool.

I had left Denver around four in the afternoon. I was across the border into Kansas by seven o'clock. Around eight o'clock, as I approached Colby, the headlights flashed along road signs that promised me the World's Largest Chipmunk. I managed to drive on without stopping.

I left the Interstate about twenty miles farther on, and picked up Highway 83, going south. It was headed for pretty much the same place that I was, and according to the map it was a good road. But I was tired, so I gassed up the car in Oakley, grabbed a hamburger, and found myself another motel.

I'd tried two or three times to telephone the hospital while I was on the Interstate, but I'd been out of range. I tried again now, lying on my "luxurious king-sized bed," and I got through. Rita's condition was unchanged.

I didn't want to call anyone else. I poured myself a heavy drink, climbed into bed, and turned off the lights.

I lay there listening to the sad groan and rumble of distant trucks barreling toward their unknown destinations.

I lay there remembering Rita.

I tried to sleep, but that white dividing line of the highway had seared itself into my retinas. Whenever I closed my eyes, it began to flicker past them, endless, inexorable.

I drank some more. Quite a bit more. I remembered Rita as she toppled to the patio. I remembered her lying in the hospital bed, the vulnerable human center of an alien network of wires and tubes.

Memories tumbled over one another in no particular order. I saw her standing in the doorway of a barn in northern New Mexico, holding the gun that saved my life. I saw her walking toward me in the moonlight, her bare skin glowing pale. I saw her sitting in the wheelchair, patiently explaining to me why I was wrong. I saw her peering out the porthole of the boat in Catalina, laughing at the fish. I saw her crying—the first time I'd ever seen her cry—as she told me she had begun to believe she would never leave the chair, never walk again . . .

I must have drifted off. Suddenly the phone rang and my entire body twitched. Blindly, I fumbled around on the bed until I found the receiver. It rang again. I flipped it open and I glanced at my watch. Ten-thirty. The hospital?

"Hello?" I said.

"Croft?" I didn't recognize the voice.

"Yeah?"

"Hey, *Josh-you-ah.* How's your girlfriend, bro?"

I recognized it then. Ernie Martinez. The man who had shot her.

18

I COULD FEEL my fingers curl around the tiny telephone as though it were his throat. If I weren't careful, Leroy's expensive toy would become a handful of splintered plastic and shattered circuits. "She's fine, Ernie," I said.

He laughed, low and gravelly. "That's not what I hear, bro. I hear she's in one of those comas. I hear she's a fuckin' vegetable. A fuckin' tomato, bro. Hey, bro, can you fuck a fuckin' tomato?" He laughed again. "Can you do that, *Josh-you-ah?*"

I kept my voice even. "I don't know where you're getting your information, Ernie. She's fine."

Another laugh. "Hey, *Josh-you-ah,* you got one of those phones tell you who's calling? Caller ID? That won't work, bro. I blocked it."

"Maybe the call's being traced."

"Cops aren't gonna set up a trace—why should they figure me to call you? Besides, you were running a trace, that's the last thing you'd want me to think about. Doesn't matter anyhow, bro. A few minutes and I'm outta here. I'm history. Just thought I'd call and shoot the shit with my old amigo."

"How's Sylvia Miller?"

"Sylvia? She's okay. Great little chick, bro. *Hot,* you know what I mean? A lot hotter than your tomato girlfriend, that's for damn sure. Hey, was that you? Called the house up in Denver?"

"That was me."

Another laugh. "You gave us a real scare, *Josh-you-ah.* Panic city. How'd you find out about Lyle?"

135

"So where are you now, Ernie? Let's get together, maybe do lunch."

Still another laugh. "Hey, bro, you should go home, get some rest. You been hangin' around the office too long. You sound a little loco these days, you know?"

"Was it you, Ernie, who called before and hung up?"

"Just wanted to see how my old amigo was doing. My old amigo *Josh-you-ah.* Hey, bro, you go home now. Or go over to the hospital, check out the tomato."

"Why don't we get together, Ernie. You and I."

He laughed once more. "I'm gone, bro. I'm outta here." And he hung up.

I took a breath. Then I poured myself a straight shot of Jack Daniel's and I took that. Quickly. My hands were shaking.

The phone call hadn't told me much. He had said "up in Denver." Most people use "up" to mean north. But some don't. Maybe he was south of Denver, maybe he was in Carlton, Texas. And maybe he wasn't.

He didn't know that I was in Kansas. He had dialed the office number and the call had been forwarded to the cellular phone. Maybe it gave me an advantage, his not knowing that I was headed for Texas. And maybe it didn't matter at all.

I first met Ernie Martinez seven years ago, at Vanessie's in Santa Fe.

Vanessie's is a big, open saloon that a local newspaper had once described as looking like a Viking mead hall. The high ceilings are supported by square, oversized wooden beams. At either end of the huge room are oversized stone fireplaces, and above each of these hangs the oversized stainless steel skull of a stylized longhorn steer. A Steinway grand piano sits against the south wall, beneath an oversized mirror and between a pair of oversized wall hangings. The big rectangular bar sits in an alcove at the north wall.

It was a Sunday night in winter, and it was late, nearly midnight. Except for some couples at the tables near the lighted fireplaces, the room was empty. There were only a few people at the bar. Gordon, the bartender, stood under the lamp by the cash register, his right foot propped against the metal rack that held the bottles. A *New York Times* magazine lay folded open on his raised thigh. Gordon worked the *Times* crossword puzzle every Sunday night, and he worked it with a ballpoint pen. I always found this vaguely annoying. I would learn later that Rita did the same thing.

Gordon looked up, saw me, put aside the magazine and the ballpoint pen, strolled over. "Joshua. How goes it?"

"Fine, Gordon. You?"

"Can't complain. Jack rocks, water back?"

"That would be extremely nice."

He smiled and turned away to make it.

I glanced around the bar. To my right, alone, sat an old man named Jonathan. I had seen him around Santa Fe, had talked to him a few times. He hadn't remembered me from one time to the next. Until the administration of the high school fired him for drinking, ten or twelve years ago, he had been a teacher. Now he shambled around town in a long black overcoat that had once belonged to someone taller and wider, and he gave away business cards that he'd typed onto plain paper and carefully cut out with scissors. I liked him for the business cards.

Across from me, toward the end of the bar, sat an attractive young blonde woman in a white cable-knit turtleneck sweater. A wing of her hair fell down along the right side of her face, concealing it. What I could see of the face looked familiar, but I couldn't hang a name on it.

Separated from her by an empty chair were two Hispanic men. The one nearest her was standing, leaning slightly toward her, his head lowered, his forearms resting on the tall back of his chair. He was saying something that the woman was doing a pretty good job of ignoring. The other man sat to his left, also leaning toward the woman. Both men were good-looking and both were in their twenties. Both had black hair, thick and shiny, combed into complex pompadours. Both wore black leather jackets with the collars turned up. Brando had no idea what he was unleashing upon the world.

Gordon brought me the drinks, the Jack Daniel's and the water. "So how's the PI business?" he asked me.

I didn't get a chance to answer. The blonde woman called out. "Bartender? Excuse me?"

Gordon turned to her. "Yes?"

"I'm sorry to bother you," she said. "But could you please ask this gentleman to leave me alone?" She didn't seem nervous. She sounded very matter-of-fact, and she didn't look at the Hispanic man as she spoke.

Gordon was tall, maybe six feet three, but in his blue jeans, denim shirt, and black vest he probably didn't weigh more than a hundred and sixty. The standing man was almost as tall, and both men were a lot broader. Even so, Gordon didn't hesitate. He walked toward them.

The standing man smiled easily. Still resting his arms against the back of the chair, hands drooping, he said, "Fuck off, bro. None of your business."

Gordon leaned forward, arms apart, and put his palms along the edge of the bar. From where I sat, his back hid the standing man. Gordon said something I couldn't catch, and the standing man must've said something in reply, because his friend laughed. Smiling, watching Gordon, the friend pushed back his chair and stood up.

So did I.

I was younger then, and I had more to prove and less to lose.

I walked around the bar. The man nearest the woman had moved his right hand off his chair and draped it on the shoulder of the shearling coat that hung over the back of hers. She was canted to the side, away from the hand and him, but she had her head turned in his direction. She didn't seem happy, but she still didn't seem nervous.

Closer up, the taller man was less good looking. His face was beginning to put on meat, and his eyes were rimmed with red.

He looked at me and he gave me the same easy smile he'd given Gordon. "You got a problem, bro?"

"I think it's time for you to leave," I said.

He nodded, pleased by the notion. "That what *you* think, bro?"

"That's what I think."

Lazily, he pushed himself off the back of the chair and turned to face me. His friend stood there, waiting, his glance flicking between me and the tall man.

The woman snatched her purse from the bar, slipped off her chair, and came around me, on my right. I heard her mutter *"Jesus,"* under her breath. She sounded more irritated than frightened.

The tall man shrugged and slipped his hands into his pockets. "Why you want to say something like that?" He shook his head regretfully. "Not very polite, bro."

"Gordon?" I said. I didn't take my eyes off the tall man.

"Yeah?"

"When he pulls his hand out of his pocket, I'm going to deck him. You dial nine-one-one."

"You got it."

The tall man laughed. He looked me up and down with elaborate amazement. "You gonna *deck* me, bro?"

"That's right."

He grinned. "Hey, I gotta tell you, bro. I'm scared. I'm quakin' in my fuckin' boots."

"Then you're smarter than you look," I said. I was younger then.

He smiled broadly. "But hey, bro," he said, "what about my friend here?" He jerked his head toward the other man.

I glanced at him. "He's probably not," I said.

He laughed again. "You're something else, you know? You insult us? You say rude things? And you gonna deck the *both* of us?"

"Right."

Grinning again, he said, "Hey, what you think? You think I

got a big ole knife in there, bro? In my pocket? All the greasers, they all carry big ole knives, right, bro? *Switchblades.*" Still grinning, he twitched his shoulder toward me, feinting a pull from the pocket.

I did nothing, and he rocked back on his heels and laughed.

I said, "Gordon?"

"Yeah."

"There's not much point in waiting. Why don't you go ahead and make the call."

"Right." Out of the corner of my eye I saw him moving toward the telephone.

The tall man grinned again. He looked me up and down again. He cocked his head. "Hey, bro, what's your name?"

"Joshua Croft," I told him.

"Josh-you-ah," he said. *"Josh-you-ah* Croft." He nodded. "I'm gonna remember that name, bro."

"Good."

"Yeah," he said, and nodded once more. "I think so." He turned to the friend. "C'mon. Maybe we see *Josh-you-ah* again sometime."

The friend glanced at me, and then the two of them walked toward the doorway, strutting—to demonstrate, to me and to themselves, that the departure was their own idea. The tall one still had his hands in his pocket. When he was nearly at the door, he stopped, turned back to me, and whipped his hand from his pocket as though it were a gun. It was empty and the finger was pointing at me. *"Bang!"* he said. He laughed once, sharply, then he turned around and sauntered off, plucking with both hands at his collar to make sure it was still up.

I turned to Gordon. He was standing at the telephone, holding the receiver. "I don't think you'll need the cops," I said.

"I never called them," he told me. He smiled. "Looked like he was going to fade."

"He's an asshole!" shouted Jonathan from the end of the bar. He cleared his throat. "Ernie Martinez. He was always an asshole. A *big* asshole. Always."

"Jesus," said the woman.

I turned to her. I was surprised that she was still there. When she slipped by me, I had thought she was leaving.

I hadn't realized how short she was, about five foot one. But she was perfectly proportioned and she was very well packaged in the turtleneck sweater and tight faded jeans and a pair of tan Frye boots. Her eyes were gray.

She said, "A person could get testosterone poisoning just breathing the air around here."

I looked at her. I smiled. "You're right," I said. "We should've let him maul you for a while. Maybe, if we were nice, he would've let us join in."

She stared at me for a moment, her lips pursed. Then, lightly, she tossed back the hair that swept down alongside her face and she raised her chin. "All right," she said. "Thank you." She turned to Gordon. "I'm sorry. I didn't mean to cause you any trouble."

"No trouble," he told her.

She turned back to me, and the hair fell into place along her cheek. "But that remark you made, about his being smarter than he looked. You were deliberately trying to antagonize him."

"Maybe a little," I admitted.

"And wasn't that just a wee bit childish?"

"Just a wee bit."

Her eyes narrowed. "What would've happened if he'd actually pulled out a knife?"

"I'd have gotten stabbed, probably."

"Lordy me," she said, smiling as she put her hand between her breasts, a parody of the Southern Belle. "An honest macho-man. There can't be too many of you around."

"Me and another guy. But he got stabbed."

She laughed. "Well, I suppose I should thank you for springing to my defense." She held out her hand. "Sally Durrell," she said.

I took the hand. "Joshua Croft." I nodded toward Gordon. "Gordon James."

"Hello, Gordon," she said, then turned back to me. "You work for the Mondragóns."

"And you're a lawyer," I said. "I've read about you."

Another smile. "Small world."

"Small town, anyway."

Someone tapped me on the shoulder. Jonathan, bundled up in his overcoat. His lank gray hair was tousled and his hollow cheeks were stubbled with white. "You did real well," he told me. "With that Ernie asshole. Here." He handed me one of his homemade cards. I thanked him and put the card into my shirt pocket. He handed one to Sally Durrell.

She looked at it, smiled, and said, "Thank you, Mr. Richards." She slipped the card into her purse.

"He was always an asshole," said Jonathan. "Wiseass little shit." Then he turned and shuffled off, out the door and out into the night.

"Time for me to leave, too," said Sally Durrell. "This has been more excitement than a girl can stand." She set the purse on the bar, came around me, lifted her coat from the back of the chair. She eased it on, the left sleeve, then the right. It was a pleasure to watch her.

I said, "Did they see you come in?"

She glanced toward the door. "Those two? They came in behind me."

"I'll walk you to your car."

She smiled. "I don't really think that's necessary."

I shrugged. "If I'm wrong, I'm the one who looks like a jerk."

She raised an eyebrow. "And does that happen often?"

"Being wrong? Or looking like a jerk?"

"Either. Both."

"All the time. You'll get to see it, probably, in a few minutes."

She sighed theatrically. The wing of blonde hair trembled as she shook her head in mock resignation. Or maybe it was genuine resignation. She picked up her purse.

Gordon said, "Joshua?"

"Yeah?"

He reached his right hand down below the level of the bar-top, brought it up holding an old-fashioned cop's nightstick. "Here you go." He tossed it to me and I caught it. "I had you covered," he said. He smiled and added, "Bro."

"Oh, for God's sake," said Sally Durrell. She made a face. "I'm surrounded by vigilantes." She buttoned up the coat, looked up at me. "This is a real treat. It's not every day I get escorted to my car by a thug with a nightstick."

"A good thing, too," I said. "Think of all the overtime you'd have to pay."

She smiled, but the corners of her mouth were slightly down-turned in irritation. "Do you have an answer for everything?"

"Not everything."

"Thank goodness." She nodded wearily. "All right," she said, "let's get it over with."

I turned to Gordon and told him I'd be right back. He nodded.

We left, walking out the door and down the concrete steps to the parking lot. I held the nightstick down along my thigh. "Which is your car?" I asked her. In the yellow light of the sodium lamps, the lot was nearly empty.

She nodded toward the end of the lot. "The Fiero."

"Okay."

We were halfway across the asphalt when they came at us from the shadows, running side by side.

19

I AWOKE AT dawn on Wednesday in Oakley, Kansas, with another hangover. I drank a couple of pints of water. I called the hospital in Santa Fe. Rita was the same. I showered, dressed, loaded the car, signed out on my bill, ate some gray bacon and some gray scrambled eggs at the diner next door, swallowed some scalding coffee. By eight o'clock I was on the highway, heading south.

Except for a big rig or two, the road was mostly clear. By ten-fifteen I was in the Oklahoma panhandle. Forty minutes later I was in Texas. The countryside around me didn't look much different from the way it had looked since I left Denver. Expanses of flat prairie or flat farmland in every direction. The occasional tiny house squatting in the middle of an emptiness that seemed infinite. The occasional tiny dust-blown town—a cluster of houses, a water tower, a grain store, sometimes a silo. But now the sky was overcast, making everything seem still more grim and bleak and oppressive. Behind me, in the north, bilious black clouds were piling up on the horizon. A storm was following me.

I thought about Rita. I thought about Ernie Martinez. I thought again about that night in the parking lot of Vanessie's.

When the two men rushed toward us, I pushed Sally Durrell forward. She stumbled and went down, her hands scrabbling at the air. Martinez had his knife out, so I slammed the stick at his wrist as I sidestepped. The knife went flying and he gasped and doubled over, clutching at the wrist as the other man dieseled into me and slammed his arms around my shoulders. I knifed the stick into his belly, below the belt, and he hissed and let me go, and I swung down and bounced the stick off his shin. He yelped once, reached for his leg, and I stiff-armed his shoulder and he went down onto his backside with a dull flat smack.

It had all taken only a few seconds.

I turned to Martinez. He was standing there, staring down at the wrist he held cradled to his chest. He looked over at me in disbelief. *"You broke it, you fuck."*

"Get out of here," I told him.

"You broke it, motherfucker."

"You've still got one left." I jerked my head. "Out. Take your friend with you."

"Motherfucker."

I slapped the nightstick against my palm. "Out."

"This ain't over, bro."

"It is for now." I took a step toward him.

He backed away. "Yeah, right," he said. "For now." He turned to his friend, who was sitting up now, rubbing at his shin. "Carlos."

Awkwardly, Carlos got to his feet. He hobbled toward Martinez. In the yellow light, his teeth showed in a rictus of pain.

Martinez said to me, "Another time."

"Sure."

"Believe it, bro." He looked at Carlos, nodded, and then the two of them walked off, Martinez holding his wrist, his friend limping.

Sally Durrell was up. She was examining a tear at the left knee of her jeans. "Damn it," she said. She looked at me. "These are Calvin Kleins."

"I'm sorry."

She straightened up and expelled a rush of air, part laugh, part incredulous gasp. *"Sorry?* You knock me down, you rip up my clothes, you rip up my knee. You make me listen to some of the most incredibly stupid, macho conversation I've ever heard. And you're *sorry?*"

"Not anymore."

"Look at that," she said, in a kind of awe. She was holding out her hand, fingers spread, and it was trembling. "That won't do," she said. She fumbled open her purse, rummaged in it for a moment, found her keys, held them out to me. "You drive," she said.

"Excuse me?"

"You got me into this. You can get me out."

"And where am I driving you?"

"Home. My house. You can take a cab back."

I nodded. "You don't want to report this? To the police?"

She shook her head dismissively. "They'd be out in an hour. Let's go."

As it happened, I didn't take a cab back from Sally Durrell's house. I stayed there that night, and in the morning she drove me to the parking lot. As it happened, we were involved for a while, and then, as it happened, we weren't. About a year and a half after the incident in the parking lot, she defended me in court when Ernie Martinez sued me for damages.

At eleven o'clock—ten o'clock in Santa Fe—I was still on Highway 83 South and I was coming up on Perryton, Texas. I tried the cellular phone. There was a dial tone, and I called Norman Montoya.

"Mr. Croft," he said. "How good to hear from you. I understand that your conversation with Mr. McBride was fruitful."

"Yes it was. I meant to call you, to thank you, but I've been running around. I apologize."

"Not at all. You've had good reason to be distracted. Mrs. Mondragón is still in the hospital, I understand. There's been no change?"

"No. Mr. Montoya, is your offer of help still good?"

"Of course. As I said, I am in your debt."

"Are you familiar with Luiz Lucero?"

"Only by reputation. A most unpleasant man."

"There's a possibility that he and Martinez may be running for Texas, or maybe for Florida. I was wondering whether you had any contacts in either place."

"Mr. Croft," he said, and I thought I could hear a smile in his voice, "you overestimate the small sphere of my very small influence. I know only a few people in Texas, acquaintances only, and I know no one at all in Florida."

"The people in Texas," I said. "Would they know anything about Lucero?"

There was a pause. "Possibly," he said at last. "I shall make inquiries, of course. What leads you to believe that Lucero and Martinez will be going to Texas?"

"They've got to go somewhere. So far as I know, Martinez doesn't have any bolt-holes. Lucero used to work in Dallas."

"So I understand. Ah, something occurs to me. My nephew, George—you remember him?"

"Yes."

"George has spent considerable time in Miami. Perhaps he knows someone. I shall ask him."

"Lucero was working for a Miami drug family, the Ortegas."

"Yes," he said. "Colombians," he added, the way a czar might've added *serfs*. "I shall speak with George," he said.

"Thank you."

"You are most welcome," he said. "But perhaps you should save your thanks until such time as I accomplish something."

"I appreciate the effort."

"It is nothing," he said. "Good-bye, Mr. Croft. And good luck."

"Thanks. Good-bye."

The big Cherokee swayed slightly as a gust of wind slapped at it. The sky out there was growing lower and darker. I wouldn't be outrunning this storm.

I made another call that I should have made earlier. It was just after nine in California.

Ed Norman was in. "What's up?" he said. "How is she?"

"The same," I told him. "I need some help."

"Anything."

"I need the name of a good investigator in Dallas, and one in Miami."

"Teddy Chartoff's in Dallas. Small agency, just him and his partner, but they're top notch. Hold on. Okay. In Miami, there's Dick Jepson. I've never met him, but I hear good things. What do you need them for?"

I told him what I needed them for.

"I'll call them," he said.

"Thanks."

"I don't care what it costs," I told him.

"Forget that. Teddy owes me. And we'll work something out with Jepson. You want their numbers?"

"Yeah."

He recited them, I wrote them down.

"One other thing," I said.

"Shoot."

"Could you ask Chartoff to find what he can on a man named Thorogood, Thomas Thorogood? Residence in Carlton, Texas." I spelled the name, gave him the street address.

"I'll tell him," he said. "What's the matter with your phone?"

"It's a cellular. The signal's breaking up. Wait." I slowed down, drove the Jeep to the side of the highway. "Ed, you there?"

"Give me your number."

I gave it to him. "I'll talk to you later," I said.

"Fine. You take care."

"Thanks."

Just as I hung up, the storm suddenly broke. Fat round raindrops shattered against the windshield and hammered against the rooftop. I turned on the wipers, turned on the headlights, pulled the lever that changed the drive to four-wheel, and drove back onto the highway.

I stayed below sixty miles an hour. On either side of me, the prairie had vanished behind swiftly shifting curtains of gray. Beneath me, the tires sizzled. Ahead, the raindrops blasted through the headlight beams like tracer bullets.

It was in the summer, a year and a half after I first met him, that I met Ernie Martinez for the second time.

By then I had worked with William and Rita Mondragón for over two years. I had learned a few things about both of them.

William was one of those people who are sometimes resented because they believe they're smarter than everyone else. They're also sometimes resented because they're usually right about this.

Personally, I liked him. He left me alone.

I had gotten to know Rita better, and I suppose we had become friends. I liked her, too, and there were times when I almost forgot that I felt something more. There were times when I thought about nothing else.

Occasionally, with the keen eye of your trained detective, I noticed tensions between them. No matter how charming he could be, and he could be very charming, William lived inside an impregnable solitude. There was a part of him, isolate and private, which I don't think even Rita ever reached, and I think this bothered her. From the other office, very rarely, I heard her snap at him. Once, when the two of them were in there, I heard her stalk from the room and slam the door behind her. No one ever said anything about the incidents. No one ever acknowledged that they'd actually occurred.

As infrequent as they were, however, they produced small blips on a radar screen at the back of my mind. I noted them, wondered how William could cause her even the slightest unhappiness, wondered how Rita could put up with even the slightest unhappiness, but I tried not to linger over them. Mostly, I succeeded.

I wasn't thinking about William and Rita, though, or at least not any more than usual, on that sunny Friday morning in June. I was parked on San Francisco Street, six blocks west of Vanessie's in the Hispanic barrio that runs between Guadalupe and Paseo, beside a low chain-link fence that surrounded a small run-down adobe house. The tiny yard was hard-packed dirt, tufted with weeds. A pair of dusty lilac trees braced the tiny wooden portico. Shades were drawn at the window. The house looked empty. But inside it, I was pretty sure, was a young woman named Nancy Gomez.

She had run away from home a week ago. She was eighteen, no longer a minor, but her father had hired the agency to find her. I had traced her here with information I'd obtained from another young woman, Rosa Sanchez. Rosa had taken the money I'd offered, but she had given me the information more out of jealousy than greed. She had been involved with Ernie Martinez before Martinez became involved with Nancy. The renter of record for the house on San Francisco was Ernie Martinez.

I had been parked outside for fifteen minutes. There were no other cars parked nearby. No one had entered or left the house. I could sit there all day, practice making stern detective faces in the rearview mirror while I waited for something to happen, or I could try a more direct approach.

I got out of the car—I was driving an old Ford back then—and walked through the opened gate of the fence, up the crumbling concrete walk. The warped floorboards of the portico creaked as I crossed them. Through the closed door I could hear the sounds of a television set. *The Price is Right.* "Lucille Baker, come on DOWN!"

I knocked on the door. After a moment it opened, and Nancy Gomez stood there. Five foot six, one hundred and thirty pounds. Her black hair was straight and shiny, hanging past her shoulders and cut in sleek bangs at her round forehead. She hadn't lost her baby fat, and maybe she never would. Maybe no one would ever suggest that she should. Like the forehead, the rest of her face was round, but it was very beautiful—poreless skin, almond-shaped dark-brown eyes, a small Indio nose, a wide red mouth. Beneath a clean white T-shirt that reached to her thighs, her breasts were plump and proud.

"Yeah?" she said. The beautiful face was slack with boredom.

"Hi, Nancy," I said. "Your father sent me."

The slackness tightened and she slammed the door on me, but it bounced against the steel-reinforced toe of a Justin mule-skin boot that had somehow wandered over the threshold.

"Go away," she said. She held the door with both hands. "You can't do nothin' to me. I got a legal right to be anywhere I want."

"That's true," I said. "But your father asked me to talk to you. So here I am."

"I don' wanna talk to you. Or anyone else. You tell him that."

"Look, Nancy," I said. "Just give me ten minutes."

"I don' gotta give you *nothin'*."

"Nancy, if you don't talk to me, your father will only send someone else." I put on my stern detective face.

She turned to her left and hollered over her shoulder, *"Ernie?"*

I should have practiced in the car.

"Hey Ernie!"

I heard him answer from somewhere within the house. *"Yo?"*

"Ernie, this guy's botherin' me."

"What guy?"

She turned again, looked back at me triumphantly, then swung the door wide open. *"Him,"* she said.

Ernie Martinez stood there, blinking sleep from his eyes. His pompadour was flattened on the right side, as though it had been ironed. His right cheek was creased. Tucked into his jeans was a T-shirt that matched Nancy's, except for the dirt. His feet were bare and they weren't any cleaner than the shirt. He had put on weight since I last saw him, but it was beer flesh, loose and pale. "Hey," he said, and pointed a finger at me. "I know you."

"Hello, Ernie," I said. "I'm working for Nancy's father. He'd like me to talk to her. Deliver a few messages."

"Josh-you-ah," he said. He was still pointing the finger. He grinned. *"Josh-you-ah,* right?"

"Yeah."

"Hey, good to see you." Nancy was looking up at him with a kind of vacant puzzlement. Still grinning, he stood back and waved a hand at me. "Come on inside, bro."

I wasn't puzzled. Once I was inside, he could claim that I was an intruder. Legally, he was allowed to defend his home by any means he chose. There are some Santa Fe cops who'll tell you that when you shoot a burglar in the front yard, you should drag him inside afterward.

"Maybe some other time," I told him. I turned to Nancy. "I'll talk to you later."

"No you *won't,* motherfucker," he said. He leaned toward me. He was pointing a finger again. "You stay the fuck away, you hear me? She's mine, bro, and she's street legal. You got that?" He stood upright and he wrapped his meaty arm around her shoulders. "You tell her father to fuck off."

Nancy smirked at me, proudly, and then she looked up at him again, with pleasure in her big sloe eyes, and admiration. Love is not love which alters when it alteration finds.

I had a notion that I could somehow shatter her admiration for the man, smash the image she held of Ernie Martinez. So I smiled and I said, "How's the wrist, Ernie? Slowing you down any?" And then I turned and walked away, offering him my back. I thought it was an offer he couldn't refuse.

I was right.

20

THE TELEPHONE STARTED chirping at about a quarter to one in the afternoon, just as I was approaching Interstate 40, south of Wheeler. I was able to see the green highway signs through the wavering sheets of rain, but nothing beyond them.

I lifted the phone from the passenger seat, flipped it open. "Hello."

"Josh." Hector Ramirez. "I've been trying to reach you all morning."

"I was out of range."

"Where are you?"

"On the road."

"Where?"

"Texas."

"*Texas?* What the hell are you doing in Texas?"

"Checking something out."

"You're thinking Dallas? You're thinking Lucero's bringing Martinez and the woman back there?"

"I don't know, Hector. I'm looking into it."

"Forget it, Josh. You don't know Dallas. Even if they're there, you'd never find them. And the place is probably crawling with Feds already. You're wasting your time."

"I've got time to waste. Has anyone spotted that RV of Sylvia Miller's?"

"Nope. It probably got dumped in a garage somewhere. But we ran a check on RV registrations, and had Motor Vehicles cross-check them against new licenses. We've got an RV registered to a Susan Sanborn, and three months ago, the same Susan Sanborn applied for a driver's license. The picture on the license is Miller. So now we know her name, and we know what kind of an RV she bought. For what that's worth."

"What kind was it?"

"An eighty-four Tioga. Twenty-two feet. But it's not on the road. Someone would've seen it."

"What did Miller use for ID when she got the license?"

"Passport. According to the Feds, she got the passport with a birth certificate."

"A dead baby."

"Yeah." You find the grave of a child born at about the same time you were, request a copy of the birth certificate from the Department of Records, and use that to obtain other ID.

"Oh," said Hector. "The Denver cops picked up something about Lyle Monroe. You remember—the guy in the house? When you made that stupid phone call?"

"I remember."

"According to his girlfriend, he was one of Lucero's investors."

"Investors?"

"Monroe would drop five, ten grand on Lucero every couple of months, according to her. Lucero used it to buy coke. He'd pay back Monroe double the money."

"Why would Lucero need Monroe's money?"

"He probably didn't. Denver cops figure he took the money to keep Monroe on a string. It never hurts to have a buddy with connections. You knew that Monroe was old money up there? Old family?"

"Yeah."

"He wasn't doing too well with that movie business of his. The money from Lucero probably helped out. *Assisted him in maintaining the extravagant lifestyle to which he had grown accustomed,* it says here. According to the girlfriend—her name's Heidi, by the way—Monroe thought Lucero was the bee's knees."

"The bee's knees?"

"That's a paraphrase."

"So why did Lucero shoot him?"

"They don't know. The Denver cops. What they're saying is, maybe Monroe balked at the game plan. Whatever it was."

"Or maybe Lucero's gun went off accidentally, while he was cleaning it."

"Yeah, there's that."

"Did the Denver cops find her safe-deposit box?"

"Yeah. Nothing in it. Tax records. Listen, Josh, why don't you get on back here? You won't be able to do anything in Dallas."

"I'm losing the signal, Hector."

"Asshole," he said, and hung up.

I flipped the phone shut.

What Ernie Martinez lacked in subtlety he made up for in stupidity. I'd gone only two steps down the concrete walkway when I heard him roar behind me and come clomping across the portico.

Ducking, I wheeled to my right, and as he blitzed past me I thumped a left into his kidney. He was moving too quickly in the same direction for the punch to do much damage, but when he spun around to face me, his face was twisted with rage.

"What's the matter, Ernie?" I said. "Wake up on the wrong side of the bed?"

He came in at me, heavy shoulders lowered, fingers clawing at the air. If I'd let him grab me, he could've torn me apart. I didn't let him. I got in a good jab at his nose, and then another. While he contemplated those, I hooked a right into his belly. Ernie hadn't been doing his sit-ups. He gasped.

I moved away, lowering my hands. "Come on, Ernie," I said. "You can do better than that. Big tough guy like you?"

From the portico, Nancy shouted, *"Kill the fucker, Ernie!"*

155

My plan was working wonderfully so far.

Martinez had seen too many movies. He lumbered in at me like a cowboy in a Western, his hands balled now, and he threw a big, sloppy roundhouse right. I stepped away from it and hooked him in the gut again. As he folded forward, I smacked my open palm against his ear.

I moved back again. "Maybe we should do this some other time," I said. "When you're feeling better."

He was still bent forward. He dove at me and I stepped aside. He landed in the dirt.

"Need a hand up?" I asked him.

He rolled over onto his elbows. The T-shirt was brown with dust. "Motherfucker," he said. But he stayed on the ground.

"You go away!" Nancy screeched at me. She hadn't moved from the portico. *"I'll call the cops!"*

"What do you think, Ernie?" I said. "Think we should get the cops here?"

Still supporting himself on his elbow, Martinez turned to her. His hair hung in thick strands down his forehead. "Shut up," he told her.

"Ernie, he's got no right!"

"Shut the fuck *up!*" he said.

I turned to her. "Nancy? You want to leave? I'll drive you. Your father just wants to talk to you."

Her eyes were slits. "You go to *hell,* mister."

I nodded. Mission accomplished. "Maybe we'll talk later."

"Never!" she said.

"Right," I said.

I went down the walkway and out to my car. Before I climbed into the Ford, I looked back at them. He was still on the ground. She was squatting down beside him, reaching out. He swatted her hands away.

Later, when I told William and Rita what had happened, neither was overly impressed.

"So," Rita said, "basically, what happened was that you bullied the man in front of his girlfriend."

156

We were in William's office, Rita in one of the client chairs, me in the other. She was wearing a lightweight pale blue top of knitted silk, V-necked, over a long flared skirt of dark blue linen. Behind the desk, William was wearing a pinstriped pale yellow Oxford shirt with a buttoned-down collar, a patterned red silk tie, and a gray suit vest. I was wearing sackcloth and ashes.

"Basically," I said, "yeah."

"Thereby," she said, "provoking her sympathy for him. That was very cunning."

"If I'd known," said William, "that you'd had an earlier run-in with Martinez, I wouldn't have let you continue with the case."

I said, "I didn't know until this morning that Martinez was involved."

He nodded. He was tapping a pencil lightly, distractedly, against the edge of the desk. "I think," he said, "that we'll let Rita handle this one from here on."

"Probably a good idea," I said. I turned to her. "Watch out for that left of his."

"That won't be necessary," she said. "I'll just shoot him on sight."

William smiled. "Joshua, why don't you write up the report. And then you can take off for the day. Oh. Could I borrow the Ford? I can get it back to you tonight."

He had borrowed my car before. His own, a bustle-back Eldorado, was sometimes a bit too conspicuous.

"Sure," I said. "Do I get the Cadillac?"

"You can take Rita's Mercedes." An old yellow sedan, as solid as a tank, and almost as fast.

"Fine," I said. I stood. "Look," I told him. "I screwed up. I should've handled it differently."

"Water under the bridge," he said. He smiled. "Do up the report and then take off. We'll bring the car over to your place. After nine o'clock, I imagine. We'll stop in and say hello."

"I'll get out the pretzels and beer." I turned to Rita. "Take care with Martinez."

She smiled. "Thanks, Slugger."

When you look back at your life, you discover, or you invent, points in time that seem to be tightly knotted nodes of possibility. Out of the seemingly endless options that present themselves in a given situation, you choose one in particular, and your life and the lives of those around you start moving relentlessly toward a particular outcome.

One of these nodes, in my life, was the moment I decided to antagonize Ernie Martinez in front of Nancy Gomez. If I'd simply walked away, I've often told myself since, things would have proceeded differently.

Another of these was the moment that I agreed, without any serious thought, to lend my car to William. If I'd stopped to consider, it might have occurred to me that Ernie Martinez would be looking for me.

But Martinez hadn't come back at me after the incident at Vanessie's, and I assumed he wouldn't come back at me now.

I stopped for lunch in Wellington, Texas, at two o'clock. Gray chicken-fried steak, gray home fries, gray green beans. By two-thirty, I was back on the road. I was about a hundred and twenty miles from Carlton. The rain kept coming.

At ten o'clock on that Friday night in June, six years ago, I was lying on the sofa in my living room when I heard the shots. They were loud, fired just outside. There were two of them, followed by two more.

I was living then in the rear half of a small house on Santa Fe Avenue. The apartment was small—the bedroom closet, where I kept my pistol, wasn't that far from the living room. But I think that at some level I already knew what had happened, knew who had been shot and why, and I didn't run to get it. I ran, instead, to the front door and out it, and down the three wooden steps to the narrow driveway.

I had parked Rita's Mercedes out on the street, so William could drive my Ford into the driveway. The Ford was there now, and there were two bodies lying in the gravel on either side of it, sprawled in the light of the street lamp like dolls cast aside.

21

I ARRIVED IN Carlton, Texas, at a quarter to five in the afternoon. The rain was still hurtling down.

I keep a small work duffle in the Cherokee. When I stopped at a Circle-K, I turned around, reached back over my seat. I opened the duffle and dug out a thermos bottle, an empty mason jar with a lid, and an old pair of Ziess binoculars. I set the binoculars on the passenger seat, lay the Mason jar on the floor mat. Cradling the thermos like a football, I sprinted through the downpour to the store's entrance. The air was warm and thick, and the raindrops that spattered against my cheeks felt like blood.

Inside the store, I filled the thermos with coffee and I bought a couple of plastic-wrapped gray sandwiches, some bottles of water, a package of Fig Newtons. I also bought a small bottle of dishwashing soap and some disposable washcloths. From the clerk, I got some paper cups and the directions to Hillside Avenue, where Thomas Thorogood lived.

Back in the car, I took the soap and the washcloths from the paper bag. One by one, I covered the interior of the Jeep's windows with a thin film of soap. To any shopper walking past, I was just a maniac from New Mexico who had a thing for clean windows.

Just as I finished, the telephone rang.

"Hello?"

"Joshua Croft?" A male voice, slow and soft and Southern.

"Yes?"

"This is Ted Chartoff? In Dallas?" He ended the sentences

with a rising inflection, as though they were questions. "Ed Norman asked me to give you a call."

"Hello."

"Just wanted to let you know that I'm on the stick here. I put out some feelers already, on that Lucero scumbag?"

"Thanks. I appreciate your help."

"No sweat, buddy. I never met that Mrs. Mondragón of yours, but I hear she's a damn fine woman."

"She is."

"Don't you worry. If the scumbag is anywhere near Dallas, I'll be camping in his asshole by the end of the week."

"Save me a bunk."

He chuckled. "I'll do that. And, lookit, I got some stuff on the guy you asked about, Thorogood?"

"Yeah?"

"His father's a big honcho, over in Wichita Falls? Owns a big frozen food company, trucks food to restaurants from here to hell and gone. Junior's a vice president in the company. Picture of him in one of the Texas magazines, last month. Got it here, you want it. You got a fax?"

I already had one photograph of Thorogood. Mr. Niederman had printed out a copy of his surveillance shot. But another picture wouldn't hurt. "Yeah. You can use the same number, after we hang up. Anything else on Thorogood?"

"He's a major pussy hound. Doesn't seem to do much of anything but chase women. Hardly ever shows up at the office, even. That house in Carlton? Used to be the family place. The father signed it over to Junior a couple years ago. I figure the kid for deadwood. Daddy keeps him on the payroll, to give him an allowance? But he sticks him out in Carlton, where he won't trip over his dick in public. But, lookit, if Junior's hooked up with Lucero, maybe he's using Daddy's trucks to move some nose candy?"

"Maybe, yeah." Lucero had apparently used Lyle Monroe in Denver. Maybe he had used Thorogood down here.

"Okay, lookit," said Chartoff, "I talked to Dick Jepson, over

161

in Miami? Ed said you were in and out, contact-wise, and he asked me to do a little liaising. Dick's on board, too. He's got your number. Anything turns up, he'll give you a jingle. He can't reach you, he'll buzz me. How's that by you?"

"Fine. Thanks. After I hang up, give me a couple of minutes to set up the fax."

"No sweat. Hang in there, buddy."

"Right."

I moved the binoculars and the Circle-K bag to the floor mat, tugged Leroy's briefcase from the back, arranged the computer and fax on the passenger seat. Five minutes later I had my second photograph of Thomas Thorogood.

A man in his late thirties wearing a tux and a big silly smile, he was sitting at a cloth-covered dinner table, raising a glass of champagne toward the camera. He had dark curly hair and a dark mustache. Sitting beside him, and trying to clamber into his lap, was an attractive woman with eager eyes and long insistent arms and a hairdo that looked like it had been carefully molded from blonde cement. The caption identified her as his fiancée, Miss Lee Ann Horsley, and said she'd won the Miss Wichita Falls title in 1990. Miss Congeniality, too, probably.

I folded the picture, slipped it into my jacket. I zipped up Leroy's case and returned it to the back of the Jeep.

Ten minutes later, I was on Hillside Avenue. If there was a hill anywhere nearby, I didn't see it. Maybe the hill had been razed, decades ago, to make room for the big frame houses. These weren't as upscale as the houses in Mr. Niederman's development outside Denver, but they weren't hovels either. It was a cozy, dozing neighborhood that had been here for a while, judging by the tall sycamores and magnolias that lined the paved driveways.

Like the houses on either side of it, 340 Hillside was a large white two-story building, taller than it was wide, with a steeply pitched roof, a covered porch, and an attached garage with what looked liked servants' quarters over it. I drove past the place for three blocks, turned around, and drove back. There weren't many cars parked in the street, but there were a few, and I parked on the side opposite Thorogood's house, and one house up.

Through the rain, I had a fairly good view across the lawn. The curtains were drawn at the large window to the left of the porch, probably the living room, and a light was on inside. Maybe someone was home. Or maybe Thorogood liked to leave his lights on.

I turned off the wipers, turned off the engine. The film of soap on the windows would stop them from fogging over, and keep the view clear. And prevent anyone who spotted the car from wondering why someone was breathing inside it. I moved over into the passenger seat, away from the driver's window, opened the thermos, poured myself a cup of coffee, and I sat back to wait.

When I came rushing down the steps of the house on Santa Fe Avenue, I heard the squeal of tires as a car roared off. I was too busy at the time to check it out.

Rita was lying facedown, unconscious but still breathing. She had been shot once, low in the back, just to the right of her spine. William had been shot twice, once in the stomach and once in the face. He lay on his back and there was a puddle beneath his head, shiny in the lamplight. He wasn't breathing.

Later, the cops worked out the way it must have happened. Back then, my name and address were listed in the phone book. Anyone could have learned where I lived. The people who rented the front of the house weren't at home that night. If it were Martinez who pulled the trigger—and I'd known, since the moment I heard the shots, that it was Martinez who pulled the trigger—he had seen the darkened front, had seen that my car wasn't in the driveway, and assumed I wasn't there.

He had waited in a car at the curb, probably parked just behind Rita's Mercedes. He had seen my Ford pull up and he had assumed that I was driving. As it turned into the driveway, he had left his own car to stalk up behind it. William was the same height as I was, and from the back he could easily have been mistaken for me. When he and Rita stepped out of the Ford, Martinez had fired.

Because Rita had been shot in the back, the police were fairly certain that she had been shot first. William had turned at the sound of the gunshots, and he had been facing his killer when he died.

No one ever knew why Martinez fired first at Rita. He never said. Maybe her presence surprised him. Maybe he simply wanted to hurt any woman he believed to be with me.

I had heard four shots. The police found the fourth slug in the wall of the house next door.

When I discovered that Rita was still alive, I raced back up the driveway and back into the house. I dialed 911.

From then on, things went very much as they were to go six years later. There were cops and paramedics, police cars and ambulances, there were questions and answers. But that time, the ambulance carried Rita away without me beside her.

After a while Hector was there. We went into my apartment. As manic lights twirled blue and red against the window, I told him about Ernie Martinez.

I spent four hours outside the house of Thomas Thorogood before anything happened. At nine o'clock, a light went on in an upstairs window.

The rain had stopped about an hour before. The night was dark, the moon a dull gray blur behind the clouds.

By that time I had emptied the thermos of coffee, eaten one of the sandwiches and half of the Fig Newtons, and used the Mason jar once.

A shadow moved in that upstairs room. Through the binoculars, all I could see was the paper on the far wall. It was printed in a floral pattern. A bedroom? Thomas was getting ready to hit the sack?

No, the lights were still on downstairs.

He and Lee Ann were together up there?

After fifteen minutes, the upstairs light went out. Two minutes later, the downstairs light went out. A minute after that, the garage door slowly swung up. The Lincoln backed out. As it came down the driveway, the white wooden door swung slowly shut. A remote.

The Lincoln backed into a turn, then headed toward me. I ducked below the dashboard before the headlights swept through the car.

Thorogood was alone. Maybe Lee Ann was back in Wichita Falls, doing her hair.

So. Follow Thomas or check out the house?

Follow Thomas. If it looks like he'll be busy for a while, come back to the house.

I started the Cherokee, pulled it into a U-turn. I could see, about seventy-five yards ahead, the bright red taillights of the Towncar. I kept my headlights off for a couple of blocks, and turned them on when he made a turn.

I followed him for about two miles through Clayton. Just at the outskirts of town, where the prairie began to stretch out into the endless empty night, he turned off the highway and pulled into the unpaved parking lot of a roadhouse. It was a long, low, cement block building, its flat roof topped with a huge red and yellow neon sign that said "Wrasslin' Randy's" in gaudy script. Standing beside that was a huge blue and yellow neon cowboy, complete with hat, hunkered down into a crouch as though about to leap forward and wreak some havoc.

The parking lot was only half full, so I drove past it, but slowly. The Towncar was parked by itself at one end of the lot, beside the pole of a solitary light, and Thomas Thorogood was getting out of it.

He was wearing a black shirt, black jeans, a pair of tan boots, and a pinto cowboy hat that curled upward along the sides of the brim.

I drove on for a quarter of a mile, made another U-turn, and drove back. I parked the Cherokee at the other end of the lot, concealing it behind the rest of the cars, and I climbed out and walked to the building.

The entrance door was metal. When I opened it I ran into a dense warm wall of sound. Garth Brooks.

The place was a large open rectangle with a low panelled ceiling. Apparently, there hadn't been much decorating money left after the neon sign had gone onto the roof. The bare block walls were painted a flat black. The floor was painted a flat burgundy, and the enamel was chipped here and there, showing gray cement.

In the center of the room was a small, scuffed wooden dance floor that held a few enthusiastic couples. You could tell that the men were genuine cowboys, because they wore hats, and they touched them often. The women had lots of hair and they all looked like Loretta Lynn. Except for one of them, who looked like Buck Owens. More couples sat at wooden tables in the corners.

I saw the pinto hat on the bar before I saw Thomas Thorogood. There were people scattered at stools along the length of the bar, but he was sitting at the far left end, alone.

I walked to the other end of the bar and slid onto a stool. The bar was curved at this end, so I had a good view of Thorogood. Which also meant that he had a good view of me. But I would've been still more conspicuous if I'd sat alone at one of the tables.

He was drinking something out of a rocks glass. Separating us along the bar were an older couple drinking Lone Star beer, two construction workers drinking Lone Star beer, a very old man drinking Lone Star beer, and a pair of women drinking Lone Star beer.

Unlike the rest, the women were drinking their beer from glasses. Both were blondes in their forties, very well preserved, who at some point had evidently taken styling tips from Lee Ann Horsley. Both were dressed hopefully in tight jeans and brightly colored Western shirts, embroidered at the yoke. So far, no one was circling. But the night was young.

The bartender waddled over to me. "What kin I getcha?"

Prematurely balding, he was an immensely fat young man in a Dallas Cowboys sweatshirt, its sleeves rolled back above pale forearms the size of Virginia hams. The sweatshirt was a necessity, because he was sweating. It was probably always a necessity.

"A Lone Star," I told him. When in Rome.

He waddled to the cooler, bent down with visible effort, opened it, plucked out the long-necked bottle, waddled back. He cracked the bottle open with a church key, set it down on the bar. No glass. Glasses were for sissy boys.

"Two dollars," he said.

I put a five on the bar and he took it, wiped his forehead with the bunched-up sleeve of the sweatshirt, and then waddled away to make change.

I sipped at my beer and glanced at Thorogood. He held a cigarette in his right hand. He was staring down at his drink, using his left hand to revolve it slowly, aimlessly, in its place on the bar top.

The bartender brought me my change and waddled away again.

"Howdy!"

I turned to my right. Another cowboy, another hat, sliding onto the stool next to mine. A pressed white cotton shirt, Western-style, and a pair of brown knit pants. He was in his fifties, as lean and weathered as a strip of jerky, and almost as dark. His teeth seemed very white and very plentiful, and he was showing them in a broad grin.

"Billy Fetterman," he said, and held out a gnarled brown hand.

I took it. "Jim Collins."

"Pleasure, Jim." He released the hand from a death grip and hollered to the bartender, "Randy?"

Randy lumbered over. Fetterman said, "Gimme a Heineken,

you don't mind, and give old Jim here 'nother bottle of that horse piss."

Randy lumbered away. Fetterman turned to me. With a stiff index finger he poked up the brim of his hat, the cowboy equivalent of taking it off. A widow's peak of wiry hair, black and white, showed just beneath the brim. "Where you from, Jim?"

"Phoenix," I said.

"Been there," he nodded. "Great little town. I'm outta Wichita Falls myself. Been there?"

"Not yet." I glanced at Thorogood. He was blowing smoke from his nostrils as he eyed the two women. He stroked his black mustache.

"Helluva town, Jim." Grinning, he shook his head. "Helluva town. Weather like you never witnessed in all your born days. I been through heat waves, ice storms, blizzards, and a coupla hellacious tornados. Course, Tuesday was a mite better."

I smiled.

The bartender set down the beers. "I do thank you, Randy," said Fetterman. Without asking the cowboy for money, Randy waddled off.

Fetterman raised his bottle. "Here's looking at ya, Jim."

I raised mine and we clinked glass. We upended bottles, we drank beer. We were bonded for life.

I nodded toward the bartender. "He's the wrestler?" I asked Fetterman.

"Him?" Fetterman guffawed. "I reckon Little Randy couldn't wrestle himself outta that tent he's wearing without a derrick and a full crew. Shoot, he must weigh pretty near a ton, bareass naked. And that's a thought to scare the crows away, ain't it? Nah, it's his daddy was the wrestler. Built this place back in the seventies, is what I hear." He took a hit from his bottle. "What kinda line you in, Jim?"

"Photography."

"No shit," he said. "Don't know a damn thing about photography. I'm in horses myself. Know anything about horses?"

"Not a whole lot."

"Lotta people, now," he said, leaning forward, into the subject, "they'll tell ya that horses are dumb. I got me a brother, Delbert. Pig farmer. He's big on pigs, Delbert is. Subscribes to the theory that they're smarter'n horses. I been tellin' him for years that horses ain't dumb, they're just pure ass ornery. And that's the truth of it. Most ornery damn creatures on God's green earth." He took a hit of beer. "So what kinda photography is that, Jim? Is that like portraits?"

"Landscapes. I'm doing some work for National Geographic."

Thorogood had gotten up. Now he walked toward the two women, holding his glass.

"You don't say," said Fetterman. "Got me about a ton of those, up in the attic at home. Think they're worth anything?"

"Hard to say," I told him. Thorogood and the women were talking. The women laughed. I asked Fetterman, "What brings you to Carlton?"

"Been here for pretty near a week now. Dickerin' with a fella 'bout a string of Appaloosas." He shook his head regretfully. "Real sweet animals, ever' one of 'em as pretty as a Paris runway model, but he's askin' more for 'em than any kinda horseflesh is worth."

Thorogood signaled the bartender and ordered a round of drinks.

I glanced at my watch. Ten o'clock. I turned to Fetterman. "Sorry, Billy, I just remembered something. I've gotta run."

Pine Avenue ran parallel to Hillside, a block south. I parked the Cherokee on Pine, across the street from another white frame house. The house was dark and its property backed onto Thorogood's. I tugged the big Beretta from under the passenger seat, stuck it beneath my belt in back. I left the Jeep and I walked, as though I were out for a moonlight stroll, up the driveway of the house and then around the building, toward the dark stand of trees that hid the house I wanted. The heels of my boots sank into the spongy ground.

I had just gotten through the trees and I was heading for the back door when, behind me, someone called out, *"Freeze, asshole."*

22

I FROZE.

"Hands behind the head."

I put my hands behind my head.

After a moment, from behind me, someone started to pat me down. Armpits, stomach, pants pockets, legs, ankles.

Maybe he'd miss the Beretta.

He didn't. I felt him jerk it away. He said, annoyed, "Look at this. He's supposed to be carrying a thirty-eight."

"He's fickle," said another voice. "Turn around, Croft."

I turned around. In the dim moonlight, I couldn't make out their features, but they were both big men. Both held guns, one of the guns being my Beretta. The man with the Beretta was wearing a suit, the other was wearing a dark windbreaker.

"FBI?" I said.

"He's a genius, too," said the one holding the Beretta.

"Put your hands down, Croft," said the man in the windbreaker. "I'm Special Agent Peterson. This is Special Agent Cooper. What you're going to do is turn around and walk. You think you can handle that?"

"Is there a prize?"

"They said you were a wiseass." That was Cooper.

"Just do it," Peterson told me.

I turned around and walked, Peterson and Cooper following. I went across the small lawn, around the garage.

"Keep going," said Peterson.

I went up the driveway. "Keep going," Peterson said. "Across the street. Up to the house over there, to the front door."

I walked across the street, down the driveway of still another white frame house, up the brick walkway. Lights glowed behind the drawn curtains.

At the front door, the other man, Cooper, circled around me and pushed the doorbell. He wasn't carrying my gun now, and probably he hadn't been carrying it since we hit the street.

The door opened. Billy Fetterman said, "Get in here." His Texas accent was still there, but it had become a lot more subdued. His hat was gone.

I stepped in, followed by Peterson and Cooper.

I said, "What'd you decide about those Appaloosas, Billy?"

He smiled. "National Geographic? Taking pictures of bridges, are we, Mr. Croft?" He nodded to the left. "Go on inside."

I said, "Could I see some ID first?"

Cooper said to Fetterman, "You want me to bounce him around for a while?" He said it casually, as though he were asking about letting out the dog.

Fetterman smiled and shook his head. "We're all friends here." He reached into his back pocket, pulled out a wallet, flipped it open to show me his ID. His name wasn't Fetterman. It was Cornwell. William Cornwell. "Is that satisfactory?" he asked me.

"That's swell," I said.

"Now would you mind going into the living room?"

"My pleasure."

I stepped into the big, old-fashioned room. A fringed Persian carpet on the dark-wood floor. Overstuffed embroidered furniture draped with antimacassars.

"Have a seat," said Fetterman-Cornwell, pointing to a plump armchair and matching ottoman.

I crossed the room and sat down. Peterson and Cooper sat on the sofa. Cornwell eased down into another armchair, facing me, and sat back, crossing his legs. Beneath the cuffs of his brown knit pants, he wore shiny brown lizard-skin boots. He said, "You're supposed to be a moderately intelligent man, Mr. Croft. You do realize that you nearly disrupted a surveillance undertaken by the United States government?"

"I do now," I said. "How long have you been on Thorogood?"

He turned to Peterson and Cooper. "He didn't get into the house?"

Cooper shook his head. He was younger than his partner, and less bulky. His hair was black and thinning, Peterson's was brown and thick. Both were pale, as though they spent most of their time indoors. "We grabbed him just after he came through the trees," Cooper said. "Piece of cake." He smiled at me. He had enjoyed saying that.

"Fine," said Cornwell. He ran his gnarled brown hand back over his wiry gray hair, turned back to me. "How long have we been on Thorogood? Since Lucero escaped from the prison. Not that it's really any of your business, but another government agency has had him under surveillance, off and on, for nearly a year."

"The DEA?" I said.

He smiled as though the idea amused him. "Now why would the DEA be watching Thorogood?"

"Beats me," I said. "Maybe he was using his father's trucks to move drugs for Luiz Lucero."

Cornwell smiled at Peterson and Cooper, and then he turned back and smiled at me. It was a friendly smile, bright white in the tanned face. "Just how did you find friend Thorogood, Mr. Croft?"

I considered the question, wondering how Mr. Niederman would feel if the FBI descended upon his house and asked to go through his rogue's gallery. I decided that Mr. Niederman would be tickled pink. I told them.

"Thorogood was in Denver in March?" Cornwell asked me. For the first time, he seemed genuinely interested. "With the Miller woman?"

"Yeah," I said. "Didn't you say that someone had him under surveillance?"

"Off and on, I said."

"Ah."

"I don't second-guess other agencies," said Fetterman. "But we're handling the case now."

"Great," I said.

He smiled. It was still friendly, but slightly less so. "Mr. Croft," he said. "When you pulled up outside there this evening, you gave us, I admit it, quite a little start. But it took us all of thirty seconds to run your license plate and learn who you were. I've spoken with Sergeant Ramirez, in Santa Fe."

I nodded. I was waiting for the punch line.

"And I can understand, from what Ramirez said, why you're so determined to locate Luiz Lucero and Ernest Martinez. I'm not an unsympathetic man. Your partner has been hurt, and you want to do something about it. That's a very natural response, a very human response. I can appreciate it. That's why we're all sitting here in a nice comfortable house, quietly discussing this like intelligent adults."

I was still waiting.

He leaned slightly forward. "But don't push me, Mr. Croft. You don't want to push me. And you'll find that sarcasm comes very close, extremely close, to pushing me. I'm sure you're aware that we can always conduct this elsewhere, in a somewhat less pleasant atmosphere."

"Let's go," I said.

Cornwell smiled. "Come again?"

"Let's go. Let's get to this other atmosphere. There's probably less horseshit there. But an old cowpoke like you, Billy, I guess you've got a real fondness for horseshit."

On the sofa, Cooper leaned forward. "You dumb fuck. We'll break you like a popsicle stick."

I smiled. "You could try."

Cooper stood up. Peterson looked at him from the couch, mildly curious as to what would happen next.

"Sit down, Jack," said Cornwell.

Cooper glanced at him, opened his mouth, clamped it shut, sat down. His pale face had darkened.

Cornwell smiled at me and said, "Make your point, Mr. Croft."

"We're sitting here," I said, "in this nice comfortable house, discussing this like intelligent adults, because you think I know something that might be useful to you, and you think this is the best way to get it out of me. And you're right. I'm as happy as a clam to cooperate with big time, gee-whiz government agents. I'll probably gush about it in my memoirs. But don't try to carrot-and-stick me. You lean on me, I shut up. Maybe you can make me talk, maybe you can't. You'll be wasting a lot of time while you find out."

"Not that much time," said Cooper.

Cornwell held up his hand. "Enough," he said. He smiled again. "All right. We've all flexed our muscles. We've all demonstrated that we're tough and dauntless. Let's have an end to it. You say you're willing to cooperate, Mr. Croft?"

"My pleasure," I said.

Another smile, very brief. "Then you can begin by explaining what led you to the woman, Sylvia Miller."

Without mentioning names, I told him about Jimmy McBride, and then I told him about the woman who lived across the street from Sylvia Miller.

"The neighbor," said Cornwell. "That would be Mrs. Rudolph."

"Yes."

"And you were led to Thomas Thorogood by the photographs of this Mr. . . . ?"

"Niederman," I said.

"Mr. Niederman. Another neighbor." He nodded. "You seem to have a way with neighbors, Mr. Croft."

"It's a gift."

The smile was still more brief this time. "All right. You mentioned a possibility before. That Thorogood was using his father's trucks to transport drugs. Whatever gave you that notion?"

"Luiz Lucero uses people. He used Lyle Monroe, up in Denver. Monroe was the black sheep in a rich family. So is Thorogood." I shrugged. "Seems to me that the best way to use Thorogood is to use his father's trucks."

I was taking credit for the idea given to me by Teddy Chartoff, the Dallas investigator. But I didn't see any reason why I should tell Cornwell about Chartoff.

"And how did you learn about his father's trucks?" Cornwell asked me.

"I snooped around. That's what I do."

"And you've done it with a modicum of success, I must admit."

"He was using the trucks," I said.

He frowned judiciously before he answered. Finally he said, "Let's just say we have reason to believe that he may've been. Tell me something, Mr. Croft."

"What?"

"It was you who brought in Ernest Martinez, six years ago. How did you locate him then?"

Sergeant Labbady, in Denver, had asked me the same question. I gave Cornwell the same answer I'd given Labbady. "An old girlfriend of his came to me. Rosa Sanchez. She told me where he was."

His girlfriend of the moment, Nancy Gomez, had gone running back to her father when she learned that Martinez had shot two people. Martinez had driven up to Truchas, in the mountains, where he hid in the house of a distant cousin. From there, he called Rosa Sanchez and asked her to bring him some things. She came to me instead.

Cornwell said, "And this Rosa Sanchez is the same woman that Martinez and Lucero executed last Saturday night in Santa Fe. Along with her husband."

"Yeah."

"Why did she divulge his whereabouts to you?"

"She was upset with him at the time."

"Why you, and not the police?"

"We had a rapport." And I had paid her, earlier, for the information she provided. She thought that I would pay her for this. She was right.

"So she told you," Cornwell said, "and you simply went out and got him."

"Yeah," I said.

"I understand that Martinez was somewhat bruised when you brought him in."

"He fell down."

"Several times, according to the medical reports."

"He lacked motor skills."

Cornwell smiled. "He attempted to sue you, later."

"He attempted to. Why don't you tell *me* something?"

"And what might that be?"

"What was the idea of the Billy Fetterman number?"

"We couldn't have you bothering Mr. Thorogood. I decided to keep an eye on you."

"What if I'd approached him in the bar?"

"I would've stopped you."

He said it as though there wasn't any question about that. Maybe there wasn't.

I said, "So who's minding the store now? Do you have someone else on Thorogood?"

"Yes." He uncrossed his legs and nodded to me. "All right, Mr. Croft. Thank you for your assistance." He smiled once more. "And what exactly do you plan to do now?"

I looked from him to Peterson and Cooper. Both were waiting for my answer. I was waiting for it myself.

Coincidences happen. The cops don't like them, I don't like them, but they happen.

Just then, a phone began to chirp. For a moment I thought it was mine, and then I remembered that mine was still in the Cherokee.

It was Cooper's. He reached into his suit coat, pulled it out, tapped a button, put the phone to his ear. "Cooper. Yes, sir. Hold on."

He stood, walked across to Cornwell, handed him the phone.

Cornwell took it. "Yes?" As he listened, his brow tightened. "When . . . ? There's no doubt at all . . . ? All right. All right, fine." His brow relaxed and he sat back against the chair. "I understand. Yes. Thank you."

He pushed a button, set the phone on the arm of the chair. "Well," he said. He looked at Cooper and Peterson, frowned. He looked at me. He said, "It seems that this has suddenly become academic. It's all over."

He turned to the other two. "They're dead. All three of them. Lucero, Martinez, and the woman. Sylvia Miller. An accident in New Orleans."

PART FOUR

23

Near the New Orleans Criminal Courthouse, the six lanes of Tulane Avenue run through a tired neighborhood of cheap motels, fast-food joints, and bail bondsmen. The signs for the bondsmen claim that they're fast, too. The courthouse itself is a big building of weathered stone that takes up a whole block, opposite a gas station and a tired-looking Chinese restaurant.

All the parking places seemed to be occupied by police cruisers. I drove around for a while until I found a spot for the Cherokee across from Police Headquarters, on Broad. I got out and walked back to the courthouse.

I was tired and hot, and everything seemed slightly unreal. The sidewalks were buckled and crumbling, as though they'd gone through an earthquake. The air was thick and it smelled of car exhaust.

I passed a large painted mural that displayed the huge faces of women peering out from beyond banana fronds. The faces were stylized and impossibly beautiful, the faces of what a friend once called "feral women"—abandoned at birth and raised by fashion photographers.

I wondered if I were dreaming. Wondered if I had fallen asleep at the wheel somewhere in Texas, and if all this—the heat, the humidity, that strange mural—were the products of exhaustion and greasy food.

There had been no seats on the flights from Dallas to New Orleans this morning, and none from Houston. So I had driven here, six hundred and something miles from Clayton. Down

Highway 287 to Dallas, where the interchanges surrounding the city made me feel as though I'd wandered into a giant pinball machine, then down I-45 to Houston. From there, I'd picked up I-10 East, heading into the morning, passing the exits for places with evocative names like Beaumont, Mermentau, Lafayette, Plaquemine.

I'd left Clayton at midnight. It was now two o'clock in the afternoon. I'd stopped only for food and gas.

And even now I wasn't sure why I'd come. There was no real point in my being here. I should've turned the car around at Clayton and headed back to New Mexico.

In the car, somewhere between Dallas and Huntsville, I'd discussed it with Rita. We had been out on the patio again, in that bright clear unchanging sunlight.

"It's over, Joshua," she said patiently. "They're dead. Come home."

"It's over when I see them dead."

"This really doesn't have anything to do with them, does it?"

I frowned at her. "What do you mean?"

"You don't think that I'm going to make it, do you? You think I'm going to die. And you don't want to be there when it happens. You're using this trip as a way to avoid that."

"You're not going to die," I said.

She smiled. "I think you believe that I am. Joshua, I'll be just as dead if you're in New Orleans when it happens."

"You're not going to die," I told her.

"Mr. Croft?"

"Yes. Mr. Carter?"

He held out his hand. "Very pleased to meet you, sir," he said sadly. The hand was white and puffy, as if it had been underwater for a very long time.

He was in his fifties. His gray hair was combed from the left over his white scalp and held stiffly in place with pomade. His face was round and dewlapped, and there were deep dark bags under his shiny brown eyes. His lower lip was pink and pendulous, with a small white fleck of something trapped at its right corner. He wore black brogues, white socks, baggy gray pants, and a zippered black jacket that hugged his bulging stomach. Beneath the jacket he wore a white permanent-press shirt. The right collar of the shirt was poking out over the jacket like the sail of a tiny boat.

We were in a hallway in the courthouse building, beside the door at which he had told me to meet him when we'd spoken on the phone. He was carrying a videocassette in his left hand.

"You do understand," he said sadly, "that these bodies are in a dreadful condition, Mr. Croft? The two men, I mean. They were very badly burned in the accident. Very badly burned indeed. The woman, Miss Miller, she was hardly burned at all."

"I understand. But I won't be seeing the actual bodies, you said."

"No, sir, you will not. As I told you, we use videotape now." He held up the cassette briefly and looked at me with a sad earnestness. "It's ever so much more humane, don't you think? For the friends and relatives?"

"Much more."

"I believe so, Mr. Croft, I honestly believe so. Used to be, they'd view the bodies close-up, downstairs, in the morgue?" Wincing slightly, he shook his head. "And that was a horror for 'em sometimes, a pure horror."

"I'm sure."

He nodded sadly. "I only reiterate that, Mr. Croft, about the condition of the bodies, because in cases like this, serious burn cases, many people are often very badly shocked by the appearance of the victim."

"I understand."

"It's nothing to be ashamed of, not at all. Being shocked, I mean. Any decent human being would be."

"Sure."

"Very well then, sir. I only wanted to assure myself, for my own sake, that you were prepared."

He opened the door and I followed him into a small, comfortable room. On the back of his jacket was the word CORO-NER.

Gray walls, upholstered furniture, a table that held a nineteen-inch television, and, below that, a VCR. To the left was another table, smaller, that held a coffeemaker and a stack of white plastic foam cups.

Carter walked over to the TV, then turned back to me. "Why don't you make yourself comfortable, Mr. Croft?"

I sat down in one of the chairs.

Carter punched a button on the television and the screen flickered to life. It was a scene from a soap opera, a well-dressed man and a well-dressed woman leaning toward each other over a table at an expensive restaurant. Well-dressed extras were chatting happily in the background. *"I don't care what Evan told you,"* the man said, his mouth grim, his eyes steely. *"Genevieve was never in Hope City that night."*

Carter slid the cassette partway into the mouth of the VCR and then turned to me.

"Would you care for a cup of coffee, sir? I made it up fresh, so you could enjoy some when you arrived."

"Thank you, Mr. Carter. I would."

"Why would Evan lie to me?"

The man smiled with a kind of knowing bitterness. *"Where was Evan that night?"*

"Sugar, Mr. Croft? Cream?"

"Sugar, please."

"He was here in Blaisedale, of course."

"Can he prove that?"

"Your coffee," said Mr. Carter. "Careful now, it's hot."

"Why on earth should Evan need to prove anything?"

"Here we go," said Mr. Carter sadly, and pushed the cassette firmly into the machine.

Multicolored snow replaced the restaurant scene, static replaced the dialogue, and then suddenly the tape came on. Mr. Carter lifted a remote control from the top of the TV.

Despite what I'd said to Mr. Carter, I wasn't prepared for what

I saw. For a second or two I didn't understand what it was. And then I did.

"Jesus Christ," I said, and my body went cold.

It was lying on a table of stainless steel, brittle and curled, looking like the charred fetus of a monkey. It was black and its skull was deformed, flattened from front to back. Its hands were clawed in front of it. Where the flesh had seared away from the body, black sections of bone were showing, like scorched twigs.

"That's Mr. Lucero," said Carter sadly. "I'll just fast-forward here, Mr. Croft."

My chest was constricted. I swallowed some coffee. It was hot and bitter, laced with chicory.

The screen flickered, then blinked, and then it showed the same object from the other side. Someone had turned it over.

The screen blinked again. Another scorched monkey, curled the same way, lying on an identical metal table. Like the first, the creature's skull was smashed.

"That would be Mr. Martinez," said Carter. "It's the terrible heat that twists them up like that, ya see. And, of course, they were seated when the accident occurred. But even with their seat belts, you can see how their skulls were very badly damaged in the crash."

I glanced away. Partly out of horror—and partly, I think, out of guilt. I had wanted Martinez dead, and now he was. But I wouldn't have wished that death on anyone, not even him.

"And this, of course, is Miss Miller," said Carter. "You knew the woman, Mr. Croft?"

I looked back at the screen. "No," I said. "I've seen photographs."

It was Sylvia Miller. She lay on another metal table, covered by a blanket, only her head and bare shoulders visible. Except for a dark indentation on her forehead, she seemed untouched.

Her eyes were open and she was staring up at the ceiling.

I remembered that unsettling house in Las Vegas, remembered that filthy room dense with the choking stench of rot. Remembered the yellow parakeet lying stiffly on the grass. Remembered the photograph in the living room—the young girl in her best Sunday dress, out on the lawn with her family, her expression unreadable.

She had been permanently wounded by her childhood, Mrs. Rudolph had said. She had grown, Mrs. Rudolph had said, accustomed to the Dark. Staring at the image on the television screen, I wondered whether Sylvia had sought out Luiz Lucero because he offered an escape from that darkness, or because he promised its continuation.

If I'd investigated the childhoods of Luiz Lucero and Ernie Martinez, probably I'd have found something in each that had caused both men to grow accustomed to the Dark, in their lives and in themselves. Something that had caused the violence they shared, or something that had prepared the way for it. But Lucero and Martinez had directed their violence outward. Sylvia had directed hers only at herself.

Back in Las Vegas, I had told Mrs. Rudolph that I felt sorry for the woman. I still did.

Sylvia had found another Dark now, and she had all of forever to grow accustomed to its secrets.

"Will that be all, Mr. Croft?" said Mr. Carter. "Shall I turn it off?"

"What? Oh. Yes. Thank you. Would you mind if I asked you some questions, Mr. Carter?"

"Not at all, sir." He clicked the remote. "Let me just rewind this." He said to me, confidentially, "Sometimes people don't, you see, and that causes all kinds of problems."

He leaned forward and turned off the television. The VCR whirred for a moment, then clicked. Carter pressed the eject button and the tape sighed out of the machine.

Holding the cassette, he sat down opposite me in another armchair. "Now, sir, how can I help you?"

"Just how did the accident occur, Mr. Carter?"

He frowned judiciously. "Have you talked to the police, Mr. Croft? I mean, I'm only the coroner's investigator. The police, now, they're sure to know more."

"I'll talk to them. But maybe, in the meantime, you could tell me what you know."

His dewlaps quivered as he nodded. "Happy to oblige, Mr. Croft. Well, sir, the way I understand it, the tanker truck got itself stalled in the middle of the road. Mr. Harper—that's the driver of the truck—he was proceeding for help, and he only just turned the corner when he saw the car coming. The convertible, the one that was carrying the victims. They were moving at a prodigious rate of speed, and Mr. Harper, he tried to wave them down, but they paid him no mind at all. Mr. Harper, he says he knew what was about to transpire, and he hollered just as loud as he could. But they never heard him, poor devils." He shook his head sadly. "And it must have been purely awful for him. Mr. Harper, I mean."

"The car hit the truck," I said.

"It surely did, sir. Tore it right open, and then the gas ignited. That Miss Miller, she was sitting in the backseat, sir, and she got herself thrown from the car when it hit the truck. That's how come she escaped the burning. But she died instantly, poor thing. Broke her neck."

"What time of day was this, Mr. Carter?"

"Round about five o'clock, yesterday evening."

While I was heading for Thomas Thorogood's house, in Clayton, Texas.

"The victims," Mr. Carter said sadly, "they didn't arrive here until about seven." He shook his head. "I never saw so much excitement in all my life. We had government people—the FBI—and we had people from the sheriff's department. We had the city police. Just about everyone in the whole entire law enforcement community. They all wanted to make sure, you see, that the victims were the fugitives everyone was lookin' for."

"How were the men's bodies identified?" I asked him. "Dental records would've been useless."

"Yes, sir, they surely would. You saw the damage to the skulls. Well, first of all, you see, they had the testimony from Mr. Harper. He saw them, clear as day, just a few seconds before the accident. And about ten minutes before that, Mr. Martinez had stopped to fill up the gas tank. So they had the testimony of the fella at the gas station. And then, of course, they had the finger."

"The finger?"

"Yes, sir. What happened was, Mr. Lucero, he was sitting in the passenger seat, you see, and he must've had his hand outside the car. His right hand? You know how people sometimes do, they put their hand outside the window, along the top of the door?" He showed me.

I nodded.

"And what must've happened, a piece of the tanker came at it like a piece of shrapnel, and it just sliced off his pinkie finger. Sliced it right off and sent it flying. The police found it at the scene. I don't know as you noticed, Mr. Croft, but Mr. Lucero's body is missing that finger."

"I hadn't noticed." And I didn't feel like checking. "The print on the finger matched Lucero's?"

"Yes, sir, it surely did."

"They had some money with them."

"Yes, sir, they did. In some metal boxes, in the trunk. Two of them. One of them blew open upon impact, you see, and the money was consumed in the flames. The other one held, and the police recovered most of what was in there. It was pretty badly burned, as you can imagine, Mr. Croft. Useless, most of it. But all told, they say, it was something like twenty thousand dollars."

I nodded. "Okay, Mr. Carter. Thank you very much."

"I'm very pleased to oblige, Mr. Croft."

I was punchy with exhaustion and with a curious kind of deflation. Martinez and Lucero were dead, and I told myself that I should feel relieved. Instead, I felt cheated, for not being able to confront Martinez—and ashamed, for feeling cheated.

For a few moments, when I returned to the car, I considered driving down to the French Quarter to lose myself in the taste of Sazeracs and the sound of jazz, in the excited mindless press of tourist flesh.

But it would've seemed too much like a celebration, and I had nothing at all to celebrate. So I drove out Tulane until it became Airline Highway. It was a seedy area, rundown hotels, young women in short skirts and halters prowling the sidewalks. Cheerleaders, maybe.

I bought myself a take-away poor boy shrimp sandwich and another bottle of Jack Daniel's, found myself another hotel room, and I crawled into bed. I called the police, talked to a Lieutenant Hanson. He confirmed everything that Mr. Carter had told me.

I dialed New Mexico information, got the number for Mrs. Rudolph in Las Vegas, dialed that. She had already heard the news.

"I'm sorry," I told her.

"It's just such an awful *waste,*" she said. "This never should have *happened.*"

"I know."

"It said in the newspaper that your friend, Mrs. Mondragón, that she's still in a coma. Will she be all right, do you know?"

"I hope so."

"So do I, Mr. Croft. And I thank you for calling me."

"You're welcome."

We said our good-byes.

So it was over.

Or was it?

The police were happy. They were satisfied with their identification of Martinez and Lucero.

But I was uneasy. It seemed a bit too pat. The identification really rested upon two things—the word of the witness, Harper, and that single pinkie finger.

Would Lucero cut off his own finger?

Maybe, if it would get the police off his back.

Or maybe I was being paranoid. Maybe I just didn't want them to be dead. Not, at any rate, as the result of an accident.

And Harper, after all, *had* seen the two of them in the car, before it smashed into the tanker truck. . . .

I could worry about it later. I was too tired to think about it now.

I ate half the sandwich, drank half my drink, and I collapsed. It was about five in the afternoon.

The chirping of the telephone woke me at eight in the morning. Automatically, yesterday, I had brought the phone into the bed with me.

I found it amid the covers, flipped it open. "Yeah?"

"This Joshua Croft?"

"Yeah."

"This is Dick Jepson, in Miami."

"Who?"

"Dick Jepson. In Miami? Ed Norman asked me to look around for Luiz Lucero. Teddy Chartoff talked to you."

"Right, yeah, I'm sorry. I'm a little rocky this morning."

"Forget it. Listen. I've got a definite spotting on Lucero."

I sat up. "What?"

"Lucero was seen last night, here in Miami."

"You know that he's supposed to be dead."

"Yeah. I read the newspapers. But I've got a definite spotting on him last night. From a reliable source."

"You're certain?"

"Would I be calling you if I wasn't?"

"Jesus."

"He's left town, him and the other one—"

"Martinez."

"—but I'll know more in a day or two. I'll call you. Where'll you be?"

"I'll be there," I said.

24

ONCE AGAIN, I couldn't get an immediate seat on any of the airlines.

I think I would've driven anyway. By then I had become accustomed to my own Dark. Sitting in the car, sharing the bitter solitude with only my memories, that was one kind of aloneness, and it was one I had come to accept. Standing in a line at an airport, or sitting cramped into the narrow tube of an airplane, surrounded by people giddy with excitement at the prospect of old friends or new adventures, that was another kind. And it was one I wanted to avoid. One I didn't think I could handle.

So I drove. I left New Orleans at nine o'clock, and took I-10 over the waters of Lake Ponchartrain, broad and flat and gray. By eleven I was passing signs for Biloxi. By one I was crossing Mobile Bay. Forty-five minutes later I was in Florida.

I explained it all to Rita.

"Obviously," I said, "they faked it. The accident."

She nodded. "If Dick Jepson's 'reliable source' is in fact reliable."

"Jepson's convinced."

"You don't know Jepson."

"Ed Norman says he's good."

"If they faked it," she said, "the witness, Mr. Harper, had to be part of it."

"Of course he was. He got paid for his testimony. And for parking the tanker there. The other guy, the guy at the gas station, he was probably on the level. They stopped there for gas so he could corroborate Harper's story."

191

"What about the money the police found? What about the finger?"

"Sacrifices. They had three or four times the twenty thousand."

"And the finger, Joshua? You're saying that Lucero cut off his own finger?"

"Or had it done for him. Under anesthesia, maybe. If the FBI and every cop in the country was on your back, wouldn't you give up a finger to get out from under?"

"What about Sylvia Miller?"

"Another sacrifice. To sweeten the story. They didn't need her anymore. They already had the money."

"How did they fake her injuries?"

"I don't know, Rita."

"And whose were the other bodies in the car?"

"Junkies, mules. Lucero's in the drug business. It probably wasn't hard for him to locate a couple of disposable people. Martinez called me, Rita. The day before he supposedly died in that accident. I think he wanted to get in a shot at me, and he knew that he wouldn't have another chance. He knew that he'd be 'dead' the next day."

"But it's all so terribly thin."

"It's all I've got."

"Joshua, I think you should come back. Before something happens to me."

"Nothing's going to happen to you."

I was about an hour past Pensacola. Green pine forest rose up on either side of the Interstate, the tree trunks tall and slender, the flat earth brown with needles beneath them. The telephone rang.

"Yes?"

"Joshua, it's Leroy." His voice was urgent. "Look, you've gotta get back here, man."

"Wait."

I braked, pulled the Cherokee over to the shoulder. An angry horn blared as a car whizzed by me. "What is it?" I said. "Rita?"

"She's bad, man. It looks like she's got some kind of infection. Her temperature's way up there, man. They're afraid it might be meningitis."

"What are they doing? The doctors?"

"*Shit,* man, I don't know."

"You have her doctor's phone number? The surgeon. What's-his-name—Berger?"

"Yeah, wait a minute. Okay, here." He read it to me.

"I'll call you right back."

"Joshua, you really should *get* here, man."

"I'll call you right back, Leroy."

I dialed the doctor's number, reached his secretary. I told her who I was. She asked me to hold. I listened to Muzak for five minutes.

He finally picked up the phone. "Good afternoon, Mr. Croft. What can I do for you?"

"You can tell me what's happening to Mrs. Mondragón."

"Mrs. Mondragón is running a temperature, and her white blood cell count is higher than we'd like it to be. There's the possibility of an infection. We've taken cultures. We expect to hear from the laboratory within forty-eight hours."

"That's two days."

"I'm aware of that."

"What could be causing the infection?"

"Until we get the lab results, we don't know that there *is* an infection. If there is, it could be any of a number of things."

"Meningitis?"

"Cerebral meningitis is one possibility, yes. But, as I say, we won't know for another two days."

"And if she has meningitis?"

"Then we have a different scenario here. But, as I told you earlier, Mr. Croft, I have every expectation that Mrs. Mondragón will recover. She's going through a crisis at the moment, yes. There is cause for concern, yes. But it's a rare brain injury that doesn't pass through some sort of crisis."

"She hasn't regained consciousness?"

"No. Not as yet."

"And she won't, either, if she dies."

"We're doing everything we can, Mr. Croft. Mrs. Mondragón is a strong, healthy woman. She's fighting this. Despite the set-back, I have every reason for confidence."

"Yeah. All right, doctor. Thank you."

I didn't know whether his confidence was real, whether it was a product of his own egotism, or whether it was a sham, designed to placate and dismiss petty annoyances like me.

I did know that even if I were in Santa Fe, there was nothing I could do to help Rita.

I dialed Leroy's number.

He picked it up on the first ring. "Yeah?"

"Leroy, I just talked to the doctor. He thinks she's going to pull through."

"Man, that guy is an *asshole.* He's just sayin' that to stop you from bugging him. Joshua, you really gotta get here. She'd want you here, man. Where're you now? Can you catch a plane?"

"Leroy, I've got a line on Martinez and—"

"What're you *talking* about, man? Martinez and Lucero, they're *dead.* You didn't hear? They were *roasted,* man, in New Orleans. They're *pork chops.*"

"I heard. It was a fake, Leroy. They're still alive. They were spotted in Miami."

There was a pause. "But . . ."

"I'm in Florida now," I said. "I'm going after them."

"But they were *identified,* man. It was in all the papers. It was on the TV."

"They set it up. They were seen in Miami yesterday."

"Where're you getting that from? Who saw them?"

"They were seen. I'm going after them. Leroy, I'll call you later. You call me if anything happens."

Another pause. Then, surly, he said, "Anything happens, man, it'll be Rita dying."

"I'll call you, Leroy."

"Yeah," he said. "Right." He hung up.

I closed the phone and set it on the passenger seat. I took a deep breath, let it slowly out.

The cops had stopped looking for Martinez and Lucero. If I didn't find them, no one would.

And there was nothing I could do in Santa Fe.

I checked the rearview mirror, pulled out onto the highway.

I was doing the right thing, I told myself. I told it to myself several times.

About fifteen minutes later, Hector called. "What's this crap about Martinez and Lucero?"

"You talked to Leroy."

"He called me. Josh, they're dead. They were positively ID'ed, all three of them. The money's been recovered."

"*Some* of the money. They had at least seventy or eighty thousand dollars, that we know of. Hector, I saw a video of those bodies. They could've been anyone."

"There were fingerprints—"

"There was *one* fingerprint. Off a finger that just happened not to get burned."

"You *want* them to be alive. You want to keep tracking them, you want revenge. So you're refusing to accept the facts. Give it up, Josh. Get back here. Rita's in a bad way."

"There's nothing I can do for her, Hector, except what I'm doing."

"You're not doing that for her, goddamit. You're doing it for yourself."

"Doesn't matter. I'm doing it."

He was silent for a moment. Then he said softly, "You do it, then. You do what you want. I'm going to the hospital."

And, like Leroy, he hung up.

A car raced by me, and then another.

I was doing the right thing, I told myself. But I flicked the switch that turned off the power to the telephone.

At five-thirty I was coming up on Tallahassee. I took the first exit available, eased the Cherokee into the first gas station I found. Stiff and sore, moving like a robot, I filled the tank.

I climbed back into the car and turned the phone back on, flipped it open. Jepson, in Miami, had given me both his office and his home number. Too late for him to be at the office. I dialed his home.

He was there. "I've been trying to get ahold of you all day," he told me. "I left a message with Ted Chartoff in Dallas."

"The phone was off. You have anything?"

"I do. I got this from a guy works for the Ortega family. They're the people Lucero used to work for, here in—"

"Yeah, I know. What've you got?"

He paused. People were pausing a lot lately when they talked to me. "The information was expensive," he said.

"You can send me a bill."

Another pause. "I'll do that," he said, and his voice had grown cooler. "All right, according to my guy, Lucero and Martinez are hiding out in the Glades. Off the Tamiami Trail, near a place called Harmony Station. You know where that is?"

"No idea."

"Where are you now?"

"Tallahassee."

"You want the cops in on this? They still think that Lucero and Martinez are dead."

"You think we can persuade them otherwise?"

"I don't know. Maybe. But I can't give up my source."

I was still angry at Hector. "Doesn't matter," I said. "I want those two myself. You're sure this guy's reliable? Your source?"

"Stake my life on him."

"Fine. But he doesn't know where, exactly, Lucero and Martinez are hiding out?"

"Somewhere near Harmony Station. Back in the swamp somewhere. But listen. I'm way ahead of you. There's a man in Clearwater—that's near Tampa. He knows the Glades. Probably better than anybody in the state. Used to live there. I talked to him. He's willing to go in there with you, help you find them, but he's going to cost."

"What's his name?"

"Carpenter. That's what he calls himself, anyway. I think the name's a flag. I'm pretty sure he used to be a spook. CIA, maybe."

"I don't care what he calls himself, so long as he can help me find Martinez."

"If they're there, he'll find them. You want his number?"

"Go ahead."

He gave it to me.

"Thanks, Dick," I told him. "Look, I apologize for being so abrupt. I've been kind of ragged lately."

"Yeah, I know. No problem. Give Carpenter a call. He's expecting to hear from you."

"I'll call him now."

"Listen, one other thing. He's a little weird. Carpenter, I mean."

"Weird how?"

"You'll find out. I just wanted to let you know up front."

"All right, Dick. Thanks. I'll talk to you later."

We hung up. I dialed the number he had given me. After two rings, a man's voice came on. "Carpenter." The voice was soft but raspy, almost a whisper.

"This is Joshua Croft. Dick Jepson said I should call you."

"Where are you now?"

"Tallahassee."

"Jepson said you left New Orleans this morning."

"Yeah."

"Get some sleep. In the morning, find Nineteen South and take that. You're about five, six hours away. Call me when you get to Dunedin. I'll give you the rest of the instructions then. Got it?"

"Yeah."

"Did Jepson tell you how much this'll cost?"

"No."

"Five hundred a day. Thousand-dollar retainer."

"Fine," I told him.

"See you tomorrow," he said.

25

I LEFT TALLAHASSEE at seven-thirty in the morning. The sun was shining brightly in a sky of blue, a blue much softer and paler than the blue that domed the New Mexico high desert. The air was warm and threatened to become a lot warmer.

For a few hours, Route 19 was mostly clear, slowly rolling over green farmland and pasture. But when it entered Pasco County, it became an endless belt of shopping centers, gas stations, automobile showrooms, fast-food emporiums, malls that ranged from strip to large to very large. The empty plains of Kansas and Texas began to seem a lot more inviting.

The speed limit was posted at fifty miles per hour, but not many of the drivers seemed to notice, probably because half of them were legally blind.

Years ago, when I was first learning to drive, someone told me that if you saw, sitting in the front seat of the car ahead, two white-haired women or a single man wearing a hat, you should start being very careful. A lot of the cars on Route 19 held two white-haired women or single men wearing hats. Some of the cars seemed to hold no one at all—until I passed them, cautiously, and looked to the right and saw a tiny old man, or a tiny old woman, leaning forward to peer over the dashboard, hands grimly clamped to the sides of the steering wheel.

I reached Dunedin at a little after one. I pulled into a 7-Eleven, refilled the gas tank, and called Carpenter. He gave me terse, whispered directions. I returned to the car and I followed them.

I got off Route 19 at Sunset Point Road, turning right, and followed that for a mile or so and then turned right again and drove past a small lake on my left, bordered with what looked like saw grass. I turned left, drove for about a hundred yards, and turned left again, into Carpenter's gravel driveway. It was hard to believe that I was within a pistol shot of Route 19 and its traffic.

It was a big white frame house with a big screened-in porch on a huge piece of property that sloped down to the flat blue lake. The sweep of lawn was very green in the shade of tall live oaks bearded by lacy wisps of Spanish moss. On the lush grass before the house stood two white statues of storks, and I was just thinking that they were a bit hokey when the statues lifted their wings in slow motion and magically rose off the ground to sail slowly up between the trees and vanish.

I parked the car beside an old gray Ford pickup, got out, walked up to the front door. I knocked at the door.

The door opened.

Carpenter was tall and rangy, in his late fifties but very fit. His square face had the kind of reddish tan you don't get from coconut oil. His white hair was closely cropped, brushed flat and forward along his scalp. He wore brown leather walking boots, neatly pressed khaki slacks, and a gray plaid shirt of thin flannel, the sleeves folded back from thick red wrists.

Across his corded throat, notching the bottom of his Adam's apple, was a thin white scar. Whatever had caused the scar had probably also caused the raspy whisper I'd heard over the phone.

He held out his hand and I took it. It was calloused and strong.

"You had lunch?" he whispered.

"No."

He nodded. "Not much in the house. I'll take you out. You want to drive?"

"You're welcome to it."

He nodded. "We'll use the truck."

★ ★ ★

Carpenter drove the truck back to Sunset Point Road and aimed it toward the west.

"What kind of food?" he asked me. "Any preference?"

"So long as it's not gray," I said.

He turned to me. "Gray?"

"I've been eating a lot from the gray food group lately."

He smiled briefly, a flicker of movement at the right side of his mouth, quickly there, quickly gone. It seemed less a sign of amusement than a recognition that amusement was expected. "Chinese okay?" he said.

"Fine."

He nodded. "I know a place."

He didn't say anything else for a while. I assumed that when he wanted to talk about Lucero and Martinez, he would.

Traffic was heavy but he drove well. We went past neighborhoods of low, ranch-style suburban homes. Past a small shopping center—a 7-Eleven, a pizza place. Past a large brick church on a broad green lawn. Past some more suburban neighborhoods. Into, and then out of, the shade of some overhanging live oaks. Past another neighborhood, this one older, the houses taller, their paint chipped and faded.

The road ended at an intersection. Beyond the cross street was the Gulf of Mexico, the blue water winking in the sunlight, a few faraway sailboats loafing across it. This was the first time I'd been near a large body of water since Rita and I had stayed in Catalina. Out there in the distance, maybe a hundred feet up, a pelican wheeled in a turn and then knifed back its wings and plunged like a rocket toward the sea.

Carpenter made a left. As we went through a short strip of cheap motels, the Gulf disappeared behind them. We drove through a quiet, slightly rundown area. Through downtown Clearwater, brick buildings, old-fashioned gaslights. Past a park on the left, a large brown hotel on the right.

Marching along the sidewalks in front of the hotel were brisk young men and women wearing what looked like uniforms, some of them nautical, some of them military.

"Who are they?" I asked him.

"Scientologists," he whispered. "The hotel, that's their international headquarters."

I couldn't tell from the whisper how he felt about Scientologists. He didn't ask me how I felt, and I didn't tell him.

We drove for another two or three miles and then Carpenter turned right. Past a golf course, down a slope through some trees, up to what appeared to be a guardhouse squatting in the center of the road. As Carpenter rolled down the truck's window, a fat man in a security guard's uniform leaned from the window of the small building.

"Lunch," Carpenter told him.

The man nodded, saluted him with a jaunty wave.

Carpenter shifted gears and gave the truck some gas. He turned to me, smiled his fleeting smile. "They like to keep out the riffraff."

"Who could blame them."

When we swung up to the right, through some more trees, I saw an enormous white building about two hundred yards away, three or four stories tall and stretching out, left and right, for hundreds of yards.

"The Belleview Mido," Carpenter said.

We parked in the big parking lot and we walked up to the entrance. Shiny glass and polished copper, it had obviously been added long after the original building had gone up.

Inside, beyond the expanse of gleaming lobby, the corridors seemed to go on forever. We finally reached the restaurant. It was a small place, elegant and subdued, done in black and dark blue. A hostess seated us and asked if we'd like a drink. I asked for a beer, Carpenter for an iced tea.

A waitress brought us the drinks and a pair of menus, left us to decide. "What's good?" I asked Carpenter.

"Most of it," he said.

Small talk evidently wasn't his strong suit.

When the waitress returned, Carpenter ordered something

with tofu. I ordered hot and sour soup and Szechuan Chicken. As she left, Carpenter sat back in his chair and said to me, "Okay. What's the story on these men?"

I told him about Martinez first. I was halfway through with it when the waitress came back, carrying our food. Carpenter held up his hand to me. "Eat now," he whispered. "Talk later."

We ate. The food was good. After the waitress had cleaned away the plates, Carpenter nodded to me. "Go ahead," he said.

I told him the rest of it. I mentioned Rita's coma, but not the fever. He listened quietly, nodding from time to time.

Then I told him about Luiz Lucero. He showed only two reactions throughout it all. When I said that Lucero had been a Marielito, he frowned slightly. When I told him about Lucero shooting his victims in the eyes, his mouth twitched in that small quick smile, and he shook his head slightly. I got the feeling that he'd made an aesthetic judgment.

"Okay," he said, when I finished. "We find them. Then what?"

"We bring them back."

"Likely they'll have something to say about that."

"We may have to persuade them."

"Uh huh. You have weapons?"

"A pump shotgun. Slugs and double ought shot. A nine-millimeter Beretta. A couple of thirty-eights."

The mouth twitched. "Loaded for bear."

"And a Swiss Army knife."

Another twitch. "I've got most of the gear we need, back at the house. You need another pair of boots. And we need some supplies. We'll get them up this afternoon."

"What's wrong with the boots?"

"They're fine for Roy Rogers. He didn't spend much time in the swamp."

I nodded. He knew the swamp and I didn't. "When do we leave?"

"Tomorrow morning, early. You have the retainer?"

"You'll take a check?"

He shrugged. "Sure." He didn't need to tell me that the check had better be good.

I wrote him a check. He used his own cash to pay for the lunch.

The air had kept its threat and gotten warmer. When we returned to the truck, the interior was as hot as a sauna. As I climbed in, I felt a droplet of sweat prickle down my ribs. I wondered what the Everglades would be like this time of year.

We drove back the way we'd come, along Sunset Point, passing the turnoff for Carpenter's place and continuing on to Route 19. In a big shopping center, we stopped at a sporting goods store. Inside, we picked up a blend of insect repellent and sunscreen, some packages of gorp, and some freeze-dried food, half of it vegetarian. I tried out a pair of comfortable walking boots, leather and Gore-Tex. As I was lugging them toward the cash register, Carpenter appeared at my side and handed me three lightweight brown and green camouflage shirts, starched and pinned to cardboard inserts.

"We'll wash them when we get home," he whispered. "Otherwise the starch'll drive you crazy. You have a cap?"

"No."

"Hang on."

I hung on.

When he returned, he handed me a floppy gray cotton hat. "The brim gives you some neck coverage."

"Yes, dear."

Now there was a hint of irritation in the quick smile. "This is why you're hiring me."

"Yeah. Personal shopper."

He shrugged, smiled. "Forget the hat. Fry your brains out."

"No." I smiled. "You're right. I'll take the hat."

I paid for everything with my credit card.

Back at the truck, we dumped it all behind the seats. Carpenter turned to me. "We'll get some food for tonight. Can you live without meat?"

"If I have to."

He nodded. "Come on." I went.

A few doors down from the sporting goods store was a Safeway. I followed him into the building. He maneuvered a shopping cart free and I followed him down the aisles.

Carpenter poked and prodded at the vegetables like a finicky housewife—spring onions, bok choy, carrots, broccoli, ginger, jalapeño peppers—before he loaded them into the cart. He lifted a brick of tofu, squeezed it gently, placed that beside the vegetables. He turned to me. "Okay. Anything you want?"

"Jack Daniel's?"

The mouth twitched, more of a frown this time than a smile. "You a juicer?"

"Would I admit it if I were?"

"I don't want any surprises down there."

"No," I said. "I'm not."

"You can live without it?"

That was his creed, apparently—if you could live without something, you did.

"Yeah," I told him.

He nodded. "Might as well start now."

I was more annoyed than I should have been.

Back at Carpenter's place, he directed me to the porch. Both of us carrying bags, we entered through the screen door. The only furniture was an aluminum beach chair and an aluminum chaise lounge. Carpenter set the groceries down on the concrete floor. "We'll bring it all in first," he said. I put down my bag.

After two more trips, one of them to the Cherokee to grab my luggage, everything was on the porch. Carpenter sat down on the chaise lounge and began to unlace his boots. He looked up at me and said, "I'd appreciate it if you'd take off your boots."

It was his house. I sat down on the chair and pulled them off.

He unlocked the door and we started to shuttle the stuff in.

The first room was the kitchen, and it was spotless. Every surface was gleaming—the tile floor, the gray marble counters, the butcher block table in the center of the room.

When all the supplies were inside, Carpenter turned to me. "Get your bags," he said. "I'll show you where you sleep."

I got my bags.

"Follow me," he said.

I followed him.

Like the kitchen, the big living room was spotless. It was also nearly bare. No paintings on the wall, no bric-a-brac, no bookcases, no rugs, no television, no stereo. There was an oak futon sofa and an oak futon chair, both futons dark blue. In one corner stood a small oak pedestal cabinet that held a framed photograph. Against one blank wall, along the shiny wooden floor, lay a black mat, about three feet by two. Atop it was a plump round cushion. I'd lived in Santa Fe long enough to know that the cushion was designed for meditation.

I was beginning to get the feeling that Carpenter didn't do much entertaining.

In the hallway, we passed one door, shut. The next door was open and I glanced into the room. I stopped walking. Every wall was covered by white bookcases, and all the shelves were filled. Not with books, though. With Barbie dolls.

There must have been thousands of them in there, blonde, brunette, red-haired, standing at stiff attention on the white shelves, wearing thousands of stiff and brightly colored outfits, none of them the same—business suits, bathing suits, cocktail dresses, summer dresses, sheaths, muumuus, jeans, sweaters, denim jackets, flight jackets, fur coats, woolen coats, wedding gowns, evening gowns, nightgowns.

Carpenter turned around, saw me staring at them. "It's a hobby," he told me. "I collect them."

I nodded.

"Here's your bed," he said, and nodded toward the next room. It was even more spare than the living room. Just a single bed, neatly made, covered with a plain white cotton spread. At the opened window, before the screen, stood a small white fan, softly whirring.

"Bathroom's there," he said, nodding to the last door in the hallway. "You want to sack out for a while? I need to make some phone calls."

"Yeah," I said. "Thanks."

"We'll have dinner when you're hungry."

"Fine."

He nodded once, then left me.

Barbie dolls? I thought.

I set the suitcase on the floor, set Leroy's briefcase beside it, closed the door, lay down on the bed.

I looked over at the briefcase. I'd put the phone inside it. I hadn't talked to anyone in Santa Fe since this morning.

I knew I should call the hospital.

But I was working now on the principle that Rita would recover from her fever. That the right thing for me to do was to continue looking for Martinez and Lucero. Calling would've been an admission of doubt—not so much to Leroy and to Hector as to myself.

So I lay there and I remembered things. And I argued with Rita.

I didn't really expect to sleep, but after a while the warm air, the drone of the fan, put me under.

I awoke suddenly, startled from some unpleasant dream I couldn't recall. I was slick with sweat. For a few moments I had no idea where I was.

The orangish light of early evening slanted through the window. I looked at my watch. Seven o'clock.

I got up, left the bedroom, walked down the hallway in stockinged feet. The first door—Carpenter's bedroom—was shut and I could hear nothing coming from inside.

I walked into the living room. No one there.

I walked over to the oak pedestal in the corner and picked up the framed photograph. It showed three people. One was a younger version of Carpenter, in army fatigues, smiling hugely. His arm was draped over the shoulders of a young Asian woman with long black hair. She wore a white blouse, a black skirt, and she seemed as happy as he did. The third person was a girl, perhaps ten years old, in a white dress and white patent leather shoes. She was grinning and she was holding both small hands up to her chest, and clutched in her slender fingers was a Barbie doll.

"My wife," Carpenter said behind me. "And my daughter."

26

M Y HEART DID a little skip. I hadn't heard him come up behind me.

I put the photograph back on the cabinet, turned to face him.
"What happened to them?" I asked.

He was standing there with the folded camouflage shirts tucked
under his left arm. "Automobile accident. Over on Nineteen."

"When?"

"Five years ago." He handed me the shirts. "Washed and
dried." They'd been ironed, too. "Wait here. I'll get the gear.
We'll pack."

I waited.

He made several trips back to his bedroom to fetch the equipment. Two external frame backpacks, olive drab. Two lightweight sleeping bags, olive drab. A ripstop nylon tent, olive drab,
tightly rolled. Two aluminum one-quart canteens in olive drab
canvas covers. Two Thermarest air mattresses, olive drab.

He didn't ask for help. When I offered it, he told me he
wouldn't need it, thanks. It seemed to me that he didn't want
anyone else in his bedroom.

When he carried in a hip holster and attached belt, olive drab,
that held a government issue Colt automatic, he said to me, "A
Beretta, you said?"

"Yeah."

He lay the gun belt along the futon chair, padded back to his
bedroom. He came back with another gun belt and holster,

empty. He tossed it to me. "Okay. You'll need three changes of clothing. Underwear and socks. One pair of pants, plus the pants you wear."

"It'll take us three days?"

"If we don't find them in two, we come out and restock. The third set is backup."

We spent the next half an hour getting organized. He stuffed more equipment into his own pack than into mine—a brass Optimus stove, an aluminum fuel bottle, a mess kit, a first aid kit, a drop line and some hooks.

"We're going fishing?" I asked him.

"If we have to."

"Have to?"

"We get stuck and run out of food."

I didn't ask him how, or why, we might get stuck.

When the pack was full, he tied the tent to its bottom, his sleeping bag to its top.

He turned to me and said, "You hungry?"

"I could eat."

He nodded.

He didn't want any help with the cooking either, so I sat there at the butcher block table while he cut up the vegetables and the tofu. When everything was chopped, he stir-fried it all in a big cast-iron skillet, seasoning it lightly with fish sauce and sake. Your strong silent types like to go light on the seasoning.

We sat at the table to eat. Once again, chat was kept to a minimum.

At the end of the meal I told him, truthfully, that the food had been good.

He nodded. "My wife taught me."

"She was Vietnamese?"

"Cambodian." He looked at his watch, then abruptly stood, lifting his plate. He held out the other hand for mine, and I gave it to him. "Time to call it a night," he said. "We're up at four."

I stood. He set the plates on the counter, turned back to me. "Think you'll have trouble sleeping?"

He still believed that I was an alcoholic. "I slept this afternoon," I said.

"Afternoons are easy." He turned, opened a cabinet, took out a small brown plastic bottle, turned back and tossed it to me over the table. He was clearly a man who liked to toss things. His aim was always good.

I read the label. Melatonin, three-milligram tablets.

"One or two of them should do it," he said. "Three, if you need it. They won't hurt you."

"I won't need them."

He shrugged. "You've got them. I'll take care of the dishes. See you in the morning."

I had been dismissed.

Maybe I'd slept for too long in the afternoon. Or maybe Carpenter was right—maybe I was a boozer. But I couldn't sleep that night.

Finally, at eleven o'clock, I climbed out of bed, turned on the light, opened the briefcase and took out Leroy's phone. I dialed his number. It was nine o'clock in Santa Fe.

"Hello?"

"Leroy? Joshua. How's she doing?"

"Her temperature's still up there, a hundred and three, but she's holding on. No thanks to you, man."

"They still don't know yet what it is?"

"Lab results come in tomorrow."

"Okay. Thanks."

"Come on back, man. You should be here."

"Soon as I finish up."

"It's not right, Joshua. What you're doing. They're dead, those two."

"I'll try to call you tomorrow," I said.

"Yeah," he said, and hung up again.

After another fifteen minutes, I took two of the melatonin tablets. Twenty minutes later, I was out.

Carpenter woke me at four. I showered and toweled myself dry. I stared at myself for a while in the mirror and wondered who I was.

After I dressed, I slipped Leroy's telephone into the left breast pocket of the camouflage shirt and I buttoned the pocket closed.

In the living room the backpacks were gone—out in the truck, presumably. Carpenter had already made the coffee, and we sat at the kitchen table to drink it.

In a neatly ironed camouflage shirt of his own, he looked more alert than I felt. But that couldn't have been very difficult.

I asked him, "How long will it take to get down there?"

He shrugged. "Six hours, seven."

That was pretty much the entire discussion. He never appeared to resent the questions I asked, but he never appeared inclined to enlarge upon his answers, either. He seemed perfectly content to sit there and stare down into his coffee cup.

After another five minutes, he drained the cup, looked at me, and asked, "You ready?"

"Yeah."

He nodded. He lifted his saucer and cup, stood, held out his hand for mine. I passed it over. He carried them to the sink, washed them, set them in a rack to dry. We went outside and I transferred the Beretta, the shotgun, the boxes of shells, and Rita's .38 from the Cherokee to the Ford, stashing everything behind the seats. I took my sunglasses from the glove compartment, put them on.

Carpenter spent a few minutes checking the packs, and then we were on the road.

There was still traffic on Route 19, even at five in the morning, but it wasn't bad. By five-thirty we were on the Sunshine Skyway Bridge, high over the entrance to Tampa Bay. To the east, the sky was growing pearly. To the west, below us, running roughly parallel to this bridge, was what looked like the truncated spur of another one.

"What happened to it?" I asked Carpenter. "The old bridge."

"Freighter hit it," he said.

On the far side, we headed east for about five miles, then picked up I-75 South.

Carpenter kept the truck at a steady seventy-four, nine miles above the speed limit, as the highway ran through the pine forests. At seven o'clock, we were passing exit signs for Port Charlotte.

At nine o'clock we were passing signs for Fort Meyers. Once we left them behind and crossed the Caloosahatchee River, the pines slowly gave way to cedar forest and patches of marshland. None of it looked very inviting.

Throughout it all, the conversation wasn't any different from what it had been since I met Carpenter. I would ask him a question—"What are those trees, down there by the water?" He would answer it—"Mangrove." Now and then, not often, he volunteered something—"See that? Sandhill crane."

About thirty miles past Fort Meyers, we took the exit for East Naples. On Highway 41, the Tamiami Trail, Carpenter pulled the truck into a gas station. While he filled the tank, I called Leroy.

Rita was the same. I told him that I'd be out of touch for a while. He said, "Yeah," and hung up again.

I put the telephone back into my shirt pocket. It would be useless in the swamp, I knew that, but it was my only connection to Santa Fe.

I ducked inside the station and bought a ham and cheese sandwich. I carried it back into the truck, ate it while Carpenter drove.

He looked over at me. I could see my reflection in his sunglasses. "You know how many nitrates are in that thing?"

"Seven," I said. I could be strong and silent, too.

He shook his head. He didn't smile.

The countryside was getting wetter. Between the stands of cedar there were sometimes acres of swamp, tall green grasses poking from the dark slick of water. Now and then, I saw a heron stalking thoughtfully through the shallows.

"Are we going to need a boat?" I asked him.

"We'll find out when we get there."

"Where is there?"

"Little ways past Harmony Station."

Just after twelve, we passed the signs for Harmony Station. Ten miles beyond, Carpenter slowed the truck and crossed the road, turning left onto a dirt road that wandered off into the cedars. We bounced and bucked down the road for a mile or two, and then Carpenter made another turn, to the right.

Two hundred yards later we pulled up in a clearing before a small shingled shack, fronted by a lopsided covered porch. Scrawny chickens fluttered and flapped away, clucking fretfully. To the right, an old Chevrolet stood on rust-stained cinder blocks. To the left, in not much better condition but on its own tires, stood an old Dodge pickup. On the porch, an ancient hound dog raised itself up onto its front legs and trembled. Its grizzled brown skin was so loose it looked as though it had once belonged to some other, much larger animal.

Carpenter turned off the engine. "You stay here," he told me.

I stayed there.

Carpenter left the truck, walked to the porch, climbed up the steps, reached down and patted the hound's head. The dog lay back down. Carpenter knocked on the front door and it opened. I couldn't see who opened it. Carpenter disappeared inside.

I waited. A mosquito bit me on the back of the hand. I waited some more. I noticed that there were no phone lines or electric lines going into the house.

Which would maybe explain why Carpenter hadn't called here before we left Clearwater.

Ten minutes later, Carpenter came out onto the porch, his sunglasses in his hand. He was followed by a short, swarthy man wearing jeans and a khaki shirt.

Carpenter waved the sunglasses at me, beckoning, and I got out of the truck. As I reached the porch, Carpenter said to me, "This is Eugene Samson. He's going to lend us a canoe. Eugene, Joshua Croft."

I shook hands with Eugene Samson. Silently he bobbed his round head at me. He looked as though he were at least part Native American. "Thank you," I said. It seemed like the thing to say to a man who was going to lend you a canoe. I turned to Carpenter. "How do you know we'll need a canoe?"

"They're in there," he said, nodding toward the forest. "Lucero and Martinez. They went in with a third man, two days ago. They were using an inflatable."

"Mr. Samson saw them?" I asked.

"His cousin did. Down the line a bit."

"We're lucky."

His smile twitched. "No way for them to get into the swamp, anywhere along here, without someone seeing them." He nodded toward Samson. "This is their territory. They keep an eye out."

I nodded. "So there are three of them."

He shook his head. "The third man came back out yesterday." His smile twitched again. "Too bad."

"You know him? The third man?"

He nodded. "I know him."

"Who is he?"

"A Cuban. Another Marielito. Name's Esteban." Lightly, he stroked the white scar at his throat. "He gave me this."

I looked from Carpenter to Eugene, back to Carpenter. "So that's it? We know they're in there? It's that simple?"

Carpenter smiled that smile. "Simple? Couple hundred square miles of swamp?"

"How long before the third guy came back? This Esteban?"

"Just under twenty-four hours, Eugene says. And the inflatable was using a trolling motor. Electric. Not much faster than a canoe."

"So Lucero and Martinez can't be more than twelve hours away."

His smile twitched. "Unless Esteban dropped them off, and they walked."

"Lot of walking room back in the swamp, is there?"

"Some." He nodded. "But likely you're right. Likely they're about twelve hours away. Thing is, we don't know in which direction."

"You don't have any ideas?"

"One or two." He looked at me appraisingly. "You ever been in a canoe before?"

"Once. A long time ago."

He nodded, slipped on the sunglasses. "Let's get the gear down to the water."

We carried the packs around behind Eugene Samson's shack. The swamp began back there, a small pond of black water, maybe thirty feet across, spotted here and there with flat green pads of lotus. At its northern end, a thin channel led off into the grasses.

The canoe was aluminum, dull and dented but watertight. Samson swung it up alongside the shore and he helped us load it, everything but the shotgun and the gunbelts. When we finished, Carpenter handed me my belt and I strapped it on.

Carpenter strapped on his own, then picked up the shotgun. "What's it carrying?" he asked me.

"Double ought."

He nodded. "I don't like loaded shotguns in a boat." He worked the pump, jacking out the shells until the action stayed open. He gathered up the shells, stuffed them into the big pockets of his field pants. He lay the gun in the canoe, beside the packs.

"Be right back," he said, and went off toward the truck. I looked at Samson. He stared back at me, impassive.

When Carpenter returned, he was wearing an olive drab field

cap and he was carrying a pair of knee pads, the kind that skate-boarders use. He handed them to me.

He said, "Canoe's a lot more stable when you kneel to paddle. These'll help."

"You brought them along?" I asked him.

"Thought we might need them."

I strapped on the knee pads.

"Where's your hat?" he asked me.

"In the pack."

"Get it out. And the repellent."

I squatted down beside the canoe, opened the pack, found the hat and the repellent. I put on the hat, squirted some repellent into my hand, slapped it over my exposed skin. I tucked the bottle into the other shirt pocket.

"Okay," Carpenter said. He handed me a paddle. "You're sitting forward. Go ahead." He held onto the frame of the canoe as I stepped carefully aboard, left foot, right foot. When I eased down onto the thwart, the canoe wobbled. Anxious ripples fanned out across the water.

"Kneel," Carpenter told me.

I knelt.

The prow of the canoe swung away from the shore, toward the center of the pool, and then suddenly the boat was drifting forward. I turned around. Carpenter was kneeling behind me, beyond the backpacks.

On the shore, Eugene Samson stood and watched us. Impassively.

I looked at my watch. One o'clock.

27

CARPENTER HAD BEEN right about the hat. Without it, I would've fried my brains. The sunlight poured down from that washed-out blue sky and streamed out along the dark surface of the still water like molten metal, yellow and dazzling, and it pressed with physical force against my head and shoulders and arms. Despite the sunscreen, my hands began to go red.

I didn't have much to do. Carpenter told me, early on, not to paddle until he said so. Not to talk, either.

So I knelt there quietly as the canoe slid along.

We sat low in the water, below the tops of the grasses. Sometimes the channel became so narrow and winding that all I could see was grass, a forest of it, left and right and straight ahead. Carpenter used his paddle to push us and I used mine to fan aside the brittle stalks as they came in. They fanned back at me and then rustled and rasped along the frame of the boat. Now and then, in front of us, something plopped into the water, startled and startling. Now and then, off to the side, something chittered and fluttered.

Sometimes the channel suddenly opened onto a small quiet lake, and a single crane, or a pair of them, flapped big astonished wings and climbed up into the sunlight. Carpenter didn't like the open water, and he kept the canoe close to the wall of grass. Occasionally a fish jumped out there, a flash of silver, a gurgling splash, rings of ripples slowly widening. Once a large dark snake swam away from the boat, its head above water, its graceful body slowly whipping back and forth beneath the surface. "Cotton-mouth," said Carpenter.

Snakes didn't bother me. We had snakes in New Mexico. What we didn't have were alligators, and periodically, in the back of my mind, it was alligators I saw, the long bodies lying motionless in the water, the bulbous snouts, the empty patient eyes. But on that first day I saw them only in the back of my mind.

There was land from time to time, low islands of tall cedar, the knobby trunks pale and spectral, like the spines of skeletons. When we came to an island, Carpenter would steer the canoe toward the bank and then paddle more slowly alongside it as he searched for signs. The thin strip of shade was welcome, but he never found any signs.

He had been right, too, about the insect repellent. Mosquitos whined at my ear, tiny eager buzz saws, but they never settled on my flesh. And he had been right about the knee pads. If I hadn't been wearing them, I would've been in agony as soon as we left Samson's. But after a couple of hours, the pressure began to get troublesome. I spent the next hour shifting my weight, as gently and as quietly as I could.

At four-thirty we came to still another island, this one tiny, only a small cluster of gray cedars soaring upward. Carpenter aimed the canoe toward the bank and then, at the last moment, swung it smoothly to the left. The right side smacked gently against the ground.

I looked back at him.

"Wait'll I get out," he said. He rose as easily from the kneeling position as he might've risen from a sofa. He stepped lightly from the boat to the shore, then stepped toward me. Squatting, he gripped the canoe's side with his left hand and offered me his right. I pushed myself up onto the thwart, took his hand, and clambered from the boat. I did it neither easily nor lightly.

"You see something?" I asked him.

He shook his head. "Time for a break."

He would get no argument from me. I put my hands against

my hips and bent my torso backward, stretching the stiffened muscles.

There was a rope at the boat's stern, long enough to reach the trunk of the nearest cedar. Carpenter tied it there, made it fast. Stepping back to the canoe, he squatted down beside it, opened his pack, burrowed around for a while. He came up with a canteen and a plastic bag of gorp.

He stood, tossed me the canteen. His aim was still good.

I unscrewed the cap, drank. The water was warm, but it was wet.

Carpenter sat down, leaning his back against one of the cedar trunks, straightening out his long legs, crossing them at the ankles. I walked over and handed him the canteen. He offered me the bag of gorp.

I opened it, poured myself a handful, gave it back to Carpenter. I sat down about four feet away, against another cedar. The ground was damp.

Carpenter took a swallow from the canteen. "How're the knees?" he asked me.

"They've been better."

He nodded. "You get used to it," he said. He screwed back the canteen's cap, set the canteen upright beside him on the soft ground. He took off his sunglasses, lay them in his lap, rubbed at the bridge of his nose.

"What do we do," I said, "when we run out of water?" I flipped some gorp into my mouth. Raisins, nuts, bits of chocolate.

His smile came and went. He nodded toward the dark channel. "What's that?"

"Polluted."

"There's iodine in the first aid kit. And some salt tablets. How's your bladder?"

"Distended."

He smiled. "Pick a spot."

"In a minute. When did it happen? With Esteban?"

He frowned, and for a moment I thought he was going to fob

me off with another curt answer. But maybe the silence of the swamp had relaxed him. Or maybe he'd grown to admire the way I caught everything he tossed.

He peeled off his fatigue cap, lowered his head, ran his hand forward over the damp white hair, raised his head again. "In eighty-one," he said. "I was working a camp over in Broward County. Training some Cubans. Esteban was one of them. We had an argument. He came at me later, while I was asleep. I woke up in time." He smiled his twitchy smile, and then scratched at the scar on his throat. "But I was a little slow."

"What kind of training?"

"Paramilitary."

"Anti-Castro Cubans?"

He nodded and then looked up into the branches of the cedars. "We've got a few hours of light left." He turned back to me. "Camp here or go on?"

"Go on."

He nodded. "There's a place, couple of miles away. They could be there."

We glided through the silence. I had only Carpenter's word for it that this part of the swamp wasn't the same part we'd covered earlier. I could see where the sunlight angled into the trees and through the grasses, so I knew where the west lay. At any given moment I knew which direction we were taking. But it all looked the same—narrow channels through the grasses, pools and ponds and lakes, sometimes a hummock of land, sometimes an island.

About an hour after we started off again, I found out why Carpenter didn't like the open water. We were sliding along the edge of a small lake when suddenly the canoe picked up speed. I glanced back.

Paddle!" he rasped, and pointed his oar toward a small opening in the grass.

I paddled, and a moment later we slipped into the opening.

Another powerful thrust from Carpenter and we rounded a bend in the channel. I glanced back again.

"Airboat," he said. "Probably a ranger."

I heard it then, a distant muffled moan, growing louder. The volume increased until it became a roar, sounding like the airplane engine it was. It passed us by on the far side of the thin wall of grass. The grass swayed and shivered, the canoe bobbed gently. Slowly, the roar faded.

"What's he looking for?" I asked Carpenter.

"Poachers, probably." He smiled. "You want to explain the shotgun?"

"Nope."

He nodded. "We'll give him a few minutes," he said.

An hour later, when the sky had grown darker overhead and the slant of the sunlight had become almost horizontal, Carpenter slowed the canoe. We were in a narrow channel, nothing but grass in every direction.

I turned around. "What?"

Far off, a bird made a whooping sound that wavered up and down the scale, then died off.

"We're almost there," Carpenter said. He lay his paddle inboard, leaned forward, lifted the shotgun and the box of deer slugs. He set the box on the top of his pack, reached into his pocket, pulled out a shot shell. He slipped the shell into the action of the gun, then opened the box, removed a slug, and slipped that in. He kept loading the weapon, alternating shotshells and slugs.

"How are you with a shotgun?" he asked me.

"Not great."

"You mind if I carry it?"

"No."

He nodded. "Get that pistol ready."

I pulled out the Beretta, worked the slide, pushed the safety.

He lay the shotgun across his pack and he picked up the paddle. "No talking."

Fifteen minutes later, we were peering through a veil of grass, across a stretch of water, at another cypress island. It was no more than twenty-five yards long. At its east end, beneath the trees, stood a ramshackle shanty of weathered planking. The tar paper of the roof lay in uneven strips down along the walls, and the walls themselves had warped, leaving gaps through which the fading light was visible.

We watched the small building for a few minutes, silently, but it was obvious the place was empty.

Carpenter paddled the canoe toward shore. We got out and took a look at the shack. Its south side was open, facing the water. No one had used it for years.

"What is it?" I asked Carpenter.

"Poacher's shack." He glanced around. "Let's make camp."

"What were they poaching?"

"Alligators."

"And we're going to camp here?"

He waved his hand around the clearing. "You see any alligators?"

"Not yet."

"Don't worry. They feel the same way about you that you feel about them."

I doubted that.

The graphite poles for the tent were shock-corded, and it took Carpenter only five minutes to have the thing up and ready. It was a dome tent, big enough for three people. He unlaced his boots, took them off, and climbed inside it. I passed in the air mattresses and the sleeping bags. When he came back outside, he put his boots back on and from his pack he took a roll of toilet paper and a black entrenching tool—a small shovel. I hadn't seen the roll of paper or the tool before—he must've slipped them in there while I was asleep.

About twenty feet from the tent, he dug a small hole in the damp earth and stuck the entrenching tool into the pile of dirt, left it there with the roll of paper. "Toilet," he said to me as he returned to the tent. "You know how to use it?"

"I can probably figure it out."

He nodded.

He lit the small Optimus stove, scooped water from the swamp, boiled it. He clipped the tops off two of the freeze-dried meals—macaroni and cheese for him, beef Stroganoff for me—then poured boiling water into the pouches and let them sit for a while.

We ate out of the pouches, using aluminum spoons. The Stroganoff was edible. Barely.

Afterward, Carpenter cleaned up, shoving the empty pouches into a grocery store plastic bag.

We sat again with our backs to a pair of cedars. The mosquitos had gotten hungrier, but the repellent was still holding them off.

"Any other possibilities?" I asked him. "Places they could be hiding?"

"One or two," he said. "A couple more, if they'd been portaging."

"They haven't been?"

"No signs of it. From what Eugene says, that inflatable's a fair-sized boat. Three men and all their gear. If they'd carried it out, I'd have seen something."

"Maybe they've got another boat."

"No way they could arrange that. Not unless they brought it in."

"Maybe they did. Another inflatable."

He looked at me.

"Couldn't weigh all that much," I said. "One guy could probably carry it."

He took off his cap, lowered his head, ran his hands forward along his hair. He looked up. "I'm an idiot," he said.

"They could've done that?" I asked him.

"They could've done that," he said. He nodded. "And if they did, I think I know where. We'll go back in the morning."

I turned in first, leaving Carpenter at his cedar trunk, staring off into the night, or off into his own memories.

I didn't expect to sleep well, but I was tired, my muscles sore, my hands sunburned, and I was out even before Carpenter came into the tent.

I awoke at dawn. Carpenter was still asleep. I climbed out of the tent, used the toilet, walked down to the shore. Looked out along the sea of grass, silent and still in the gray of morning. Looked down at the murky pool of water before me. And I saw, lying out there as though it had been waiting for me all night, twenty feet away in the flat unmoving water, the alligator.

I had been imagining alligators so often that for a moment I thought I imagined this one. But it was real. I could make out, clearly, only the snout and the round dark eyes. I couldn't determine exactly how large the animal was, but the snout looked big and so did the eyes. Maybe seven feet long, maybe eight, maybe longer.

Neither of us moved.

And then I jumped, as Carpenter said, beside me, "That one's a baby."

Maybe the animal heard him, and took offense. The snout and the eyes dipped beneath the surface, and then the water behind them seemed to bulge slightly upward and thicken for a moment, as though it were about to solidify, and then it smoothed out again and there was nothing.

"You ready for breakfast?" Carpenter asked me.

Breakfast was instant coffee and gorp. Carpenter broke down the tent, folded it, rolled it, tied it to his pack. He emptied the shotgun again, slipped the shells into his pockets. I slapped on my insect repellent. He slapped on his. We climbed back into the canoe.

He had said we were going back, but, once again, I had to take his word for it. For hours we drifted through a landscape identical to the landscape we'd drifted through yesterday. Water and grass, grass and water, islands, channels, more islands, more channels.

At around ten o'clock we were approaching still another island, the ghostly cypress looming over us. Carpenter slowed the canoe, swung it around, brought it up against the bank. He stepped from the boat, then helped me out. "Wait here," he told me.

He moved off slowly through the trees, stalking roughly parallel to the bank, his head bent forward as he studied the ground.

I sat down against another cypress, felt the moisture seep almost immediately into the seat of my pants.

Fifteen minutes later, he was back. For the first time since I'd met him, he smiled a full smile. "Esteban is good," he said. "But one of the others screwed up." He nodded toward the canoe. "Let's go."

We sailed for maybe a hundred yards along the bank of the island, then Carpenter brought the canoe back to the shore. We left the boat and he bent forward, snared my pack, turned, and handed it to me. "We'll carry all the gear first. Then the canoe."

He grabbed his pack, swung it on. I wrestled my arms into the straps of mine. He squatted, raised the shotgun. Carrying the gun at port arms, he set off. I followed. We trudged over the spongy ground, around the gnarled trunks, under the faraway canopy of branches, for maybe a hundred yards, until we came to another patch of still black water. More grass out there, more channels. Carpenter unsnapped the straps of his pack, shrugged himself free, set the pack up against a tree. "Now the boat."

Half an hour later, we had the canoe back in the water and the gear back aboard. Standing beside it, Carpenter began to load the shotgun, once again alternating shot with slugs. "We're about half an hour away," he said.

I loosened the Beretta in its holster.

Carpenter moved into a squat, supporting himself with the barrel of the shotgun, the butt against the ground, and signaled for me to come down to his level. I did. "Okay," he said. He took a ballpoint pen from his pocket, used the rear end of it to draw in the damp ground. "We're here. If I'm right, they're over here, on this island. It's another shack. Set back from the front of the island, in the trees. What we do is circle around the island and come in from the rear. There's a steep bank back there, five or six feet, good cover for the canoe. We've only got about twenty yards of open ground to worry about. But there're no windows at the back of the shack. We'll get to them before they know we're there."

I nodded.

He looked over to me. "You ready for this?"

"Not really."

He smiled that quick smile. "Then let's do it before we change our minds."

It took longer than half an hour, but within forty-five minutes we were slipping across a fifteen-foot swath of open water, toward the bank Carpenter had mentioned. Its top was above the level of our heads, and I couldn't see much of the island, only that it stretched off, left and right, for a hundred yards or so.

Carpenter brought the boat against the shore and we stepped out into the mud, both our boots sinking up to the ankles. We kept low.

Holding the shotgun, Carpenter nodded his head toward my Beretta. "Up over the bank, and then across the clearing, to the right. Got it?"

I nodded. I pulled out the Beretta, released the safety.

"Go," he said.

We scrabbled up the bank, out in the open. The shack was maybe thirty yards away.

The first bullet took Carpenter. He went backward, into the water. The second and the third bullets took me, a punch in the arm that lost me the Beretta, then a punch in the chest, and then I was down.

28

JOSH-YOU-AH," said Ernie Martinez. "It's good to see you again, bro." Standing over me on my right, holding my Beretta loosely in his right hand, he grinned down at me. "Long time, hey?"

He was wearing blue jeans and a denim shirt, the tails hanging loose. He was in better shape than he'd been when I'd seen him last, in civil court, six years ago. His heavy stomach was gone, his chest was full. Prison had apparently agreed with him.

He was also in better shape than I was. I was lying on the ground and the upper part of my right arm was on fire. I reached over with my left. The sleeve was wet and sticky. Hole in the front, hole in the back. The bullet had gone through.

I felt at my chest. Leroy's telephone was smashed. A hole through the shirt pocket, a long ragged tear, but no bullets in there.

"Hey," said Martinez. He kicked me. In the right arm, where the bullet had hit. "What you got there?" He came down to me and rammed the barrel of the pistol against my temple. "Don't move, asshole."

Using his left hand, he opened the pocket of the shirt, jerked out the telephone. I felt bits of it fall to my chest. "What's this, bro?"

"What's it look like?" I said.

He stood up and kicked me again. I hissed.

He turned to his left. "Hey, he's got a telephone," he said. "Maybe he called someone."

"Let me see it," said another voice. I lifted my head.

Two men were approaching across the clearing, one of them Luiz Lucero. The other had to be Esteban. He had returned here sometime this morning, before Carpenter and I arrived.

He was a short man, very dark, wearing camouflage field pants and an open field jacket, also camouflaged, unbuttoned. Beneath the jacket he wore a blue undershirt. He was carrying an Uzi.

It was Lucero who had demanded the telephone. Tall and slender, he held a Colt Python revolver in his left hand, probably the same Python that Sylvia Miller had bought in Las Vegas, weeks ago. He wore a tan guayabera shirt, dark twill slacks, and a pair of ornate leather sandals over a pair of white silk socks. It wasn't an outfit I would've worn in the swamp. But it wasn't an outfit I would've worn anywhere else, either.

His right hand was bandaged, cotton gauze wrapped around the palm. His pinkie was missing. Even so, he used this hand to take the phone from Martinez. He examined it for a moment. "A cell phone," he said. "Not worth shit out here." He put the shattered phone to his ear and made his face go goofy. *"Hello, Mom? This is E.T."*

Martinez laughed. Esteban smiled.

Lucero turned to me and shook his head. He tossed away the phone. *"Lucy, Lucy, Lucy. How many times I got to tell ju to stay away from de clob when de band is rehearsin'?"* He kicked at my feet. "Get up."

I rolled over onto my left side, pushed myself up, slowly, awkwardly. I stood, wavering a bit, forward and back. I felt blood trickling warmly down my right forearm, down along the palm of my hand. I looked toward my feet. Bright red droplets were pattering against the brown earth.

Trickling was okay. Pattering was okay. The bullet hadn't hit an artery. Not that it mattered, in the long run.

With my left hand I reached again for the wound.

Martinez slapped the barrel of the Beretta against my left knuckles. *"Bleed,"* he said. "It's *good* for you, bro."

"You know this one?" Lucero asked him.

"Sure," said Martinez, and grinned. "This is my old friend *Josh-you-ah. Josh-you-ah* Croft. This is the one I told you about." Still grinning, he slammed the gun barrel against the wound.

Lucero stepped up to me and smiled sweetly. He was a handsome man, a strong chin, feline cheekbones. But his dark eyes were bright, the pupils contracted, and I wondered whether he had been sampling the goods he once marketed. He shook his head again, with elaborate regret. *"Holy moley, Lucy,"* he said. *"Ju and Ethel have been makin' a terrible mess again."* He raised his pistol, put it almost gently against my forehead. *"So now ju tell me, Lucy, who was Ethel, eh?"*

Spooky, Jimmy McBride had called him, back in Santa Fe. Spooky was right.

"A guy named Carpenter," I told him.

Without removing the gun from my forehead, Lucero nodded, turned to Esteban. "You called it," he said. He looked back at me and smiled sweetly again. "And now," he said, "you've got two seconds to tell me how you found us."

"A friend of Carpenter's saw you come into the swamp. An Indian. Carpenter knows the area. He's the one who found you."

He cocked his head, grinning idiotically. *"And who else did ju tell, Lucy? Ju tell Fred?"*

"No one."

He swiveled the barrel slightly and fired. I had time to close my eyes, but the sound was deafening. I felt the muzzle blast sear along the side of my skull. My ear rang and I could smell the stink of scorched hair.

"Babalu!" he said, and laughed. Then he narrowed his eyes. *"Don' lie to me, Lucy. Ju know how dat makes me crazy."*

"It's the truth," I told him.

Lucero glanced at Martinez and shifted abruptly from his Ricky Ricardo mode. "Would he do that? Come in here on his own? No backup?"

"Josh-you-ah? Sure he would. *Josh-you-ah's* a Boy Scout. Aren't you, *Josh-you-ah?"* He tapped at my wound.

Lucero turned to Esteban. "Go find the other one. Make sure he's dead."

Esteban nodded. Carrying the Uzi, he stalked off toward the bank.

Martinez said, "You made a big mistake, *Josh-you-ah,* coming here." He tapped the gun barrel at the wound again.

I turned to him. "Why don't you try that without the gun?"

Martinez grinned. He tapped the wound. "You a little pissed off, *Josh-you-ah?* You think you can take me?"

"I always have."

"I been practicing."

"You're still a loser."

This time he whipped the barrel at me. My knees nearly gave way.

"Who's the loser now?" he said.

I turned to Lucero. "Can I ask you a question?"

He grinned at me. "Absolutely, Lucy."

"Why did you kill Sylvia Miller?"

He laughed. He put his left hand on his hip, the Python pointing to the rear, and he spoke in a lilting, high-pitch lisp. *"This is the scene where I tell you everything. Right? Like on Rockford Files."* He lowered his voice, made it smooth and silky, like a television announcer: *"Isn't that right, Jim?"*

"I'm just curious."

He dropped his hands and now he spoke with a German accent: *"Ah, vell, Jim, dot curiosity, dot's vot killed de cat, you know."*

"I figure you just got tired of having her around."

He winced with impatience. "She was a freak. A plain freak. Talk about a loser." He grinned suddenly. *"Well, you got it outta me, Marshall. But, please, don't let the boys know I squealed."*

"I've got another question."

"What's that, Jeopardy Man?"

"You're supposed to be a pretty smart guy. How'd you get involved with a moron like Ernie?"

Martinez pounded at me with the gun barrel again.

232

I turned to him. "Come on, Ernie. For old time's sake. Try it without the gun."

Lucero said, "You want to fight him, Ernesto?"

"Sure he does," I said. "That's what this is all about. That's why he shot my partner. That's why he called me a few days ago."

Lucero looked at Martinez and waggled a finger at him. "Ernesto. You've been a very naughty boy. You weren't supposed to call anyone."

"Just him," Martinez said. "He's the only one. And it was before New Orleans." He turned to me. "Hey, you hear about your girlfriend, *Josh-you-ah?* Your girlfriend, the tomato, Rita what's-her-name, she kicked off."

I looked at him. "You're lying."

He shook his head earnestly, eyebrows raised. "No, bro, that's the straight shit. Ask Esteban when he comes back. He found out this morning. Really a shame, huh?"

"I don't believe you."

He shrugged. "Don't matter to me, bro. She's still dead."

I took a breath. Ignore that. Focus on the important thing. Causing Martinez some pain.

"C'mon, Ernie," I said. "Without the gun. You afraid your boyfriend will see you get your ass kicked?"

"Fight him or shoot him," Lucero told him. To me, in an English drawl, he said, *"This all grows so terribly tiresome, don't you think?"*

Martinez grinned. "I fight him." He handed the Beretta to Lucero. He clapped his hands.

Lucero said, "Fine." Sticking the Beretta into his waistband, he turned to me. "Now, Jeopardy players, listen carefully to the rules—"

Martinez leaped at me, wrapped his thick arms around mine, and squeezed. A flame of pain flared through my arm. He spun me around and flung me loose, toward the ground.

I landed on my left side, hard, and I knew I had to keep moving, because Martinez would be coming in with his feet. I used the momentum of the fall to roll away from him, and pain flared again as I flattened my right arm, and then I felt another pain, in my gut, as his foot ripped up and crashed into me, slamming the air from my lungs.

I kept rolling—I had no choice—and he came rushing in again. But this time his kick missed and I grabbed at his foot as it came whistling past and I shoved it skyward as I lumbered up off the ground. Off balance, Martinez toppled over. Now he was on the ground and I was standing, and I moved in for a kick of my own. Lucero's pistol boomed and a slug went zipping past my face.

"Now now now," he said, and he cocked his head and waggled that finger. *"Ju got to play fair, Lucy."*

I stepped away.

I had rolled toward the house, away from the water. Martinez was between me and the shore. If I could somehow maneuver this thing closer to the bank . . .

Martinez pushed himself off the ground. He dusted himself off and then he grinned at me again. He raised his fists. "You're going to die, *Josh-you-ah.*"

I raised my left hand. I had no right. That arm was useless.

Martinez had been telling the truth. He had been practicing. He came in like a boxer, heavy on his feet but with his shoulders hunched, his fists moving in small tight circles. He feinted a right at my face and then he pounded a quick left at my wounded arm.

I managed to stumble back, away from him. And away from the water.

He came in again, grinning, and he hit me with a solid right to the chest, and then he punched again at the wound. I backpedaled some more. He shuffled in, feinted a left, feinted a right, then smashed a left at the wound. I gasped, and he drove a right into my face. I felt my lip split. I staggered back.

Boxing wasn't going to work, not for me.

I squeezed the fingers of my right hand. No power in the arm at all.

When he came in the next time, I threw the right at him. It was slow and it was puny, and he knocked it aside as though he were swatting a fly. But that left him open, and I jabbed a hard straight left at his nose. It was a good hit, and it caused him some pain. He forgot about the boxing and he roared and grabbed at me again, wrapping those powerful arms around me. His finger found the hole in my arm and dug into it, prying at the flesh.

My vision was blurring as I raised my foot and then drove it, all my weight behind it, down onto his instep. He gasped and let me go and I walloped my knee into his crotch and then, as he doubled over, I knifed the knee up into his face.

He exploded upright, arms flapping, and then he went back and down. I stepped forward and out of the corner of my eye I saw Lucero raise the Colt, and I think he was going to kill me this time. It was just at that moment that Carpenter came sprinting around the side of the shack, the shotgun held low. Lucero tried to bring his pistol to bear, but Carpenter was already firing and the big double ought slugs pocked sudden dark holes in his handsome face and then a deer slug slapped into his chest and he took a step backward as another round of heavy shot peppered him, and then he dropped.

I looked at Carpenter. He was upright now and walking toward me, watching Lucero, the gun still ready. He was soaking wet and the front of his shirt was smeared with blood and mud. Somewhere he had lost the sunglasses and the hat.

"Esteban?" I said. I was panting.

So was he. "Finished," he said. He looked down at Martinez, who had rolled into a ball and who clutched with both hands at his groin. "So," said Carpenter. "We end this now, or we bring him back?"

It was tempting. I considered it. After a moment I said, "We bring him back."

His mouth moved in a twitch. "That's the hard way," he said.

"Yeah."

EPILOGUE

MARTINEZ HAD BEEN lying about one thing. Rita was alive. I learned that by using the first telephone we came to, when Eugene Samson drove us to Coral Springs.

The fever had passed, Leroy told me. There was no infection. The doctors had discovered that both the fever and the increased white blood cell count had been caused by a small mucus block trapped in her lung. It had been removed. Her temperature had returned to normal. She was still unconscious, but she was stable.

Carpenter used another telephone, this one at the hospital in Coral Gables, to call in the Feds.

Carpenter had been shot in the right shoulder, and his wound was more serious than mine. A couple of times, as we'd come out of the swamp, he'd blacked out. We had all been in the inflatable—him, me, and Martinez. If I hadn't been able to revive Carpenter, all of us would still be back in there somewhere.

The Feds came in, lots of them, and they took Martinez. For the next couple of days, from hospital beds in different rooms, Carpenter and I answered their questions.

On the third day, Billy Fetterman/William Cornwell showed up.

The knitted slacks were tan today and the pressed white cotton shirt had short sleeves, but he was still as dark and weathered as a strip of jerky. He wasn't wearing a hat. Maybe he'd left it in the car.

"Hey, Billy," I said from the bed. "How are brother Delbert and the pigs?"

He smiled. "You're recovering, it seems. Do you mind if I sit down?"

"Why would I mind? Everybody else has."

He lowered himself into the plastic chair and looked over at me. "I thought I'd bring you up to speed on Martinez. I felt we owed you that."

"He's been talking?"

"In torrents."

"Why?"

"He seems to believe that we'll go easy on him if he tells us what happened."

"And will you?"

"Not likely." He smiled. "I can't imagine where he got the idea."

"What's he say about New Orleans? Who were the two men in the convertible?"

"A pair of nobodies. Small-timers from Miami. They drove up to New Orleans and met Lucero and Martinez at the site."

"How did Lucero and Martinez fake the deaths?"

He crossed one leg over the other. He was wearing the same shiny lizard-skin boots he'd worn in Texas. "Harper was paid to drive the truck to the site, and paid for his testimony. We've got him, and he's talking. The four of them, Lucero and Martinez and the small-timers, stood in the convertible and held Sylvia Miller by her arms and legs and tossed her out onto the street. Martinez says that Lucero was laughing while he did it."

"Harper confirms that?"

"He showed up later. So he says. Martinez says otherwise."

"Was Sylvia alive at the time?"

He shook his head. "Lucero had already broken her neck. She was out cold when he did. They'd gotten her drunk."

And she had slipped, unknowing, from one Dark to Another.

"Then what happened?" I asked him.

"Then, according to Martinez, Lucero took out the two from Miami."

"By himself."

"According to Martinez. A couple of karate chops."

"You believe Martinez?"

His square shoulders moved in a comfortable shrug. "It hardly matters, does it? He's an accessory. He certainly didn't try to stop Lucero. Not then, and not when Lucero worked on their faces with a baseball bat."

"Who cut off the guy's pinkie?"

"According to Martinez, Lucero did. With a cleaver. Then he cut off his own. He bandaged the hand up and used a few grams of cocaine as an anesthetic. Afterward, they drove to a doctor who cleaned the wound."

"You find the doctor?"

He nodded.

"When did Harper and the truck show up?" I asked him.

"Just as Lucero was wrapping up his hand. Once again, that's according to Harper. Martinez puts him there for the entire time."

"So then," I said, "after they get the bodies arranged in the car, Lucero and Martinez set the car running toward the tanker truck. It explodes, and they drive merrily away. In the car the Miami men brought."

He nodded again.

"Pretty complicated plan," I said.

Another nod.

I said, "And they had to pull it off quickly. They needed the confirming testimony from the guy at the gas station."

"That's right."

"Kind of hard to believe, isn't it?"

"What is?"

"That they *did* pull it off. That Lucero's pinkie finger exactly matched the missing finger of the guy in the car. That an autopsy couldn't determine that Sylvia's neck was broken before

239

she hit the ground. Or that the faces of the guys in the convertible had been smashed before the car hit the truck. And what about DNA testing?"

Smiling, he tipped his head forward slightly in agreement. "It does stretch credulity a bit, now that you mention it."

"Uh huh. So when did you people realize that the bodies weren't Lucero and Martinez?"

He was still smiling. "Maybe an hour after you left Texas."

"You kept quiet about it. You never told the newspapers. You were thinking that if Lucero figured he'd gotten away with it, fooled you, he might make a mistake."

"And he did. But you were the one who caught it. You did a good job, Croft."

"Jeeze, Billy, thanks."

He smiled again, but now the smile was tight.

"Tell me something," I said.

"What?" He glanced at his watch. I'd hurt his feelings. He didn't like sarcasm.

"Why did Lucero kill Lyle Monroe, in Denver? It was Lucero who killed him, right, and not Martinez?"

"According to Martinez it was. He claims that Monroe had promised money to Lucero, and then reneged."

"Martinez was pretty much an innocent lamb in all this."

"According to him." He stood up. "Well," he said, "it's time for me to go, I'm afraid."

"What does Martinez say about shooting Rita?"

"Ah," he said, and nodded. "He does admit to firing the rifle. But he says he was aiming for you." He smiled another tight smile. "Ironic, don't you think?"

He seemed to feel that this was a good exit line, because he tapped his finger at his forehead, adios, and turned to leave.

Just as he reached the door, I said, "It was pretty much a win-win situation for you, wasn't it?"

He turned. "What was?"

"The faked deaths. If you people managed to find Lucero, you could claim afterward that you hadn't been fooled. And if Lucero managed to get away, it didn't make any difference—he was already dead."

He looked at me for a moment. Then he said, "You're a cynical man, Mr. Croft."

"Yeah," I said.

While I was still in the hospital, I received phone calls from Hector Ramirez, Norman Montoya, Ted Chartoff in Dallas, Ed Norman in L.A., and from some other people, including Mr. Niederman, the computer expert in Denver. Mr. Niederman thanked me for putting the FBI in touch with him.

Dick Jepson, from Miami, stopped by to introduce himself. At my request, he brought along something I wanted to give Carpenter. It set me back a fair amount—I had no idea that a Barbie doll, even a rare one, could cost so much.

On the day I left the hospital, I spoke with Leroy. Rita had begun to come out of the coma.

She was still on the respirator, and she would slip in and out of consciousness, but she had been lucid enough to write down questions for the nurses. The first question was "What happened?" The second question was "Joshua?"

I said good-bye to Carpenter that day, and Eugene Samson drove me back to the house in Clearwater. I picked up the Cherokee and I started the trip back.

On my second day of traveling, I spoke to Rita. She had been taken off the respirator. Her voice was threaded, sandy, and she couldn't talk much above a whisper.

"You're in all the newspapers," she said. "My hero."

"How are you?"

"Like a little baby. It's very . . . frustrating. I try to say something, and sometimes I can't come up with the right word. Things come and go."

"I'm one of them. I'll be there in a day or two."

"I'll be there. *Here*. I mean *here.*"

"Wherever. I'll see you soon."

★ ★ ★

I spoke with her again the next day, and the day following.

That night was the night I came home.

I sailed over the hill at La Bajada at a little after ten o'clock—too late to go to the hospital—and I saw, stretched ahead of me, the far-off twinkling lights of the city. No matter how often I complain about the place, the sight of those familiar lights in the darkness has always given me a lift. It was a signal that the journey was nearly over. And this time it signaled a great deal more than that.

If someone had been standing at the Cross of the Martyrs that night, looking off to the south, he would have seen my headlights as only one more droplet in the stream of lights that poured into Santa Fe.

I saw her the next morning, at eight. They had moved her from Intensive Care into a private room.

Her head was still bandaged and her skin was still whiter than it should have been. But she was sitting up, her back propped against the pillows, her arms outside the covers. She smiled at me when I came in.

I bent down and I kissed her. "Hello," I said. Once again, I was having some difficulties with breathing.

"You look pale," she said. "The newspapers said you'd been wounded."

"Not badly." I sat down on the bed, took her hand.

She smiled wryly. "Just a flesh wound?"

"The bullet bounced right off."

She reached up and touched me, just below the stitches on my lower lip. "What's this?"

"It's nothing, Rita. I'm fine. How are you?"

She frowned. "I'm still disoriented sometimes. The doctor tells me that I'll be that way for a while."

"How will we know?"

She smiled, squeezed my hand. "Listen," she said. Her face went very serious for a moment, as though she were concentrating with all her effort. Then she looked at me directly and said, "You did the right thing."

"Which right thing?"

"Leroy told me what happened. And I've read the papers. If you hadn't gone after them, Lucero and Martinez would've gotten away."

"Maybe. Who knows?"

"Leroy told me that he gave you a hard time."

"He was worried about you. Everyone was."

"But you did the right thing. I want you to know that I know that."

"I had to believe you'd come out of it. That you'd get better."

"I know that."

I said, "Look, I'm not supposed to stay very long. But suppose I start making some plans. For the two of us. As soon as you get out of here, as soon as you're able, we can go away for a while. Maybe back to Cancun. Or back to Catalina. Someplace new, if you want. It's up to you."

She frowned again, and looked away. "This is going to be difficult."

"What?"

Once again, she looked at me directly. "Joshua, I want you to understand that this has nothing to do with you. With us. And certainly nothing to do with your going after Lucero and Martinez."

"What are you talking about?"

She looked away, looked back at me. "When I get better, I need to go away for a while, on my own. Without you."

"Without me."

"I need to be on my own for a while."

"On your own?" I was beginning to feel like an idiot, repeating everything she said.

"It's something I've been thinking about for a long time," she said. "Since before . . . this." She moved her hand limply, to indicate the hospital room, the shooting, the two of us.

"For a long time now," she said, "I've been thinking that I needed to go off and do something for myself. Being here, lying here hour after hour in this ridiculous bed, in a way that's helped me think about it more clearly. Become more focused about it. Joshua, for most of my adult life I've been a part of something else. The marriage to William. The office." She smiled. "You."

"There's nothing necessarily wrong with being a part of—"

She squeezed my hand again. "I know that. I know that. But I've never really had any alternative. And I need it, Joshua. It's time for it. I need to put myself in a place where I can do something on my own. Entirely on my own. I'm not even sure yet what that place will be. But I know I have to put myself there. I know I have to find it."

"Rita, we can talk about this when you get out of here."

She smiled another wry smile. "I'm sure we will. But I want you to understand that I'm going to do this."

"Leave me," I said. "Leave Santa Fe."

She nodded. "Yes."

"For how long?"

"I don't know. However long it takes."

"Rita—"

"You have to understand that my feeling for you hasn't changed."

"Sure, that makes sense. That'd be why you want to take off."

She shook her head. "This isn't about you. This is about me."

"This is not making me very happy, Rita."

"It's not making me happy, either. It's going to be very difficult for me. But it's something I have to do. Will you at least try to understand?"

I looked away. "Shit," I said.

Once again, she squeezed my hand. "Will you at least *try?*"

I looked at her. "I'll try," I said.

★ ★ ★

But later, when I went to the office, I knew that no matter how hard I tried, I would never understand.

There was a bottle of Scotch in Rita's desk. Single malt, expensive. It had been there for months. The time was only nine-thirty, early in the day for a drink. But it was early in the day for desolation, and I was having plenty of that already.

I opened the bottle, poured myself a drink, sat down behind Rita's desk. A film of dust lay along everything, the desktop, the computer, the keyboard.

And it lay, too, along the corridors of my heart. A film of dust and soot and bleak gray ash.

I took a sip from the drink.

I thought about the way she looked that day, years ago, when she stood in my room at the De Vargas Hotel. I thought about the way she looked that night when she walked toward me, white and sleek, through the pale light of the moon. Thought about her face, the dark eyes, the small ironic curl at the corner of her mouth. Thought about her hair, tumbling sleek and black to her shoulders, sheened like a raven's wing.

I wouldn't let it happen, I told myself. Somehow I would talk her out of it. I would convince her, somehow, to stay.

I took another sip.

I *would* convince her.

I had to convince her. I knew that being without her, being alone, was a Dark to which I could never grow accustomed.